Contents

Cover Credit
Title Page
Copyright
Dedication
About This Book
Chapter 1
Chapter 2
Chapter 3
Chapter 4
Chapter 5
Chapter 6
Chapter 7
Chapter 8
Chapter 9
Chapter 10
Chapter 11
Chapter 12
Chapter 13
Chapter 14
Chapter 15
Chapter 16
Chapter 17
Chapter 18
Chapter 19
Chapter 20
Chapter 21
Chapter 22
Chapter 23
Chapter 24
Chapter 25
Epilogue
From The Author
About The Author

Cover Credit

Christopher Coyle

darkandstormyknight.com

Thank you for adorning my words so beautifully.

Sandra R Neeley
P. O. Box 127
Franklinton, LA 70438
authorsandrarneeley@gmail.
com

82,856
words.

Haven 4: AVOW

by Sandra R Neeley

For my dear friend Kimmie.

Thank you for always supporting me, always being there for me no matter how long it's been since I reached out, and for never judging.

Would that everyone could have a friend like you.

About This Book

General Lo'San is second in command on Command Warship 1. Refusing the matriarchal ways of his home planet, he broke all ties and left for Cruestace in the hopes of joining their military and building a better life for himself. He's kept his singular focus pinpoint sharp. One's integrity, one's honor, one's duty is all that matters. Warriors aboard his warship have found and claimed their females. He however, has no interest in such emotional matters of the heart... they dim one's focus. Then a human female with eyes of blue and sparkling, silver highlights in her hair catches his eye. She's reserved, beautiful and smart. He made it clear he'd be receptive to her advances, and now he waits. Unable to understand why the hell she won't claim him!

Synclare was one of multiple females rescued from a slaver's ship by the Cruestaci people. Those not claimed by their mates were anxious to get back to Earth. But not Synclare. She had nothing to go back to. Raised a trust-fund baby, she's never had people that cared for her instead of her wealth. Even her own family were more interested in her money and what it could do for them, than in Synclare. As she waits with her friends for their transport back home to Earth, she notices a strong, stoic, beautiful male. His white hair, silver skin and gray eyes captivate her. He's quiet and serious, commanding and sure, but makes every effort to let her know he sees her, and he's interested. She begins to believe that he may be her future, and she lets him know she's interested. Yet no matter how often she puts herself in his path, he just won't claim her!

Among General Lo'San's customs and people, it is the place of the female to claim and mate her male. He cannot imagine doing it any other way. Synclare's customs indicate that the male should claim and mate his female, and she won't do it differently. It is not her place to tell an Alien General that he is hers — it's all on him to take that stance. While they try to find their way through their confusing clash of customs, a manipulative danger lingers on the horizon disguised as family. This danger could cost Synclare her life if they aren't careful. Will Lo'San recognize the danger to his beloved Synclare before it can steal her away from him, or will he continue to fall under the plan of deception that's been woven for him?

Warning: Intended for mature audiences. This book contains abuse both real and implied, and sexual situations that may be disturbing for some readers. If you are offended by these subjects, please do not buy this book.

Chapter 1

General Lo'San examined his reflection in the mirror in his bathing chamber. He'd purchased the mirror just recently. It was the one luxury he'd allowed himself — a mirror, like those the human females of Earth had in their quarters. He much preferred it to asking Missy to scan his image and show it to him as a hologram. Not to mention, if he did that, everyone who had access to Missy's files would know he'd requested to view a hologram of himself, and what kind of respectable General, or warrior for that matter, did such things? Certainly not him, and certainly not until recently.

Lo'San had never cared about such things as the appearance of his hair, his smile, or if he looked appealing. All that mattered to him was that his military dress was on point. Other than being completely perfect for military inspection, he'd never given it a thought. His clothes were kept clean and neat, pressed perfectly by those on board that were responsible for such things. His boots were always polished to a high shine and free from scuffs. Well, except for when he was returning from battle, but then he always made sure to polish, or replace them, whichever was most applicable at the time. His hair was never a consideration because it was kept shorn on the sides and back, with just enough on top to give an indication of its white color.

Sink Lar had called it a 'flattop' whatever that meant. And he'd been content to present the exact same military persona each and every day. Until now. When spending time together Sink Lar had remarked once on how beautiful his hair color was, so he'd decided to let it grow out a bit on top so that she could see more of it. But his hair was thick and wavy, and the thick tresses of his snow-white hair required some finessing to keep it from flopping about carelessly. He still kept the sides and back shorn, but, he was waiting for the day Sink Lar would comment again to let him know that she liked it or desired it longer. So he had to take extra care in the way it looked.

He also practiced his smile. He'd heard Sink Lar and Sirena Vivian speaking of the males onboard Command Warship 1, and how their smiles looked more like a grimace than a smile. Lo'San hadn't noticed. A smile was something he paid no attention to. Until he'd seen Sink Lar's smile. Sink Lar smiled with her entire face. Her beautiful lips curved up, making the small indentions on either side of her mouth dip in, and her eyes sparkled, letting whoever was the recipient of the gift of her smile know that she was truly happy. His smile wasn't like that. It was mechanical, and forced, and while it wasn't quite as much of a grimace as his Sire and most of the Cruestaci, it still wasn't warm and pleasant like hers, so he'd been practicing smiling at himself in the mirror.

Lo'San looked at himself in the mirror again and smiled. He shrugged. He was in a sour mood again. He'd done all he could to let Sink Lar know that he was interested. He'd made a gift of the sweet cakes they both loved so much. He'd told her that he'd had no interest in females until just recently, stopping just short of saying it was her in particular he was interested in. He'd even been so bold as to tell her that she was never a nuisance and always welcome to visit him. He'd even wiped a bit of frosting from her lip and licked it off his own finger. They'd shared meals together, and he'd spent time giving her tours of the ship. These things would have been scandalous on his home planet. There, the females chose their intended male and with much insistence and proclamation let that male know he was their intended. If the male wasn't interested, it was his responsibility to remove himself from society for a full revolution in order for the female to find a replacement before he once again showed his face and caused her humiliation at his refusal of her desire to mate him. He'd done all except declare that she was his. He'd stopped just short of that, and was waiting patiently for her to make the final step, but so far, she hadn't.

It seemed no matter how much he'd hinted to Sink Lar that he was interested, or how many meals they shared, she simply never took it to the next level. She had never claimed him, nor

9

even alluded to the fact that she thought of claiming him. So, he'd gradually stopped expressing so much interest himself. It was embarrassing that she'd never vocally made any proclamation where he was concerned. But he couldn't forget her. Even though he'd taken a step back from her, he couldn't make his mind stop thinking of her. And Sink Lar seemed to be happy whenever they happened on one another. She smiled, and gazed at him, and was very receptive, but she never exercised her right to make him her male. It was frustrating. He just wasn't sure how to proceed. Which brought him to tonight. He'd decided that he would have to press the issue before someone else tried to claim her for their own. He was dressed in his dark gray dress uniform, and ready, planning to go to the commissary and wait for her to come in for her evening meal. He'd ask to join her, tell her that he'd be receptive to her claim should she want to make one, then wait to see what her response would be. The idea of what he was about to do was not at all acceptable according to the customs of the matriarchal society he grew up in. If the females of his line ever heard of his outrageous behavior, they'd be shamed that he'd had to ask a female to claim him.

He looked at himself once again and straightened his high necked collar. "She is not from your world, Lo'San," he whispered to himself in the mirror. "You must make your desires clear to her." Satisfied that he was as presentable as he was going to get wearing the same military uniform he always wore, he walked out of his tiny bathroom and into his very small one room quarters. She was worth the risk of refusal. He simply had to have faith that once she knew he cared for her, she'd accept him and take him for her own. The commissary was waiting, he'd been practicing his smile all afternoon, and there was nothing more to be done until she'd either accepted or rejected him. "It is time," he said aloud.

"General Lo'San, your presence is requested on the Command Deck, sir," Missy said.

"I am off duty this eve," General Lo'San answered.

"Sire Zha Quin Tel Mo' Kok requests your presence," Missy advised. "He asks that you come right away."

10

"Thank you, Missy. I will be there momentarily," Lo'San answered.

~~~

Synclare laughed as she walked into the commissary, arm in arm with Elisha and Vivian. They'd been planning to have a girls' night for the last several weeks, and finally, this was their night.

"I'm so excited! I've never been out to dinner and dancing with just my girlfriends in my entire life!" Vivian said happily.

"Nor have I. But, that's probably because I pretended to be a male most of my life," Elisha said.

"I have many times. But, this time, I'm truly with friends, so that does make a difference," Synclare added.

As they walked into the commissary and got in line, Synclare's eyes scanned the crowd already there and having dinner.

"Who are you looking for?" Vivian asked, knowing exactly who Synclare was looking for.

"No one. Just looking," Synclare lied.

"Uh-huh," Vivian said, grinning at Synclare. "I know who you're looking for. He's around somewhere. He's off tonight since Quin is on duty."

"Doesn't matter. We're just friends, and I wasn't looking for him anyway," Synclare answered.

"Go ahead and tell yourself that," Vivian teased.

"I honestly don't know what to think," Synclare admitted. "I thought we liked each other. We were getting along wonderfully. We spent time together, shared meals, laughed. I thought he was interested, but then nothing, nada. He just stopped making any effort, other than watching me every time we happen to be around one another. Maybe I just read him wrong. Maybe he's got a girlfriend or something. Maybe he's more interested in one of the other females that came on board recently," Synclare said.

11

"Those females are part of the crew, and from what I understand, Lo'San is not mated, and is not interested in anyone but you," Vivian said.

"Then why did he run hot, then so cold?" Synclare asked.

"Just ask him, only he knows," Vivian said. Vivian looked around herself then, noticing Zahn and Rel sitting inconspicuously off to one side of the commissary. "At least we should have a decent night. I told Quin that he's not allowed to come find me, send for me, or do anything that would interrupt my time with my friends."

"You think he's going to listen?" Elisha asked.

"Yes. Zahn and Rel are just over there, acting like they're not watching. If he was coming, they'd not be on duty."

"Are they on duty?" Synclare asked.

"Yep. They can pretend all they want, but I know they're overseeing my safety," Vivian said confidently. "I gave them the night off, but I'm sure Quin sent them."

"I told Ba Re' that if I saw him following me tonight, I'd ignore him for a full month," Elisha said, laughing.

"You're both lucky to have males that are concerned for your safety, crave your attention and want your company," Synclare chided gently with a chuckle.

"These Cruestaci are a bit controlling," Elisha said. "No matter what I plan to do, Ba Re' is trying to convince me to stay in our quarters. If I go out anyway, he's constantly checking in on me, what I'm doing, or who I'm with. He seemed to support me wanting to further my career but now I'm not so sure."

"He will. He's a good male. He's just a little more stubborn than most," Vivi said. "And they all mean well," Vivian said. "In my case I know that I have to be alert and protected at all times, even on the ship. But, since we've downgraded the ship's status to a diplomatic envoy from a battle vessel, there is always someone aboard that does not live here regularly. So, I do understand their desire for all the security, and for me because of my position, but sometimes I just want a break from it all. I just want to be Vivian, you know? Leaving the Sirena part behind for a bit."

"I can imagine the stress," Elisha said. "It must be very trying."

"It is. But you get used to it," Vivian said, shrugging, "I just need a little break once in a while. But, that's going to happen more now that the two of you are here full time. It's nice to have friends again."

"Yes, it is, but you'd be lost without Quin," Synclare said.

"Yeah. I would. I don't even want to consider not having Quin at my side. He's everything that keeps me steady and strong now. Makes me feel safe," she admitted in a soft voice. "Lets me know I'm loved."

Synclare nodded and reached out a hand, laying it on Vivian's shoulder. She and Vivian had similar stories, something that Elisha would never understand even if they'd explained it all to her. Elisha had worked her way through the ranks and was now employed by the Cruestaci as a translator and liaison for visiting dignitaries, or was at least training to be. She'd never been exposed to the abuse both Synclare and Vivian had survived.

"We're going to have fun tonight," Synclare said, returning the conversation to their evening plans and yanking Vivian into the here and now.

"Yes, we are!" Vivian seconded. "Let's hurry up and eat so we can get over to the club. I want to dance until I can't move!"

~~~

The doors on the Command Deck swooshed open and General Lo'San stepped through.

"Sire?" he asked, walking toward Quin who sat in the command chair, looking at the tablet in his hand. Lo'San grinned when Kitty went from a lying position at the side of Quin's chair to sitting up anxiously to see who'd stepped onto the deck. Quin had waved the shraler back to the floor and ordered him to lie down.

"Lo'San," Quin said, looking up at Lo'San's arrival.

"You requested that I join you?" Lo'San asked.

"Yes. I need you to trail Vivi tonight," Quin said irritatedly.

"Trail Sirena Vivian?" Lo'San asked.

"Yes."

"Does she not have her guard with her?" Lo'San asked, not understanding Quin's request at all.

"She does. But, she's been known to slip away from them," Quin replied.

"Where is she going that she needs to be watched over?" Lo'San asked.

"Girls' night," Quin said, his nose scrunching up with the term.

"Girls' night? What is girls' night?" Lo'San asked.

"It is a night that human females look forward to, on which they leave their males at home, forbidden to accompany them and unable to protect their females from any who might wish them ill."

"And it is a night used for...?" Lo'San asked.

"I know not. Except that it involves dancing, and imbibing of behavior altering beverages, and ordering their males to stay far away," Quin said, clearly unimpressed with the whole thing.

"Surely you could insist on accompanying her for her own safety," Lo'San suggested.

"I tried. She simply ignored me. Finally stating that if I were to follow and ruin her fun that she would be very disappointed in me. I cannot have my Vivi disappointed in me. So, I've devised an alternative plan. You will watch over her activities unbeknownst to her this evening."

"Surely she will notice that I am there," Lo'San objected.

"Yes, but she will not know that you are watching her. She will simply think that you are enjoying your time off duty. She intentionally planned this on an evening that I am on duty, so it will make sense that you are taking full advantage of being off duty and recreating in her new Dance Club."

"You could insist that she cancel and wait for another evening," Lo'San said.

"You clearly do not know, nor do you understand my Vivi," Quin grumbled.

Lo'San looked around the Command Deck, noted that all on deck were doing their level best to pretend they weren't listening, and to be on top of their responsibilities even more so than usual. Their behavior could only mean that Commander Zha Quin Tha was in a sour mood. "Would you like me to take the Command Deck so that you can attend with your Ehlealah?" Lo'San offered.

"No. She would not allow me to attend regardless," Quin replied. "Which is why you must pretend to have plans of your own and follow them," Quin said smiling widely.

Lo'San looked at Quin's smile, realizing it did look very threatening instead of pleasant, just as the females had been discussing when he'd overheard them. "Do you not think that Sirena Vivian would become quite upset if she were to find that I was following her?" Lo'San said, repeating himself in an effort to make it known he wanted no part of this, but not being willing to outright refuse Zha Quin.

"That is why you must not make it obvious that you are following her. You must make it seem as though you are having a night out yourself," Quin insisted.

"Dancing," Lo'San said.

"Yes, dancing," Quin agreed.

"I'd had tentative plans this evening," Lo'San tried to object gently.

"With a female?" Quin asked.

"Not exactly," Lo'San admitted, knowing he'd not made firm plans with Sink Lar in a while now.

"You should spend more time with a female. Find yourself a female. There is an available female with Vivi this night. You should dance with her," Quin said. "You are safe from a forced mating here. We have none of your females aboard. You should find a female that you enjoy and... enjoy her," Quin finished.

"Thank you, Quin, but I have a female in mind already," Lo'San said. "I'm just not sure that she's interested in making her claim."

Quin was surprised that Lo'San was entertaining ideas of a female. He'd never been one to spend much time on anything other than military strategies. Quin knew it was because of the strong matriarchal society he'd left behind when pledging his loyalty to Cruestace, that he refused to even consider a relationship with a female. He'd left his homeland as a young man when his family tried to force him to accept a place among the chosen husbands of one of their own nobility. Lo'San had refused and left his planet the next morning for Cruestace and a career with their military. "Which female do you have in mind?" Quin asked, his own mind momentarily distracted from his own motives with the unexpected admission from Lo'San.

Lo'San didn't answer right away. He pursed his lips and thought about not answering Quin. But, Quin was not only his friend, he was his direct Commander and his Sire. Finally he huffed out a breath. "The human, Sink Lar. She is much on my mind."

Slowly a devious smile curved Zha Quin's lips. "This is very fortuitous, my friend. She is one of the females accompanying my Vivi on this girls' night. She will be dining and dancing with my Vivi."

Lo'San's senses came to attention at once. "She will?"

"She will. She may even find males who wish to share her company and dance," Quin suggested.

Lo'San's expression hardened. "I think I shall honor your request. I will watch over Sirena Vivian and her friends as they enjoy their girls' night."

"Excellent! I am quite pleased that you've agreed to watch over my Vivi. I will not forget your assistance," Quin said.

"I'll take my leave now," Lo'San answered.

"Thank you, Lo'San. Remember, I have nothing to do with you choosing to dance in Vivian's club this night," Quin said conspiratorily.

"She will not know that I watch over her. I give you my word," Lo'San promised.

Lo'San turned and left the Command Deck, but glanced back when he heard Quin scold Vivi's shraler.

16

"Stay! Lie down, Kitty. You are not allowed at girls' night either!" Quin insisted.

Kitty's chest rumbled when Quin scolded him.

"Do not growl at me!" Quin ordered Kitty as the doors swooshed closed.

Lo'San smiled. Vivian had not only made plans without Quin, she'd made sure he understood he wasn't invited, and left him to babysit her shraler. Then he thought of Sink Lar. He wasn't sure he could stand by and watch Sink Lar dance with another male. It was a good thing he'd promised Quin that he'd pretend he was there for his own reasons. He might have to dance with Sink Lar to keep any others away from her. Now, if he only had someone to teach him to dance so he didn't look foolish...

Chapter 2

Lo'San hurried to the commissary, hoping to intercept Sink Lar. He knew his main objective was to watch over Sirena Vivian, but, Sink Lar was foremost in his mind. As he rushed through the hydraulic doors when they slid open, he paused briefly to look around the large room. A large number of their personnel were already seated and having their evening meal. But neither Sink Lar, nor Vivian was among them.

Satisfied that he must have beaten them to the commissary, Lo'San went through the line, chose his meal from all the different foods they had available, and sat near Vivian's usual table at the far side of the room. He smiled to himself as he settled down to enjoy his meal, knowing that his evening would be spent with the female who'd stolen more of his attention than anyone else ever had. Lo'San paused for a moment and thought about it, before shaking his head in disbelief. Sink Lar wasn't just the woman who'd taken more of his attention than any other, she was the only woman who'd ever taken his attention. He'd never given any female a passing thought, regardless of who they were, or what they offered. He'd even run far and fast from his home planet the moment he was chosen by a noblewoman to be one among her husbands. He'd thought it was because he wasn't meant for mating. Soldiering was all he'd ever felt called to, but he'd been wrong. That female simply wasn't for him. And further, since finding the one who was, he'd determined he would not share his female, and she would not share him. That went against everything in the society he grew up in. But it didn't matter. All that did matter was guiding Sink Lar to claim him, if she thought of him that way.

He just didn't know how to do it, other than presenting himself for claiming and then waiting for her to do it. He'd thought he'd done so, but, apparently, he'd not been clear enough. He thought of Sink Lar, the sparkles in her hair, the bright blue of her eyes. Two things filled his consciousness, always. His duty as General of Command Warship 1, and Sink Lar. His duty he saw to every day, and Sink Lar he thought of every moment that he wasn't seeing to his duties. He thought about that... no, that was not true. He thought about her even when he was performing his duties. He wanted her to think about him as he thought about her - incessantly. He wanted her to put him first in all things — as he'd begun to do for her. He wanted her to crave his company — as he craved hers, and he wanted her to need him as he'd begun to need her. He looked down at his plate and realized he'd finished his food, and hadn't even noticed. His heart rate had risen with his anxiousness and he made a conscious effort to calm it. He was beyond excited about speaking with Sink Lar and letting her know he was ready for her to claim him. Then he'd have to have the conversation about her not claiming any other but him, and him not accepting any but her. Hopefully, she'd agree. They'd sought each other out to share company several times, but their flirtation had never moved beyond that — just a flirtation. Tonight though, he'd find out if she was truly as interested as he.

"Lo'San!" a familiar voice called out.

Lo'San looked up and found Rokai ahl and Rosie coming toward him as they wove through the tables to reach him.

Lo'San raised a hand in greeting, and smiled as he relaxed, thankful for the distraction Rokai provided while he waited for the females to arrive in the commissary.

"Why do you sit here alone all the time? You should give yourself some recreation!" Rokai said as he approached.

"I'm busy. I don't have much time for recreation," Lo'San answered.

"You should make time. I make time. Don't I, Rosalita?" Rokai asked, looking down at his Ehlealah, who stood at his side as Rokai held her hand tightly in his.

Lo'San took a minute to look at Rosalita and realized the female was sweating and slightly out of breath. "Your female appears to need a rest, Rokai."

19

Rokai looked down at Rosie again, then back at Lo'San. "We have just come from Vivian's dance club. It is very crowded there tonight. Many males and females are taking advantage of the recreation and exercise," he explained. "You should go there."

"I thought I might. I haven't attended since Sirena Vivian opened its doors. She promised that it would be a good option for all of us to expend some energy and have fun. It is past time that I attended," Lo'San said.

"Oh, there's a lot of energy being expended in there tonight. Vivian and Elisha are dancing together. I think most males know not to invite Vivi or Elisha to dance — Quin and Ba Re' would most likely punish them for dancing with their females, but I saw six different males alone ask Synclare to dance. Poor female doesn't even get a chance to rest between dances!" Rokai exclaimed.

The smile fell from Lo'San's face at once. "They are already there? And dancing?" he asked, getting to his feet.

"Yes. And yes," Rokai answered with a glint in his eye.

"But they have not had their dinner yet. I've been here all evening," Lo'San said.

"Oh? Were you waiting for them to arrive?" Rokai asked innocently.

"Well, no!" Lo'San denied. "I'd simply noticed that she'd, I mean they'd, not entered the commissary," Lo'San said, not wanting Rokai to know he was actually waiting for Sink Lar and Vivian to arrive.

Rokai leaned closer and feigned a whisper. "If you were waiting on Synclare to arrive here, you should have planned to be here much earlier. She's had dinner, and now she's searching for dessert."

"Dessert?" Lo'San asked.

"Yes! A male, to sweeten her evening," Rokai said, grinning ear-to-ear.

Lo'San's chest rumbled and he rushed away from Rokai and Rosalita, leaving his dishes on the table in a completely uncharacteristic move.

"I shall take care of your dishes, since you seem to be in a hurry!" Rokai called out.

Lo'San didn't even turn around, he just disappeared through the doors of the commissary on his way to the dance club.

Rosie shook her head slowly as she watched Rokai with a smirk.

"What?" he asked, still grinning.

"You know what," she answered.

"I have no idea what you are referring to," Rokai answered haughtily.

"Yes, you do. You came in here to find him and tell him Synclare is dancing with six other males," Rosie accused.

"And the problem with that would be?" Rokai asked.

"She hasn't danced with anyone! She's just sitting at the table and sipping her drink!" Rosie said.

"Exactly! While Vivi and Elisha dance, she's simply sitting, waiting — for him!" Rokai said.

"You don't know that," Rosie argued. "Just because she likes him doesn't mean she's waiting for him."

"I do. And I'm tired of watching them look at each other like dogs, while neither are willing to make the first step. So I've made the first step. He will now go to her and stay there, perhaps even do something other than offer her a cake. Perhaps he'll even actually speak to her, even dance with her!" Rokai exclaimed.

"Like dogs?" Rosie asked, still trying to understand the analogy he'd used.

"Yes, when males and females look at one another with love in their eyes and silly smiles on their faces. Vivi says they look at each other like dogs," Rokai said confidently.

Rosalita thought about it, then, she realized what he was trying to say. "With puppy-dog-eyes? Do you mean they look at each other with puppy-dog-eyes?" she asked.

"Yes. That is exactly what I said," Rokai claimed.

"It is not."

"Yes, it is."

21

"No, it's not," Rosie insisted.

"Does it matter?" Rokai asked. "Truly, does it matter? I caused Lo'San to finally go after his mate. He will thank me later," Rokai said, nodding as he walked over to deposit Lo'San's dishes on the conveyor taking all the dishes to the back of the galley to be washed. "Shall we see what they have to offer now," he asked, looking toward the serving line and changing the subject.

"We already ate," Rosie objected.

"Yes, but dancing is very physical. It's like sex. It uses up all your energy. I find I need more food," Rokai answered.

"Or we could go back to the dance club and see if Lo'San and Synclare spend any time together," Rosie suggested.

Rokai looked down at Rosie. "You are right. We should go watch." Rokai took her hand in his again and led her out of the commissary, on their way to see if Lo'San and Synclare would finally make their flirtation official.

~~~

Lo'San threw open the double handled, glass doors that Vivian had installed in place of the standard hydraulic ones used in every other doorway on the ship, and stormed inside the dance club. His emotions had gotten the better of him on the way from the commissary and he was not at all happy at the thought of Sink Lar dancing with six other males.

Lo'San stood his ground, his sharp, gray eyes taking in everyone he gazed upon until he finally found her. She was standing at the bar, speaking to the bartender. As he started toward her, he realized he was supposed to be watching over Vivian as well, and searched for her. Finding her dancing and laughing with Ba Re's mate, he relaxed marginally, and continued toward Sink Lar. He could see her throwing her head back and laughing. He could hear the melodic sound filling his heart and making his body react in ways he'd not expected, yet relished.

As he approached, she turned to see what the bartender looked at over her shoulder and the smile on her face caught him off guard. That smile should only be for him. No other. He reached her side and took the drink from her hand slamming it down on the bar top, then took her by the hand. "He will not be dancing with you. Neither will any of the others!" he growled, pulling her behind him to the edge of the dance floor.

Lo'San stood there, holding Synclare's hand in his own tightly. His eyes tracked the couples as they moved around the dance floor. He studied the males' movements as they swung their partners around the floor. As luck would have it, they were playing a slow song. Deciding he'd learned all he needed to from watching them, he strode out onto the dance floor, pulling Synclare behind him.

"What are you doing?" Synclare asked, her forehead wrinkled from her irritation with his behavior.

"Dancing. You will not need to dance with the others," he repeated.

"What others?" she asked, as he took her in his arms, glancing toward the males already dancing to be sure his arms and hands were placed right.

Lo'San looked down into her face as she gazed up at him. Rather than argue with her about dancing with other males, he simply shook his head and began to move her around the floor.

Synclare wasn't sure she wanted to dance with Lo'San. She'd always considered him a gentleman, and was drawn to his kindness and his calm nature, but tonight his behavior was reminding her more and more of Vivian's husband, and Rosie's. He hadn't asked her to dance, he'd practically forced her to the dance floor all the while proclaiming she didn't need anyone but him to dance with.

"I don't think I want to dance anymore," Synclare said, her steps coming to a stop.

Lo'San looked down at her again. "Am I not performing the steps properly?" he asked.

23

"You're performing them fine. I just don't want to dance," she said, pulling her hands free of his and stepping back from him.

"Yet you had no problem dancing before I arrived."

"I don't know what you're talking about," Synclare said. "And I'm not sure I like this side of you."

Lo'San took a step back. "There is no side of me. I simply am me, always."

"I'm going back to sit at the table with Vivian," she said, looking at him over her shoulder with a confused expression as she walked away.

Lo'San stood in the middle of the dance floor for only a moment before following her. As he approached the table he bowed. "Perhaps I was not clear with my intentions, Sink Lar," he said, making eye contact with her as she slid onto the stool between Vivian and Elisha who'd sat down only moments before Synclare had returned to the table.

"What exactly would those intentions be?" Synclare asked.

"I am prepared to dance each dance with you, that you will not have to dance with others. I have studied the dancers and feel that I can dance as well as they," Lo'San explained.

"It seemed to me that you were more than a little put out that you had to be here at all. If you don't want to be here, go back to the Command Deck. I'm here with Vivian and Elisha anyway," Synclare answered.

"I am aware. And I came so that you will not have to spend time with other males," Lo'San insisted.

"Have to? I don't have to spend time with any males. And what other males do you mean?" Synclare asked, her irritation beginning to grow.

"The other six that you have already danced with!" Lo'San answered. "I do not wish to watch you dance with more males than the six you've already allowed to hold you!"

Synclare opened her mouth to respond, but no words came out.

Vivian leaned over toward Synclare while continuing to watch Lo'San. "I think he thinks you've been dancing all night, and he's jealous."

Synclare looked at Vivian, who nodded at her to confirm her point.

Synclare returned her attention to Lo'San. "I... Lo'San, I haven't danced but once, and it was with Vivian and Elisha," Synclare said.

"Where would you get the idea she'd danced with six different males?" Vivian asked.

Slowly Lo'San turned and surveyed the room until his gaze landed on Rokai and Rosie sitting at their own table on the other side of the room. He glared at Rokai, and Rokai grinned at him and waved animatedly. Lo'San sighed, let out a deep breath and turned back around to face Synclare. "I must offer you an apology. It appears I was falsely led to believe that you had spent the evening in the company of several different males."

"And would it matter if I had?" Synclare asked indignantly. "I am not promised to anyone. I can freely spend time with anyone I choose."

Lo'San stared into Synclare's eyes. She'd just basically put him in the position of having to admit his feelings for her or deny them altogether. He thought about his options, determined that no matter what happened, he didn't want to give Sink Lar any indication that he might not care for her, and decided to be honest with her.

"Yes. It would matter if you had. To me, at least," he answered.

"Why?" she pressed.

"Because, Sink Lar. I would be most unhappy to see you in the arms of another male. I wish for you to be in my arms only," Lo'San admitted.

"You do?" Synclare asked, her eyebrows rising, her heart stuttering.

"I do. I have spent a great deal of time thinking of you. I do not think of you with other males, only myself."

The irritation on Synclare's face melted away and a sweet smile replaced it. "I didn't know you thought of me that way. I mean, at one time I thought maybe, but then you never made any other effort so I thought you'd changed your mind."

"No, I have not changed my mind. I'm simply no good at expressing my interest in females," Lo'San said defeatedly. "It is not my way."

"Why is that?" Synclare asked.

"Until you, I've not been interested in establishing a relationship with a female."

Synclare's mouth fell open. She slipped off her stool and walked around the table. "So, you're telling me you've never had a real relationship."

Lo'San thought about it. "Yes."

Synclare stood before Lo'San, realizing that if he did really care for her, he had no idea how to proceed. "The best thing to do is to ask — not demand — if the female you like would like to spend time with you."

Lo'San clacked his heels together and crossed his forearm over his chest as he gave her a single nod of understanding. "Will you please dance with me, Sink Lar. It is for this reason only that I came to this club tonight."

"I will. I'll be very happy to dance with you, Lo'San," Synclare said, holding her hand out to him and allowing him to escort her back onto the dance floor. The couples around them all gyrated to the music that had turned into a peppy dance tune, but the two of them danced slowly together, as though they were the only two that could hear a waltz playing.

As that song ended and another began, Synclare stepped back and picking up the pace, started to move rhythmically to the music.

Lo'San watched with wide eyes hungrily devouring her every move. "Yes, it is necessary that you do not dance like this with any other male. Please," he added for the sake of not wanting to sound like he was telling her what to do.

"As long as you're here to dance with, I won't," she answered, feeling a little flirty and a little powerful now that she understood he was jealous of any other male dancing with her.

Lo'San nodded and began to imitate her movements, dancing opposite her. His body moved in a manner that made Synclare think of the male strippers from the '80's back on Earth. Lo'San could have put them all to shame.

"If you let me know when you wish to dance, I will escort you," Lo'San said.

"You will have to invite me. That's how it works. The male asks the female for a date. That's how she knows he's interested."

Lo'San stopped dancing. His brow was furrowed. "On my planet, the females pursue the males, obsessively. They choose the one they want and make their intentions known," Lo'San said.

Synclare stopped dancing and looked at him curiously. "I'm not from your planet. I will not pursue you like that. If you want me, you'll have to let me know."

"I have already indicated that I would like to dance with you. If I am more bold and you do not agree, how should I proceed?" he asked, worried that she'd expect him to leave Command Warship 1 as the females on his planet expected a male to exit societal circles for a year to save them embarrassment if the male rejected them.

"I'll let you know if I don't agree," Synclare answered. "But if you don't take the lead and make an effort to show me you want me, we'll never have a chance."

Lo'San thought about it, then gave her a single, sharp nod. If she required that he make it official, he'd make it official. "I am General Lo'San, second in command of Command Warship 1. It is my intention to have you claim me as your male. It is my intention that you will never have reason to consider any other male. I will never consider another female. It is my intention that we have a bond not unlike Zha Quin's and Vivian's."

Synclare stood there smiling and blushing. When he was finished with his declaration, she didn't hesitate. She stepped up

27

to him and reached up, pulling his face down to hers, then pressed her lips against his. Lo'San slipped a hand around her waist and pulled her as close to him as possible, pressing his lips to hers for as long as she'd allow. When they finally released one another's lips, Lo'San stared into her eyes, still only inches from her face. "Are my intentions acceptable?" he asked.

"Yes, very much so," Synclare answered.

Chapter 3

Synclare and Lo'San spent the evening dancing and laughing. Every time Vivian and Elisha stepped onto the dance floor and Synclare would move closer to them, Lo'San would step back to allow her to dance with her friends. Not only out of observance of the fact that she'd come to dance with them this night, but because he didn't want Zha Quin or Ba Re' questioning why he was dancing with their females.

It was during one of these times that Rokai wandered over to where he stood at the girls' table.

"What do you want, Rokai?" Lo'San asked irritatedly.

"I came to ask how your evening is progressing," Rokai said, watching Rosie dancing with Vivian and the rest of their friends.

"Sink Lar did not dance with six other males," Lo'San said, his irritation clear while still staring straight ahead as he watched over the females.

"No, she did not. But, it certainly got you here in a hurry, didn't it?" Rokai asked, grinning.

"Why would you tell such untruths?" Lo'San asked.

"Because it's past time for you to claim Synclare."

"She will have to claim me. It is our way," Lo'San said. "I've made my intentions known, now it is in her hands."

Rokai's brows shot up and he regarded Lo'San with a shocked expression. "She is not like you! She is human. You will have to claim her, or you will not be claimed!"

Lo'San snapped his gaze to Rokai and watched him thoughtfully. "I've just told her it is my intention to have her claim me, and she said it was acceptable to her."

"Listen to me, Lo'San. You left your world because you didn't agree with its societal rules. As much as you profess to dislike where you came from, it's apparently still ingrained in you! Do not enforce them on your chosen mate. Abide by the ways of her people — not yours. Tell her she is yours. Tell her that you are claiming her and if she does not agree, ask her how to sway her intentions. Do not let her slip through your fingers as you cling to a practice that is responsible for you leaving your home world," Rokai said firmly.

Lo'San didn't say anything for a few moments as he thought over Rokai's words as he once again watched Sink Lar, Vivian, Elisha and now Rosie as they laughed and danced, raising their hands into the air and jumping in time to the music. Then finally, when he couldn't think of any way to refute Rokai's statement, he decided to question his knowledge. "And now you consider yourself an expert, I assume."

"In the ways of females?" Rokai asked, chuckling confidently, "I am extremely well versed. More well versed than I should be. But in the ways of human females? I only know that it is a mistake to expect them to understand our ways. It is much easier to tell them you want them, claim them, and follow their traditions."

Lo'San turned to look at Rokai finally, but didn't say anything.

"I have a very strong willed human Ehlealah, I speak from experience. Do not equate them with females we have been familiar with in the past. Human females are much stronger and will bow to our ways only if they choose to. And they will not ever do what you expect them to. Tell her you are claiming her. Take her for your own. Waste no time," Rokai said.

"Why do you care?" Lo'San asked.

"My Rosalita has said that Synclare wishes for your attentions. I've seen you watching her. If you don't want her, don't pay my words any notice. If you do want her, you need to make it known. You are running out of time."

Lo'San glared at Rokai, then followed Rokai's gaze back to the bar where two of the Elite Warriors of Rokai's team stood watching Sink Lar as she sang and gyrated to the music with her friends.

"They are good males. Either would make a good mate to her. I've heard them both expressing an interest in taking a

30

human mate. They would never force her, but now that you've stopped escorting her about the ship, they see their opportunity. If you don't want her, one of them will surely claim her," Rokai said. "It is why I came in search of you in the commissary when they both arrived here earlier — to give you a chance before they move in to ask for her attentions."

"She will not have them," Lo'San insisted. "She would never accept two warriors, even if they are Elite."

"They've agreed to let her choose after each taking a turn to spend time with her," Rokai explained. "I am many things, Lo'San, but I'm not a fool. I know what I've seen between you and Synclare. Rosalita confided that Synclare longs for you. And I saw, and still see the way you look at her. My warriors are interested and feel they've given you opportunity to claim her. You didn't and now they plan their attempts to win her over. Act on it or not, but when you lose her, remember I gave you warning."

Lo'San stood where he was for only a second longer, then he looked toward Rokai once more. "Thank you."

Rokai gave Lo'San a nod and watched as Lo'San walked out onto the dance floor to claim his female before someone else did.

~~~

Synclare spun in her dance and stopped suddenly when she felt someone standing right behind her. She turned to find Lo'San standing there, perfectly still, waiting for her to notice him.

"Lo'San?" she asked, looking up at him.

"Forgive me, Sink Lar," he said.

"For?" Synclare asked, canting her head to the side curiously.

"For this," he said. He stepped into her body, hooking his hand behind her head and brought his lips down on hers. He kissed her passionately, forcing her mouth open and plundering her with his tongue, doing what could only be described as making love to her mouth with his before pulling his lips away

31

from hers just enough to be able to speak clearly while she struggled to catch her breath.

"Sink Lar of Earth, I claim you for my mate. I will have no other, nor will you. I give myself and all that I am to you only and vow to stand beside you for eternity. You will never want for another, or for anything, for any reason. I am your male."

Synclare's eyes were wide as she watched Lo'San vow to be her male for eternity.

When she didn't answer Lo'San, he grew impatient. "What say you, Sink Lar?" Lo'San prompted.

Synclare licked her lips and swallowed before she was able to find her voice. "You didn't say anything about love," she said shakily. "I want love. I deserve love."

Lo'San smiled down at her, his heart in his eyes. He raised his voice to be clearly heard by all. "I have loved you since you first arrived on this ship. I have never loved another, and will never love any but you, Sink Lar."

Synclare grinned and glanced shyly away from him. "I love you, too," she admitted.

"Do you accept my vow?" he asked with a smile.

Synclare nodded. "I do."

"And?" he asked.

"Psst!" came a sound from a few feet away.

Synclare looked toward the sound.

"You have to claim him back," Rokai mock whispered.

"Oh!" Synclare said, looking back up at Lo'San. "I claim you, too. And I promise to always love and honor you."

"Only me?" Lo'San asked, making it a point to spell it out.

"Only you, forever," she answered.

Lo'San smiled at her, satisfaction clear on his face. Then he kissed her again, lifted her into his arms, which caused her to squeal in delight, and carried her from the dance club.

A moment later he reappeared in the doorway. "Rokai!" he shouted.

Rokai looked up at him.

"You will watch over Sirena Vivian and Elisha?" Lo'San asked.

Rokai snapped to attention almost comically. "I will!"

Lo'San gave a nod, turned, and was gone again as Rokai made eye contact with Vivian.

Vivian raised her eyebrow in question at Rokai saying he'd watch over her.

He simply grinned at her and crossed his arms over his chest, legs braced, his feet shoulder width apart, his gaze not wavering from the small group of females as he mimicked the behavior he'd seen Vivian's guard display while on official duty.

He heard the grumbling complaints of his Elite Warriors discussing the evening's developments.

"We allowed Lo'San too much opportunity!" Re'Vahl complained.

"And now I've lost my chance. It should be me carrying her away," Ne'Shear said.

"She would not have chosen you!" Re'Vahl insisted.

"Enough!" Rokai snapped. "She would not have chosen either of you! Lo'San has claimed her. As my Rosalita says... Deal with it and move on!"

"What does that mean?" Ne'Shear asked.

"It means it's finished. It's done. Find another focus," Rokai said, his eyes still glued to Vivian, Rosie and Elisha dancing. He didn't need to watch them so closely, but, since it seemed to irritate Vivian, and Rosie was from time to time glaring back at him, he got a certain amount of satisfaction out of it, and smiled widely each time they turned to stare at him — he was Rokai after all.

"He has a point," Re'Vahl commented.

"He does indeed. Is there another human aboard that is yet to be claimed?" Ne'Shear asked.

~~~

Ba Re' jumped to his feet and used his body to block the security screens he was monitoring when the door to his private office swooshed open without warning.

Zha Quin stood just inside the office regarding Ba Re' curiously with one eyebrow raised as Kitty moved away from Quin's side to prowl around Ba Re's office.

"Don't look at me like that! You could have been Elisha!" Ba Re' snapped.

"Is your Ehlealah not allowed to enter your work space?" Quin asked.

"Of course she is, but she'd have been irritated, and I do not like when she is irritated with me. She makes me sleep on the sofa in our quarters," he grumbled, moving away from the screens he was blocking and retaking his seat. "And she never does a thing I tell her to do," he added.

"I do not know how you can concentrate on work anyway. Our females are spending the evening without us! How can you work productively?!" Quin snapped.

A slow grin formed on Ba Re's face. He lifted a hand indicating the multiple screens before him.

Quin stepped closer and focused on the screens before chuckling. "Ah, I see we are of the same mind," he said, grabbing a chair from a work station beside Ba Re's and sliding it into place beside Ba Re' as they prepared to watch their females on the ship's security monitors.

"Do you see why I moved to hide the screens when you came in unannounced?" Ba Re' asked.

"Yes, yes I do," Quin answered. "But would you not know your Elisha was on the way here if you are watching her?"

"The lighting is dark inside the club. From time to time they move out of view. It would not be entirely impossible for her to make her way here without me noticing."

"Change one of the monitors to the corridor leading here," Quin said, scoffing.

"I can only watch so many at one time. If I do that, I will have to lose one of those in the club. I wish to see from all angles."

34

"I see," Quin said, nodding and peering closely at the monitors all giving him a different angle inside the club. "It is dark there. Where is Lo'San?" Quin asked. "I sent him to watch over Vivi."

"He is there," Ba Re' said, pointing to a table in the corner where Lo'San stood speaking with Rokai.

"Good, he watches. He is very efficient," Quin commented.

"Zahn and Rel are moving slyly among the crowd, and Rokai is in attendance as well. Zahn and Rel would immediately spirit Vivian away if needed, but surely despite his tendency to manipulate most situations, Rokai would stand for the other females if necessary," Ba Re' commented.

"He would, no doubt," Zha Quin answered, watching the image of his Vivi as she danced and laughed with her friends. He smiled as he watched her lift her arms in the air and clap her hands over her head. "I love to see her happy and carefree," Quin said.

"I'd prefer mine in our quarters where so many unmated males are not readily accessible," Ba Re' grumbled. "She just does not understand that she has no place wandering this ship. There is no reason for it if she is not in training. And even the training is not necessary! I will provide for her!"

"That is because you have not been forceful enough. You have not claimed your female. Mine is claimed," Quin said confidently.

Ba Re' glanced over at Quin. "Yes, she is, and I remember a particular Sire wandering around the ship trying to locate his errant Ehlealah because she kept escaping him at every turn. So do not speak to me of how perfectly you claimed your female!"

"The situations are very different, Ba Re'. You know that," Quin said.

Ba Re' sobered a bit. "Yes, yes they are. Vivi had much to overcome."

"Exactly. Yours is just stubborn," Quin commented.

"And yours hit you with a cooking pan! At least mine has not attacked me!" Ba Re' snapped.

"Why are you so irritable?" Quin asked, turning to look at Ba Re' with a scowl on his face.

Ba Re' didn't answer, just glared at Quin silently.

Quin watched him for a moment, then he noticed the dark circles under his eyes, the tension around Ba Re's mouth as he pursed his lips. "What is the problem, Ba Re'?"

"She will not accept my claim. She has stated that she will not do more than sleep beside me until she has established herself in her professional capacity among our people. She wishes to be independent and self-sufficient before she will accept my claim."

"That is good, she is strong, wants to learn to stand on her own. Vivi is strong and is happy to be proving herself as well," Quin said.

"She is driving me insane. I need to touch her. I need to bond myself to her. I can't sleep. I don't eat. All I do is sit here and watch her go about her days. She refuses to stay in our quarters. I have to work and am unable to accompany her. I need... I need..." Ba Re' stopped speaking to search for the words he wanted.

"An intervention," Quin supplied. "Vivi would say you require an intervention. You have completely focused on that which you cannot have at this moment, and it is all you can see. We shall stage an intervention," Quin said, nodding.

"I don't need an intervention! I need my Ehlealah to accept me!" Ba Re' insisted.

Quin watched the screens as Lo'San rushed back onto the dance floor and spoke to Synclare before kissing her.

"Ah! Lo'San has decided to make his wishes known!" Quin said. "Do you see? Synclare is receptive!" Quin said, pointing to them on the monitor as Lo'San lifted Synclare and carried her off the dance floor. "You should do that. You should explain exactly what you want, and what not having her is doing to you. If she understands the importance of your need to bond with her, perhaps she will comply," Quin said with a huge smile. "She is seeing things as they would have pertained to her former life on Earth. They just aren't applicable any longer. Make her see that.

But not right away," Quin said thoughtfully. "I'll need your assistance on the Command Deck if this development with Lo'San is what I think it is. Lo'San will need to be given his time to bond properly."

Ba Re' scrubbed a hand down his face and watched another of his shipmates claim his female. "I'll do what I can. And perhaps you're right. I should just sit her down and explain what her insistence at keeping me away from her is doing to me. I'd thought to allow her time to come to me willingly, but I do not know how much more of this I can take."

"Communicate with your female," Quin suggested, laying a hand on Ba Re's shoulder.

Ba Re' nodded. "How did you become so understanding?"

Quin smiled. "My Vivi. She is very perceptive, and I am learning."

Quin turned and looked at the monitors again. "Where did Lo'San go?" he asked, looking for Lo'San and Synclare on the dance floor and then at the table Lo'San had been standing near earlier.

"They're gone. He left the club with Synclare in his arms," Ba Re' answered.

"He is supposed to be watching Vivi!" Quin said irritatedly. "Wait... he's back," Quin said watching the screen again. "What is he..." Quin started to ask, watching Lo'San standing in the doorway to the club and speaking to someone. He watched as Rokai answered, then took up a protective stance beside the dance floor as Vivi and Rosie both glared at him, while he grinned in response.

"It would seem Lo'San has just asked Rokai to guard Vivi in his absence," Ba Re' commented.

Quin sighed, and sat back in his chair. "Vivi is going to be angry," he said, resigning himself to the fact that his secret effort to watch over her through Lo'San had been revealed.

Chapter 4

Lo'San strode to the lift that would take him to the residential floor and his quarters. He wore a smile, and rumbled a purr-like sound the entire time. Synclare had her arms around his neck, her face tucked into the crook of his neck, and he loved it. She didn't let him go or change her position the entire time he carried her to his quarters. And he in turn held her tightly, securely in his arms.

He paused in front of his quarters long enough to tighten his arm where it looped beneath her, keeping Synclare secure against his body, then reached out with his other arm to allow the sensor next to his door to scan his hand to confirm his identity and grant them access. He stepped into his quarters and set Synclare on her feet.

"This space is assigned to me. It is small, and sparse. I've never needed much. But I make a promise to you now that I will provide you with better quarters. You will have luxury such as Vivi and Elisha have. You will not have to make do in this small space."

Synclare did not look around the room as she turned toward him, her eyes were only for Lo'San. Though she now stood in front of him, she had not released her hold on him. "I'm not concerned about any of that. All I want is to be yours."

Lo'San looked down at her and smiled gently before lowering his lips to hers again. "You have made me the proudest of males," he admitted before kissing her.

Synclare smiled shyly at Lo'San after he kissed her innocently. "I've wanted you to make me yours for so long now. I wasn't sure what I'd done to make you lose interest. I was so mistaken," she admitted.

"Why didn't you tell me?" Lo'San asked, stroking her cheek with his thumb as he gazed into her eyes, still awestruck that she'd accepted him, and claimed him as hers.

Synclare gave a half shrug. "It's just not my way. I'm not that forward. I figured if you wanted me, you'd have to let me know. The other males all wander around growling 'mine' with no hesitation. So, I thought after the first few times we spent together, you must have decided you weren't sure you wanted me."

"Oh, Sink Lar, you were so, so wrong. My want for you, my need for you has only grown over time. I was waiting for your claim," Lo'San explained again.

"Why? Why wouldn't you just say you wanted me? Why expect me to do it?" Synclare asked. "If Rokai hadn't stepped in to make you think others were interested, we may not be here now. In my culture, the male makes the first motions toward commitment."

"Commitment?" Lo'San asked.

"Claiming. And in your culture, if I'm understanding properly, the females make the first motions toward claiming," Synclare finished.

"Yes," Lo'San agreed. "They are the driving force behind our culture. They decide who and when to mate. They also determine the size of their households."

Synclare thought about it. "You don't mean children, you mean husbands. They are allowed to take more than one."

"Yes. I wanted no part of it. I did not like being told what I was to do and how to behave by females that had no respect for me or my desires," he said, taking her by the hand and leading her toward his bed.

"Were you ever chosen?" she asked, the emotion in his voice giving her the indication that maybe he had been. She sat beside him on the foot of his bed and gave him her undivided attention as they got to know each other a bit better.

Lo'San nodded slowly. "Yes, when I was younger. I refused her, and based on the rules of our culture I had to hide myself away for a period of one revolution to avoid humiliating the female who chose me. Rather than abide by those rules, and to prevent myself from ever being claimed again, I left Eschina. I petitioned to be accepted by the Cruestaci military, and have never looked back. They are the governing force in our solar system and very highly respected — and feared," he admitted. "I knew that if I became one of their own, my family and the ways of my people could never be forced upon me. I suppose I'd not realized just how much of their beliefs had been ingrained in me. I find my female, the only one I want, and I foolishly fall into old habits, waiting for her to make her claim."

"It's alright, I'm just as responsible. I could have told you how I felt and didn't. I just assumed you'd be like the Cruestaci."

"I am as Strong as one of my Cruestaci brothers, but being raised on Eschina put me at a disadvantage where females are concerned, I'm afraid."

"Eschina... that's the name of your planet?" Synclare asked.

"It is," Lo'San said, nodding gently as he ran his fingers through Synclare's hair, his eyes taking in all her features over and over again as she sat beside him, facing him.

"Are they prominent like the Cruestaci?" Synclare asked.

"They are an agricultural world. But the females govern the planet and the males do their bidding. The males are raised to believe that it is an honor to be chosen as part of a household by any of the more successful families and some actually vie for those positions."

"I can't imagine having more than one male. I can only love one. If I were to allow another to touch me, I would feel that I'd been unfaithful to the other. It makes no sense to me," Synclare said.

"There are many farming communities on Eschina, but only a handful of prominent families. It is not uncommon for the males vying for positions in these families to carry out any demand the females may request of them. It can become quite petty, and very cutthroat. It is the very reason I sought out the Cruestaci above all other options. The Cruestaci are a strong people, and not afraid to fight against any unfairness they happen to encounter. They prize their Ehlealahs above all else, and would never compromise those they love in any way. They have a great integrity."

"I have seen the same things in my time here with them. They are a very strong people with very strong convictions. They defend any who need it, and treasure their females more than their own lives."

Lo'San nodded, pleased that she respected the people he'd dedicated himself to as much as he did.

"Do your kind recognize your mate as the Cruestaci do, and just have more than one?" Synclare asked.

"No, they are more like humans I think. They choose their mates," Lo'San said.

"I'm very pleased you chose me," Synclare said. "I think it makes it more special," she admitted. "You don't have to have me, you choose to have me."

Lo'San smiled and nodded. "I agree. And so that you know… I knew you were meant for me the first moment I saw you. I could not stop thinking of you. I was drawn to you. As I got to know you, it only confirmed what I already knew — I wanted you for my own," Lo'San said.

"I wanted you, too," Synclare admitted.

Synclare reached for him to kiss him again. "I love you," she whispered, kissing his lips but not being brave enough to open her mouth to him.

"I love you, Sink Lar. You will never know what it is to be unloved. We are each other's family now," Lo'San said.

"I'm sorry you had to leave your people," Synclare whispered, knowing for him to say they were one another's family, he must miss his own.

"I'm sorry you were taken from yours. If you ever wish to visit your world, I will escort you. Consul Kol Ra' Don Tol is stationed there and would readily accept our request to visit, I'm sure," Lo'San said.

Synclare shook her head. "I am here with you, where I was meant to be. My life is good now. I have no desire to go back."

"If that should change…" Lo'San said.

"It won't, but I'll let you know just the same," she said.

41

Lo'San looked down at his female, so trusting and loving as she looked up at him with her beautiful blue eyes. It wasn't so long ago that she'd been brought aboard with the other females rescued from Malm's ship. They'd all been afraid and traumatized, yet here she was, giving him the gift of trust and love. "I admire your strength, my Sink Lar. You are an amazing female. I am honored that you chose me."

"I see you the same way. You could have chosen anyone you wanted."

"No, you've held my heart since you first looked my way," he admitted.

Synclare looked down at their clasped hands, ran her other hand across his. He couldn't help but think of the circumstances that brought her to him, and he was angry with himself for not considering that she may not be ready for what he'd selfishly assumed would happen between them this night. "Sink Lar, I did not consider that you may need more time. If you can't bond with me this night..." he started to say out of concern for his female, but she cut him off.

"Hush," she said gently as she pulled her hand free of his and pulled his face down to hers to kiss him, finally brave enough to nip at his lips until he opened for her to allow her to slip her tongue into his mouth to play against his own.

All words stopped forming in Lo'San's brain. All he knew was that his Sink Lar was tasting him, kissing his mouth, and it was the most wonderful thing he'd ever experienced, even better than when he'd kissed her this way before. This kiss, this tasting his mouth, she'd started, she wanted, and it made him deliriously happy. His purr kicked up again and he felt Synclare smile against his lips. "Why do you smile?" he whispered.

"Are you purring? Does that mean you're happy?" she asked.

Lo'San smiled. "The rumble? It does. I can try to silence it if you'd like it to stop, but I'm not sure that it won't start again," Lo'San said, thinking she didn't like it.

"No!" Synclare said, shaking her head quickly. "I like it."

Lo'San grinned happily and kissed her again.

"I love your kisses. Your tongue is..."

"Is what?" he asked when she stopped speaking.

"It's got ridges," she finally answered.

"Is that alright?" he asked.

"I think it's going to be amazing," she answered, confusing him.

While he tried to figure out what she referred to she spoke again.

"Lo'San?" she asked.

"Yes, my Sink Lar."

"I don't need time to adjust. I've had time. Plenty of time, and what I need now is to feel loved and valued. By you. I want you, and I need you to want me, too," she confessed.

Lo'San's gray eyes seemed to darken as he looked down into her very blue ones. His fingers grazed her collarbone as they found their way to the buttons of her blouse. "I have never wanted anything more than to complete our bond!" he insisted.

"Then do it," she invited.

"May I remove this?" he asked as his chest rumbled, ever the polite gentleman despite his apparent need.

Synclare placed her hands on top of his and gazed intently at him. "You don't have to ask me for permission."

His brow wrinkled as he thought about not asking if he could touch her.

"I love that you can be so strong in your profession, demand such respect in all that you do as a General, demand others carry out your commands, and then be so gentle with me." Synclare smiled at him. "You're such a contradiction. But, I won't break. And I trust you. If you want to undress me, undress me. I want to experience the passion you hide behind that control you've mastered so well."

"I don't wish to make you fear me," he admitted.

"You won't. I'm yours, as you are mine," she said. "We've just promised that." And to prove her point, she dropped her hands to the hem of his shirt and grasped it tightly before pulling it up over his chest.

Lo'San was surprised that his female was trying to undress him, and once he realized what she was trying to do, his purr grew deeper as he lifted his arms over his head and leaned slightly toward her so she could remove his uniform shirt. When he looked at her again, she was staring at him with her mouth hanging open.

"Sink Lar?" he asked.

Synclare heard him call her name and met his concerned gaze. "Oh my god. You're so beautiful!" she said, as her eyes left his face and she allowed herself the privilege of examining every inch of his exposed body.

Lo'San couldn't help himself, he sat a little straighter, puffed his chest out a little further, proud as she proclaimed her admiration for his appearance.

"I've never, ever seen a male like you," she said, reaching up to touch the ridges that followed the curve of his shoulders. They started at the shoulder joint and protruded in an uneven line all down his shoulder, to about mid arm, even with the beginning of where his bicep was. They were several shades darker than the silvery gray of his skin and tipped with white edges and points.

Synclare hesitated before she touched him, looking to him for confirmation that it was safe to touch them.

"May I?" she asked.

Lo'San chuckled at her and guided her hand to his shoulder. "Now who is asking for permission to touch that which belongs to her?" he teased.

Synclare ran her hands over the ridges, as she explored his body. "They aren't sharp," she commented.

Lo'San shook his head. "When in battle, they will sharpen and enlarge somewhat. But they will never do so when you touch me. They will not harm you."

Synclare allowed her fingers to trail from his shoulders down his arms and over the dark patches of skin that were scattered over them. "These are beautiful, too. I thought they'd be hard," she said, touching the darker patches of skin that scattered over his silvery flesh. "They look like armor plating."

"When in battle they do harden to protect me."

44

Synclare stroked the roughened patches on his arms again as her eyes followed the path to the rest of the darkened patches on his body. His lower belly was covered in them as well.

Lo'San's breath caught when she dragged her fingers over the darkened patches beneath his navel.

"They're just a little rougher than your skin," Synclare remarked.

Lo'San held himself tightly in check as his mate ran her hands over his body, touching and exploring. The lower part of his belly where the darker, rougher skin was, was extremely sensitive.

"Do these patches keep going beneath your clothing? Even lower, I mean?" she asked.

Lo'San swallowed audibly before giving her one single nod.

Synclare's eyes flared with excitement. "I want to see," she said on a hushed whisper.

Lo'San wasted no time in standing before her and unfastening his pants. He shoved them down his legs and stepped out of them, kicking them aside to stand proudly before his Sink Lar.

Synclare stroked his lower belly, watching as the darker plates on his skin rippled with her touch. Loving that his skin was so responsive to her touch, she didn't stop there, she continued her exploration, slowly, agonizingly slowly, to his long, swollen member, which was standing up rigidly, waiting for her attention. The dark skin stopped just at the base of his cock, the length of it the same silvery skin as most of his body.

"It would be too much for a female if my battle plates extended over my length," he said, as he watched her stroke his cock from base to tip.

His breathing grew ragged as she tortured him oh so sweetly with her touch.

Then she reached out with her other hand, tracing a line down from his navel to the base of his cock. "On Earth some of our males have a line of hair that grows here, in the middle of where your plates are located. We call it a happy trail."

45

Lo'San gave a lopsided grin. "Because what lies at the end of the trail can make you happy?" he asked.

"Exactly," she answered. "You, though. You give a whole other meaning to the phrase happy trail."

Synclare licked her lips as she held him in her hand, barely able to hold him still when he throbbed in response to her touch.

"I want to taste you, I want to feel you inside me, I want to fill my body with your scent. I want your claim, your mark, your scent enveloping me. I want to forget that anyone other than you ever touched me. Will you do that for me, my mate?" Synclare asked, canting her head to the side as she released her hold on him and hurriedly unbuttoned her shirt and dropped it to the floor before pushing her body hugging leggings down her legs.

Lo'San's purr stuttered into a soft growl. "Do you promise you will not be frightened of me?" he asked as he caught his lip between his teeth as he watched her reveal her body to him.

"I promise. Don't hold back," Synclare begged as she tried to fight free of the leggings still encircling her ankles. "I need to lose myself in you."

Chapter 5

Lo'San lunged for Synclare and she just managed to grab hold of him as one moment she was seated at the foot of the bed, and the next she was flat on her back — her head cradled on his pillow as a naked Lo'San held himself above her. With a steady growl, he ripped her tangled leggings away from her ankles, tossing them over his shoulder. He didn't speak, he didn't ask permission, and he didn't give it a second thought. His mate had asked him not to hold back, and he wouldn't.

Lo'San looked down at Synclare and ran a single finger down her body from her collar bone to her hip. Then he pushed himself back, sat on his heels and looked down at Synclare spread before him, panting, aroused, waiting for him to take her. He grasped one of her ankles in each hand and lifted them up and out, opening her to his perusal. "I have touched many females over the years, but never one such as you. Humans are not common this far from Earth," he admitted, letting go of her right ankle. "Hold your leg up," he instructed, so sure she'd do it, he didn't even check to be sure she complied. His eyes were glued to the soft flesh between her legs as he dragged his fingers through her folds.

Synclare smiled at the way he took control though just moments before he'd been asking for her permission. Control was more of a way of life for him than he realized, and it excited her more than she'd imagined.

The dampness that coated his fingers as he stroked her drew his attention. There were a few other species that self-lubricated, but for the most part, he hadn't even noticed if other females responded to him this way or not. Males of his kind provided a prelubrication that was ejaculated just prior to pushing their way into whichever female was willing to accommodate them. This made it possible for immediate mating should their female be attempting to accommodate more than one male in a short time span. In addition to that the fact that most females of his own species didn't enjoy sex unless they were in heat made the males' ability to lubricate the female themselves very handy. Lo'San pushed his fingers into Synclare and pulled his lips back in a snarl of arousal at the feel of her squeezing him. He experimented with her body to see how far she'd stretch before withdrawing his fingers and licking them clean.

Synclare began to pant more quickly, and her hips lifted toward him. "Oh my god, Lo'San," she whimpered.

"You are finding pleasure with me," he said, thrilled that she wanted him to touch her and wasn't just submitting. "What do you need to achieve release?" he asked, clearly not familiar with a human female's body.

"Touch me here," she whispered, rubbing her swollen clit.

Lo'San gently, but firmly, moved her hand away with his own, experimenting, applying pressure as he touched her, then stroking more lightly to find just the touch that made her moan the loudest. Once satisfied he knew the best way to stroke that part of her, he laid himself out on the bed and engulfed her with his mouth. Synclare cried out and pulled at the longer lengths of hair on top of his head as she held him to her. "Yes! This, I need this. I knew your tongue would be amazing," she said, rocking her hips to move her pussy against his tongue as he lapped at her. Lo'San licked and nibbled every part of her sensitive flesh he could find before finally settling in to concentrate on that one part of her body she'd indicated would bring her satisfaction. He used the fingers of one hand to press on either side of her swollen nub, making it stand out from her body so he could drag his tongue over it again and again until she was trembling and begging him to make her come.

He didn't let up, just continued with the constant stimulation his tongue gave her until she clamped her thighs down on either side of his head and a very sexy, very enticing keening sound found its way up and out of her throat. Lo'San kept licking her until her breathing began to settle, her thighs released him, and her hands moved from his head to his shoulders. He glanced from his new favorite place in the universe — between her legs — to see her expression.

Synclare was looking down at him as she licked her lips. Her hips were rocking gently as her body invited him to take it in any way he wanted. Synclare reached down and slipped her slender fingers around his bicep and pulled, letting him know she wanted him to move up her body.

As he did so, he stared into her eyes, stopping to kiss her stomach, dip his tongue into her navel, swipe his tongue across her pale nipples and watch them harden in response. Lo'San thought about Synclare telling him to take her, to mark her and make her his. She didn't want him to ask for permission, she just wanted him to take what was his. So he did.

He settled into place above her, looking down on his mate, loving the way she writhed beneath him waiting for him to possess her. He tilted his hips to adjust the heavy weight of his cock as it probed her body, looking for the entrance he knew was waiting for him.

As the swollen, wet slit of her body cradled his cock, he pulled back until the rounded head of his penis was stretched open at its own slit and a smaller, pointed gland, looking much like a longer, more pliable version of the ridges on his shoulders pushed through the opening.

Synclare's eyes widened as she watched the gland stretch itself toward her.

"I will not ever cause you pain," Lo'San promised.

Synclare didn't take her eyes off his cock, and she didn't indicate she heard, but she didn't flinch away, so surely some part of her had heard him. As she watched, the gland that extended from the head of his cock swelled and seemed to glisten and undulate, then released a slippery, clear substance, shooting several strong jets of it to completely cover her pussy in whatever the liquid was.

"To be sure you are ready, and that I don't tear you," he said before he rubbed himself in the liquid, then angled his hips again, and once lined up with her body shoved his way inside her with one strong thrust.

Synclare screamed when he entered her body, not accustomed to his girth or length, though the liquid did make entry slippery smooth.

Lo'San froze, looking down at her when she screamed. "Sink Lar?" he asked urgently.

"I'm okay. Just give me a second," she said, clenching and unclenching her vaginal muscles as she held him tightly inside her.

"I can expel more..." he said.

"I don't need it. Is that what it does, prepare me in case I'm not aroused?" she asked. But even as she said the words she felt the effects of whatever he'd doused her in. A deep-seated need began to gnaw away at her womb, her clit felt fevered and actually had an itching sensation growing inside or on it, or both, she wasn't sure exactly where the sensation was centered. Her nipples hardened and the tips needed to be touched so badly she teased them with her own fingers. Her eyelids became even heavier, dropping down halfway and shuttering her eyes as she pushed her hips up toward him. "It's like... organic Spanish fly," she said.

"Spanish fly?" he asked on a groan as she thrust against him again.

"A drug that makes you want to have sex," she explained on a whine. "It doesn't matter. I needed you before, but now I need you even more. Please, please hurry, you have to move, why aren't you moving?" she begged, letting go of her nipples to grab his head and stare into his eyes as she rocked her hips against him.

"Oh my gosh!" she said, realizing as she rubbed herself against him, that the rough plates on his lower belly and just above his cock stimulated her clit when she moved her hips just right. "This is so fucking good," she said, watching herself rub her clit against what was in effect his body armor.

"You cried out," he said. "Did I hurt you?"

50

"I'm going to cry out for a whole other reason if you don't move. Now. Hard. Fast! Now!" she demanded.

Lo'San pulled his hips back and thrust himself back inside her.

Synclare moaned and moved her hands to his hips, pushing him away from her before tightening her grip and pulling him back again. "More," she demanded.

Lo'San followed her lead, and it took only a few more thrusts until he was leaning over her, holding himself above her, forcing his cock inside her faster and harder than he even hoped he'd be able to. She was small. She was frail in comparison to females he was accustomed to that did this kind of thing for a living. He'd expected to have to be careful with her. But he'd been so wrong.

Synclare was like a wild thing, snarling and holding her upper body up off the bed with one arm so she could stare into his eyes as she met him thrust for thrust, making sure to press her clit against the plates right above his cock with each stroke. "Harder," she demanded. "Fuck me harder, harder!" she insisted, biting his lip between her teeth when she finally felt herself slipping over the edge into complete bliss.

"Don't stop, don't stop," she begged as she allowed her eyes to drift closed and her head to fall back as her body contorted and she came screaming his name as her muscles clamped down on his cock.

Lo'San shouted her name as he filled her full of his release, unable and unwilling to hold back.

Synclare's eyes popped open when she felt something she didn't expect as he filled her. His release was hot, hotter than her body temperature, so she'd felt him when he started to come. But, her eyes widened and she looked at him in shock as she tightened her thighs around his waist. "Oh my god," she whispered as the small swollen gland she'd watched bathe her pussy in his own personal lubricant, pushed its way deeper inside her and began to flick back and forth over her cervix. It was a feeling unlike any other she'd ever experienced. Then she felt it begin to push. "What's it doing?" she whimpered before it finally made itself so slender it was able to force its way into the opening of her tightly closed cervix. It could only be described as pleasure pain.

"I'm not finished," he whispered. "I'd hoped..." he started to say, but gave up all chance at speech when she tightened up around his cock again. He snarled and began to pump his hips again, filling her all over again. They stared into each other's eyes until she could take it no more, and slipped into another orgasm.

Only momentarily satisfied, Lo'San's breath was ragged as he held himself just far enough above Synclare so that he didn't crush her, but he stayed buried deep inside her. He rested his forehead on the pillow she lay on, and waited for her to recover enough for another round. There was no way he was even close to being done for the night, and from her exuberance he was pretty sure she wasn't either.

Lo'San sent up a silent thought of thanks to whichever creator made his female, this female. She clearly took pleasure from his touch, which was something completely unexpected. Most males of his kind never knew what it was like to have a female crave their touch, to beg them to give them more and more pleasure. Females of his kind only ever had sex when they decided they wanted to procreate, or when they wanted to tempt a male into doing their bidding. Lo'San took a deep breath, and shivered in surprise when Synclare pressed a kiss to the space between his neck and his shoulder. There was only a small bit of flesh there, nearer his neck, without his battle ridges, and she'd managed to find it.

"That was amazing," Synclare said huskily.

"I have never experienced such a thing," he admitted. "I have been blessed by the universe," he said, kissing her reverently.

Synclare savored his kiss, feeling her body come to life again. "The..., gland thing, what was it doing?" she asked.

"Bonding us, filling your most sacred places with my essence," he answered. "It is new for me, too," he admitted.

Synclare smiled at him and caressed his face. "Because you've never bonded with another," she said.

Lo'San nodded and kissed her.

"What was that liquid you put on me? Is it to make women unable to control their desires? Does it make me want to have sex?" she asked.

"No, it simply provides lubrication so that your body will accommodate mine. It happens naturally when I prepare to enter a female, I do not control it," he explained.

"Well, it does quite a bit more to me," Synclare said, tightening around him again.

Lo'San hissed as she squeezed him. "I'm... sorry?" he asked, not sure if she was unhappy about it or not.

"Oh no, no no. Don't apologize, just do it again. I want you again. I've never ever felt such pleasure, such ecstasy!" she admitted.

Lo'San wasted no time as he pulled out of her tight, hot sheath and rubbed himself against her again. All he had to do was poise himself to reenter her and his body should comply. If she wanted him to lubricate her again, he would. He'd give his female anything in any world that she wanted. "I don't know if you will have the same reaction or not, but I know that my body will lubricate yours each time I prepare to enter."

"Wait," Synclare said, pushing him up and off her.

Lo'San didn't hesitate to stop. He would never, ever force his female to take him if she didn't want to. He got his knees under him and sat back on his heels, waiting for her to finish adjusting her position as it seemed she was wont to do.

"Okay, now, hold still," Synclare said, her eyes flashing mischievously as she leaned over and took his cock in her hand at the same time she brought her mouth down over and around it.

Lo'San let out a surprised growl as he lifted up on his knees at the same time he thrust into her mouth. "Sink Lar!" he exclaimed, holding her head gently in his hands as she worked him with her lips and tongue and he gave short little thrusts, careful not to go too deep. "I cannot... possibly... hold... still!" he panted out as she increased the sweep of her tongue on him.

Synclare chuckled and took him so deep he was concerned, then she started humming, which added vibration to the feeling of her mouth on him.

"Sink Lar," he said on a hushed breath.

Synclare didn't respond, she just kept sucking and humming.

"Sink Lar!" he said more urgently. "You must stop, now!" he insisted, though the thrusting of his hips had picked up speed.

Finally, he braced his hands on her slender shoulders, forcing her to look up at him. "I need to be buried inside you. NOW!" he growled.

Synclare's eyes widened when she took in the sight of her male. His body had almost completely covered itself in armored plates, the ridges on his shoulders had risen further out of his skin, and the darker, shadowy spots she'd just barely been able to make out before on his temples and cheeks had gotten darker.

She let his throbbing cock pop free of her mouth. "I wanted to finish you this way," she said, looking at his beauty in awe.

"Next time. This time, I need to be inside you again," he growled.

Synclare nodded as he picked her up and deposited her onto her back again. He lined himself up with her body and rubbed against her for only a second before that same gland extended from the head of his penis and covered her in what he called lubrication.

Almost immediately Synclare began to feel the effects just like she had the first time. Her womb practically throbbed with need, her clit started to swell again and that deliciously insane itching sensation had returned to that tiny swollen bundle of nerves. She slid her hands up her body to her nipples and rolled them between her fingers. "Oh my god! It's happening again!" she said, throwing her head back and moaning as Lo'San pushed inside her.

Lo'San immediately started up a fast pace, hammering away as deeply as she could take him. "I think I will never get enough of you," he rushed out as he adjusted his hold on her to be able to push even deeper inside her. "Prepare yourself, Sink Lar. We may never leave this room!"

Chapter 6

Ba Re' had been relieved by one of his up and coming engineers, Gaishon, and returned to his quarters to wait for Elisha to arrive. It wasn't very long before he heard giggling outside his quarters, then the doors opened to reveal Vivian and a very inebriated Elisha.

"Hello Ba Re'," Vivian said, laughing when Elisha mimicked her greeting.

"Hello Baaa Raaayyy!" Elisha said. "Baaa Rayyyy. Kinda sounds like Barry, don't you think?" Elisha asked Vivian. "Barry!" Elisha called out, trying the name on for size. "Baaaarrrrryyyyyy!"

Elisha was leaning against Vivian and clearly was not in control of her faculties. "That's it! Your name is now Barry," she said, grinning at Ba Re'.

Ba Re' sighed. "How much did she drink?"

"Not enough to be dangerous. I think though, that maybe she didn't realize how much she was drinking because we were dancing so much. It seemed to really affect her once we started on our way back here," Vivian answered. "But don't be too angry. She's never been out with her friends before. She deserved to let go and have some fun."

Ba Re' nodded. "I am aware," he said tiredly.

"You alright?" Vivian asked.

"I will be. Just need some rest," Ba Re' answered, not wanting to burden Vivian with all the emotional fallout of living with an Ehlealah that had not allowed you to establish a bond.

"Alright. I'll leave you to it then. Make sure that she has some aspirin available when she wakes. And something sugary with electrolyte replacement in it. It will make her feel better sooner," Vivian said, chuckling when Elisha let go of her and reached out for Ba Re', clinging to him with one arm as she turned to face him, practically hanging off him as she grinned up at him. "Hi Barry. I love you. Do you know I love you? But my god you drive me insane sometimes!"

Then she turned to look at Vivian. "Is it just all the big, horny males around here? Are they all so damned possessive and grumbly?" Elisha asked.

Vivian nodded and laughed. "It's part of their charm."

"I think you need to get laid," Elisha said, focusing on Ba Re' again. "Let's get laid together," she said, letting go of Ba Re' and grabbing the hem of her shirt and trying to pull it off over her head, but got stuck inside it instead, as she stumbled around and Ba Re' tried to balance her.

"On that note, I'm going to leave the two of you alone," Vivian said.

"Good night, Vivian," Ba Re' said, guiding his still stuck Ehlealah toward their bedroom.

"Bye!" Elisha called from inside her shirt as the doors to their quarters closed behind Vivian.

"Elisha, Ehlealah, let me help you before you trip and fall," he said, grasping her arms where they stuck out of the top of her shirt and one at a time removing them from her shirt before pulling it off her body.

"Oh my gosh! Thank you! I thought I was just going to have to live in there!" Elisha said, throwing her arms around Ba Re'. "You know? You're pretty sexy, Barry."

Ba Re' smiled despite himself. "I am happy you think so. Now, let's get you into bed."

"Ooh, yes. Bed. Tell me, Barry, what do you plan to do to me? All the wicked things I've heard males like you want to do?"

Ba Re' shook his head as he guided her to their bedroom. "A month of nights would not be enough to allow me to do all the things I want to do to you, and have you do to me. But this is not the first of those nights," he said, removing the rest of her clothes and literally lifting her off her feet and placing her in bed.

"But why not? I want you. You want me. We are always talking about mating, but there's always a reason we shouldn't. No more reasons why we shouldn't. Let's just do it. Now! Right now! Take me, Barry!" she said, throwing the covers off her body and flinging her arms and legs out to her sides.

"It's Ba Re', Ehlealah. And I can't. You must accept my claim as readily as I give it. It would not be honorable for me to extract that claim from you while you are not thinking clearly."

"You're going to miss your chaa-aance!" she singsonged on a yawn.

Ba Re' smiled down at her as he covered her once more and tucked her back into bed.

"Sleep, Ehlealah. We will speak when you wake." He pressed a kiss to her cheek as she closed her eyes and quieted almost immediately. Ba Re' went into their cleansing chamber, gathered two aspirin from the small bag she kept her toiletries in and placed them on the table on her side of the bed, then he went to their galley and retrieved a sugary drink as Vivian had directed him. He placed it on the bedside table as well. Ba Re' looked down at his sleeping Ehlealah for only a moment longer before deciding to go find something to keep his mind off Elisha for a little while.

"Missy?" Ba Re' said as he walked through their quarters.

"Yes, Lieutenant Commander Ba Re' Non Tol."

"Is Sire Zha Quin Tha still on duty?"

"Yes, Lieutenant Commander, he is."

"Thank you. I am leaving my quarters to return to duty, please monitor my Ehlealah in my absence. She is sleeping. If you detect that she needs anything, please let me know."

"Of course, Lieutenant Commander."

"Thank you, Missy." Ba Re' left his quarters knowing that if he stayed, and Elisha continued to offer herself to him, he might just take her up on it. It was better for them both if he left her to sleep off her state of inebriation, before he did something irreversible and they both ended up resentful.

~~~

Vivian stopped outside the door to the quarters she and Quin shared. She placed her hand on the scanner at the same time she glanced over her shoulder toward what appeared to be an empty corridor. "You can go home now," she called out.

It was only a moment before a male with deep violet colored skin and bright amethyst eyes stepped out of the shadows to face her. "You know we can't leave you unattended. Sire Zha Quin Tha is not here, and we are sworn to protect you, Sirena," Zahn said.

"I'm perfectly safe aboard this ship, Zahn. It's not necessary for you to have to babysit me at all times," Vivian said.

"It's my job, Sirena, and I'm sworn to perform it. Please allow me to," Zahn said, matter-of-factly.

"I know. I just feel bad that you're always standing around waiting for me. Or for danger."

Zahn had taken over leadership of Vivian's private guard when Vor met his Ehlealah. It should have only been a short while until Vor and Li'Orani bonded, and Vor would have returned. But Li'Orani wanted to go home to visit her mother before accepting any further changes in her life, much the same as Ada Jane had wanted to go home before bonding with Kol. So, Vor had escorted her to her home planet. He would be back, without a doubt he'd be back, but until then, and maybe afterward depending on Vor and Li'Orani's needs, Zahn had stepped up and done a wonderful job.

"You are always safe here, Sirena, because we do our jobs well. Feel thankful. We do," Zahn answered.

"Alright, then. Thank you for all you do, Zahn. Good night," Vivian said.

"Good night, Sirena. Sleep well," Zahn answered.

"Good night, Rel," Vivian added as her doors opened to grant her entry.

"Good night, Sirena," Rel called out, yet remained tucked away in the shadows.

Vivian smiled then walked into her quarters allowing her doors to close and Zahn and Rel to get down to the business of guarding her.

"Missy?" she said, as she walked through her home, taking off earrings and undressing on her way to the cleansing chamber.

"Yes, Vivian," Missy answered.

"Please let Quin know that I'm home," Vivian said.

A few moments later Missy spoke again. "I've advised Commander Tel Mo' Kok that you are home."

"Thank you, Missy. Good night," Vivian said as she stepped into the shower.

"Good night, Vivian," Missy answered.

~~~

Quin was surprised when Ba Re' walked through the doors of the Command Deck. "Ba Re'? Are you still on duty?" Quin asked.

"I'm back on duty, here to relieve you. Go home," Ba Re' answered.

"You've been on duty as long as I. Go back to your Elisha. Speak with her as we discussed," Quin said.

"This is not the time. She returned from her girls' night inebriated and offering herself to me," Ba Re' explained.

"Was Vivi inebriated as well?" Quin asked, standing from his command chair, concerned about her getting home safely.

"No, she was not. She escorted Elisha home, then left to go home herself. You should go home to your Ehlealah," Ba Re' said.

"You should go home to yours," Quin countered. "I have worked much longer shifts than this. It is not a hardship for me."

"Commander?" Missy asked, interrupting their conversation.

"Yes, Missy," Quin answered.

"Sirena Vivian wishes that I advise you she is home and safe."

"Thank you, Missy," Quin responded, smiling to himself at Vivian's thoughtfulness to let him know she'd returned to their

60

quarters. He returned his attention to Ba Re'. "You see? My Vivi is home, I can stay here."

Ba Re' shook his head. "It's best for me to be away from Elisha. She is not thinking clearly and it's very difficult to continue to refuse her... offers."

"It will not last, Ba Re'. She will come around," Zha Quin promised.

Ba Re' simply nodded, unwilling to discuss it any further. "Go home to Vivian," he repeated.

"If you're sure," Quin answered.

"Absolutely. Go home."

"Very well. Thank you, Ba Re'. I will not be long. I will take a short rest and return before Lo'San is scheduled to return to duty in the afternoon."

"Do not rush. I am in no hurry. I cannot rest anyway, I may as well be here," Ba Re' answered.

Quin patted his old friend on the shoulder. "It will get better," he said encouragingly.

"It has to," Ba Re' answered.

Quin turned and headed toward the doors.

Ba Re' looked down at the sleeping mountain of spotted fur on the floor beside the Command Deck and called out. "Quin!"

Quin paused and looked back at Ba Re'.

"You forgot your Kitty."

Quin shook his head. "Kitty!" he said loudly enough to wake Vivian's pet.

Kitty opened his eyes but gave no indication that he planned on moving.

"Come, Kitty," Quin insisted.

Kitty yawned and stretched, but otherwise didn't move.

"Fine. Stay here, I'm going home without you," Quin snapped and walked through the doors that whooshed open at his approach.

Kitty scrambled to his feet and bounded after Quin, knowing that home meant Vivian. Finally his person would be there waiting for him and give him lots of pets and scratches.

~~~

Synclare gradually woke and stretched her body as she turned over beneath the heavy warm blankets covering her. She settled back in to sleep a bit longer, then became acutely aware of a warm body right behind her. Her eyes popped open and her breath caught as it took her a moment to remember the last evening's occurrences. Lo'San. Her Lo'San was at her back, sound asleep.

Synclare smiled to herself as she turned to look at him, laying her head on the pillow beside his. He was beautiful. His gray lashes lying against pale silver-gray skin, and the messy tousle of his tuft of white hair put her in the mind of an angel asleep in the bed next to her. His cheekbones were chiseled and high, yet not so prominent that they looked unnatural. His lips were only a bit darker than his skin color and pursed in his sleep like a petulant toddler. And as she admired him, his eyes fluttered open and focused on her.

"Morning," she whispered.

"Good morning, my mate," he responded, reaching out a hand beneath the covers to curl around her waist and pull her closer against him. Lo'San kissed her forehead and curled his body around hers, preparing to drift off to sleep again. Then his eyes popped open again. "I should be on duty!" he said urgently.

"Well, can't you call them or something?" Synclare asked.

"It is Sire Tel Mo' Kok I relieve from duty! I must report at once," he said, jumping from bed and scrambling to pull his clothes on.

Synclare sat up in bed, holding the blankets against her chest to cover her nakedness, and watched him hurry to dress.

Once he'd finished, he rushed to the door, then rushed back, taking her face in his hands and kissing her passionately. "I love you, my Sink Lar. I'll make arrangements for a bigger home for us, and I'll request time off as is allowed to all newly mated males aboard this ship. But I must go now. I will return as soon as I can," Lo'San promised.

Synclare kissed him back and smiled at his promises. "It's alright. Do what you have to and find me when you're done."

Lo'San nodded and kissed her again before rushing away.

Synclare looked around the small, cramped room Lo'San had chosen for his own, and realized there was nothing at all personal about the room. The only thing that showed it was lived in were the extra blankets on the bed, and the clothes in the storage unit. All else was regulation as it had been built. "I'll make him a real home," Synclare said to herself as she got out of bed and walked the few steps into the cleansing chamber. She got cleaned up, put her clothes from the previous night back on, and made her way to the quarters she'd been assigned. They were small, too, but not as military regulation as Lo'San's were. Once there she changed clothes, brushed her teeth and headed to the commissary for breakfast, all the while wearing a perpetual smile. She was a mated female now. Married for all intents and purposes, and very happily so — she loved her husband dearly.

~~~

Lo'San went straight to the Command Deck, surprised when he stepped through the doors and found Ba Re' at the helm.

"My apologies for arriving late," Lo'San said, striding toward the command chair.

"What are you doing here?" Ba Re' asked, turning from where he stood over Vennie examining a chart Vennie had prepared for him to view.

"I'm on duty. I was to relieve Sire Tel Mo' Kok. It is my responsibility you had to be called in my stead. I offer my sincere apologies, Lieutenant Commander," Lo'San said.

"Unless I'm sadly mistaken, you claimed your mate last night," Ba Re' said.

Lo'San couldn't help but grin, and he gave a single nod as he stood ramrod straight, his stance one of military precision just as he was known for. "I did."

"Then you have time alloted to you to complete that process. Go back to her. Now. I'm on deck until our Sire returns."

"But..." Lo'San said, not quite sure how he felt about not having received formal approval to take leave to tend his bond with his mate.

"Quin and I both watched our females last night. We saw you leave with Synclare. We are aware of your mating. You should be with her," Ba Re' said. "And congratulations, General. I personally wish you every happiness."

Lo'San smiled. "Thank you, Lieutenant Commander."

"While normally, I wouldn't consider ordering you about for any reason... you do outrank me," Ba Re' said, "But under the circumstances — Go! You have no business on duty for at least a week. Leave me!" Ba Re' ordered, pointing to the doors.

Lo'San grinned. "Understood. And thank you." Lo'San spun on his heel and wasted no more time arguing about where he should be at the moment. He knew exactly where he needed to be — beside Sink Lar. Then he remembered his quarters and the fact that they were far from sufficient for his female. "Oh!" he said, turning back to Ba Re'. Ba Re' was head of engineering. His department included assignment of quarters, though he did not handle it personally — he had those who handled such things for him. "I will be applying for new quarters this day."

"There are several available in the same corridor as Quin's and Kol's quarters. We are holding Kol's quarters for his eventual return, but, other than that, any other empty one is available. Stop by my offices and get a list to review. I'll let Gaishon know you'll be in and that you are to be assigned any you choose," Ba Re' said. "It's about time you upgraded to one suiting your position anyway."

Lo'San gave a nod. "Thank you."

Ba Re' stood watching Lo'San as he turned and headed away from the Command Deck as quickly as he'd rushed onto it. He was happy for the male. Lo'San was a very private, very controlled male, but none better in character and loyalty could be found. He deserved good things.

Chapter 7

Quin reached out in his semi-sleep state and attempted to pull Vivian to him, only to find her place beside him warm and fluffy. He opened his eyes to see Kitty lying on his back with his feet in the air, looking right back at him.

"Why are you in my bed?" Quin grumbled.

Kitty simply mrowled at him and swished his tail.

Quin muttered under his breath about furry shralers that didn't know their places as he climbed out of bed and went in search of his Ehlealah.

Vivian was sitting on the sofa sipping her litah and reading one of her old, faded, paperback romance novels when she heard Quin enter the room. She turned to watch him walk toward her and sighed happily. "You are quite a sight to see," she admitted, watching the huge, red, horned male she called mate as he made a beeline for her.

"Is that good?" he asked, sinking down on the sofa beside her and planting his head on her lap.

"It's very good," she answered, leaning over to kiss his lips before sitting up again.

"Did you enjoy your girls' night?" he asked.

"I did. Very much. But the next time you send someone to watch over me, in addition to the guards already intent on following me, I'll not be giving you a good morning kiss the next day."

Quin considered feigning surprise and denying the whole thing, but almost as quickly gave up the pretense. "Fine. But in my defense, you tried to give your guards the evening off. So I had no choice other than to make other arrangements."

"And those arrangements were assigning Lo'San to babysit us," Vivian said.

"At least I did not tag along myself. I thought it more acceptable if someone else did it," Quin answered.

"It was. Thank you for that much. But, that club was filled with your males, Rokai's Elite team members, and Zahn and Rel. No one there wishes me harm. You are too paranoid," Vivian said. "Had we been elsewhere, I'd have asked you to assign more security, but here, no one wishes to hurt me, Quin."

Quin nodded. "True, but, we very often have dignitaries aboard, and they can be from any variety of places, and have differing beliefs. Not all are as closely allied as we'd like. It is best if we never, ever relax our security measures. Do you understand my concern for your safety, Ehlealah? I would be inconsolable and uncontrollable if anything ever happened to you," he said, sitting up so he could look at her and take her hand in his.

Vivian nodded. "I do. I just get tired of all the security sometimes. I just want to be plain old me once in a while," she answered. "It gets tiring having to make such an event out of just going to get something to eat at the commissary. Sometimes I just stay here all day because it's not worth the effort to let everyone know I'm preparing to leave here, and all that it entails."

"I do understand, Vivi. I do," Quin said.

Vivian smiled at Quin and closed her book, leaning over to place it on the coffee table before getting to her feet. "Would you like a cup of litah?" she asked.

"If we have some left, I would prefer a cup of your Earth coffee," Quin answered.

"We do. I'll get you some," she answered, walking into the galley. Minutes later she was back with two cups, one refilled with litah for her, and one with coffee for Quin. She handed it to him and then sat beside him. "Have you heard from General Lo'San?" she asked.

"No, but I believe he and Synclare are finally mated," Quin answered.

Vivian's brows scrunched low over her eyes as she regarded him. "How do you know that?" she asked.

Quin didn't answer right away, then decided honesty was best, or at least semi-honesty. "Ba Re' was watching on the security screens because Elisha has not allowed him to claim her yet and she insisted on going with you on your girls' night."

Vivian shook her head. "You Cruestaci give a whole new meaning to the word stalker, ya know?" she asked.

"What is a stalker?" Quin asked.

"You, minus the love and devotion," she answered. "Anyway, back to the point. He's going to get time off even though he's your second won't he?" Vivian asked.

"He will. Each male gets ten days, unless there are extenuating circumstances which dictate he needs more."

"Like what?" Vivian asked.

When Quin didn't answer because he was trying to find a way to explain it that wouldn't directly point out what Vivian and most of the humans aboard had lived through, Vivian figured it out herself.

"Like me, you mean," she said. "If the woman needs more attention or care because of what she's been through."

Quin nodded. "I am not sure how recovered Synclare is. Lo'San may need more time with her..."

"She won't. I mean, he may want more time, but Synclare has had her eye on Lo'San for a while now. She's a lot stronger than you'd imagine. She was used to spending time on Earth alone, and relying only on herself. She's always had to deal with people around her because they wanted something from her. She's a survivor," Vivian said.

"Good. With Kol on Earth, and Ba Re' struggling with his own Ehlealah, it makes covering the Command Deck difficult at best. I am pleased to know that Lo'San will have an easy transition and be able to return to duty in the standard amount of time," Quin said. Then he heard himself. "I must consider the ship, you understand?" he asked Vivian. "It is not that I am not concerned for our people, or intolerant of their matings and needs."

"I understand, Quin. And you care more about your people than anyone I know. I completely understand."

Vivian set her cup of litah on the coffee table and stood up. "Do you have time to have breakfast with me in the commissary?"

Quin smiled broadly, causing her to chuckle because it still looked like a grimace to her. "I will be most happy to share breakfast with you."

~~~

Synclare had just taken her seat at the table she always shared with her friends when Lo'San entered the commissary on the hunt for his mate.

"Sink Lar!" he called out as he quickly covered the distance to where she was sitting alone.

Synclare rose from her seat and met him a few feet from the table, throwing herself into his arms as he kissed her. "That was fast!" she said.

"Ba Re' had already relieved Zha Quin when I arrived. They were aware of our mating, and insisted I return to you for our standard mating period."

"Really?! I get to have you all to myself for a few days?" she asked excitedly.

"Ten days," he confirmed.

"Yay!" she said, looking up at him as she beamed with happiness. "Are you hungry? Do you want breakfast?" she asked.

"Yes. Very hungry," he said, his eyes flaring as he thought about why he'd awakened so hungry. "You stole all my energy," he teased.

Synclare smiled up at him not even blushing as she too remembered their night together.

"You sit," he said, indicating the table she'd left her food on. "I'll get my meal and be right back."

"Okay," Synclare answered, going up on tiptoe so he'd lean toward her and allow her to kiss him.

"After we eat, we will go choose our new quarters. It will be in the same corridor as Zha Quin and his Ehlealah."

69

"Yes! I'm so excited! Is there one we are assigned to?" she asked.

"No, we can choose any available in that corridor," Lo'San answered, happy to see her excitement at the idea of choosing their home together.

"Hurry! Get your food! I want to go find our new place!" Synclare said.

Lo'San chuckled at her exuberance and went to the serving line to get his meal. Moments later he was seated beside Synclare as they whispered and flirted over their meals. They were so focused on one another they didn't notice Quin and Vivian as they walked by.

"Congratulations, Synclare and General Lo'San," Vivian said.

Both looked up at her. "Thank you!" Synclare said.

"Thank you, Sirena," Lo'San said, getting to his feet respectfully.

"I'm just Vivian," Vivian said. "Especially if you're going to be mated to Synclare, calling me Sirena all the time will just make it all feel more formal."

"Then I am simply Lo'San. General is just as formal," Lo'San said, giving her a quick, little bow.

"Deal," Vivian agreed.

"I wish all happiness upon you, Lo'San, and you as well, Synclare. You are truly blessed."

"Thank you, Zha Quin," Lo'San answered.

"Thank you," Synclare echoed.

"In the event you've not been advised, you are officially off duty for your mating period," Quin informed him.

"Lieutenant Commander Ba Re' advised me this morning. I reported for duty and he promptly sent me back to my mate."

"Only you would claim your female and try to report to duty the next morning," Quin said with a smile.

"Not true, you did the same," Lo'San pointed out.

"I have no choice," Quin pointed out. "You do. Take the time, my friend."

"I will. Thank you, Zha Quin."

As Quin and Vivi walked away to sit at their own table, Quin stopped and looked back. "Your quarters, Lo'San," he started.

"Already addressed. We are going to tour several near yours as soon as we finish our meals," Lo'San said.

"You should have upgraded sooner," Quin said, shaking his head.

"Wasn't necessary. I was only there to sleep. Now I have a reason," he answered, looking lovingly at Synclare.

Vivian waved at Synclare as she placed her plate of food on her favorite table top and Quin finally took his place beside her. Synclare waved back and then completely tuned out everything else as Lo'San whispered something in her ear and she giggled in response.

"Do you think we look like that to others?" Vivian asked as Quin reached over taking a small bite of her omelet, before sampling the other foods on her plate.

Quin followed her gaze and smiled when he saw Lo'San and Synclare totally oblivious to everything in the room but one another. "No," he said. "We look even more lost in each other. Our love is the greatest of all, there is no equal," he said, placing his hand under her chin to pull her closer for a kiss. "None greater," he repeated as he kissed her senseless.

~~~

Lo'San followed Synclare into the first apartment they'd toured. They'd walked up and down the corridor and each time Synclare had paused outside its door. She was pulled toward this one it seemed.

"Oh, Lo'San, I love this one!" Synclare exclaimed. "It's got more room than we'll ever need. And it's got a kitchen! I could cook for you! Well, if I learn how to cook," she confessed.

Lo'San laughed. "We call it a galley. And it is not necessary, my Sink Lar. We can take our meals in the commissary."

"True, but, there may be times we don't want to leave home. Maybe I'll learn to cook just a little," she said, rushing back to Lo'San and hugging him as he pulled her in to him.

He looped his fingers with hers as they walked through the apartment, looking into the cleansing chamber. "It has two showers rather than a tub," Synclare observed.

"I believe Zha Quin has begun to install both our cleansing units, and a shower which functions on water in each family living quarters. Not all have baths, but we continue to look until we locate one with a bath if you'd prefer."

Lo'San watched Synclare walking around the bathroom, running her fingertips over the counter top before shaking her head. "I don't need a bath. I actually prefer showers."

They walked into the bedroom and Synclare gave a squeal of delight as she ran across the room and threw herself onto the larger than king sized bed. "This bed is huge!" she exclaimed.

"Do you like it?" he asked.

"I do, but, maybe we should try it out together to make sure there's enough room," Synclare teased, giving him a sultry look.

"That can be arranged," Lo'San answered, lying beside her and quickly rolling her beneath him.

Synclare smiled up at Lo'San looming over her. She raised a hand to cup his cheek and closed her eyes when he lowered his head to kiss her. Synclare kissed him slowly, enjoying every sensation to be had from their shared kiss.

Lo'San finally pulled away just enough to look into her eyes. "I still cannot believe that you are mine," he said.

"Forever and ever," she said, smiling up at him.

"Do you like this home, Sink Lar? Or would you like to see others. There are more in this corridor, and still more on the next corridor over," Lo'San said.

"I like this one. I like the location, and I like the feel of it. Both times I walked past I felt the need to stop here. It feels right."

"Then it is ours," Lo'San said, kissing her again before sitting up and sliding off the bed as he pulled her behind him.

"We will return to Engineering to have it officially assigned to us."

Synclare followed along happily. "I'm so excited!"

"We can order supplies for our galley, our cleansing chamber, and anything else you may want, then return here to put our belongings away," Lo'San said as they walked out of the bedroom.

"Wait, what's that door go to?" Synclare asked, noticing another door down a short hallway.

Lo'San followed her and stood in the doorway as she walked around the smaller room.

"Is it another bedroom?" she asked.

"It is. These are the family living quarters in this section of the ship. It is assumed those quartered here will have, or already have young ones," Lo'San said.

Synclare's smile lost some of its luster as she looked around the room.

"Sink Lar?" Lo'San asked, hurrying toward her. "Why have you stopped smiling?"

Synclare opened her mouth to answer as she shrugged but nothing came out. She wasn't exactly sure how, or if, she wanted to explain.

"Tell me, Sink Lar. There is no reason for sadness. If you do not wish to have the extra room, we can find another place the size of Zha Quin's. His quarters are larger even than these, yet they have no extra room."

Synclare shook her head. "Do you know how old I am?" she asked.

Lo'San shook his head, confused at her question. "I do not. It matters not."

"But it does — it might," she said.

"It does not," Lo'San said firmly.

"I'm past my child bearing years. If it's a family you want with children, I most likely won't be able to give you that," she said solemnly.

"Sink Lar, I did not bond with you for the sake of young ones. I bonded with you because I could not bear the thought of

73

waking without you at my side ever again. I was not whole."
Lo'San took her in his arms. "Now, with you in my arms, standing beside me, I am whole."

"But, what if you want children one day? What if you want a family and I can't give you that. I'm not as young as some of the other women rescued..."

Lo'San looked at his mate. He listened to her words, and watched her face when she spoke and realized this was about more than what he might want. "Do you wish to have young ones, Sink Lar?"

Synclare shook her head sadly. "I don't think I can. It's too late for me. But can you be happy with that?" she asked.

"I am happy as we are. But I think you have become so comfortable here that you've forgotten something," he said with a hint of a smile.

"What do you mean?" Synclare asked.

Lo'San grinned. "Look around you, my female. You are not on Earth. If you wish for a young one, our healers can give us young ones. It is a simple thing, really."

Synclare's face registered surprise. "They can?" she asked, tears beginning to shimmer in her eyes.

"They can. It is a common practice among females who are not able to easily conceive. If you want young ones, we will have young ones," he insisted, still holding her in his arms.

Synclare looked around the room again before meeting Lo'San's gaze. "So, this could be our nursery, for our babies?" she asked excitedly.

Lo'San looked around the room then smiled at her while nodding. "This is our nursery for our young ones. Our babies," he said. "However many you wish to have."

"Do you want children... young ones?" Synclare asked.

"I have never considered it. But with you at my side, I find I wish for a family with many young ones," Lo'San answered.

"Me, too," Synclare confessed. "And I never really wanted children until I met you. Back on Earth I had everything money could buy, and more money than I'd ever need, but my family, my so called friends... all they wanted was that money. They didn't care about me, or anything I felt or needed, as long as I continued to provide for them. I couldn't see bringing a child into a family like that."

"It sounds as though you never had a family. I sometimes feel I did not have one either."

"I didn't, not really. At least not after my father died. He loved me. He left everything to me when he died, and he was extremely wealthy. My stepmother, my aunt, and all my extended family, all they wanted was what I could give them."

"It is sad for them that they never took the time to see you as the female you are. But I am not that unfortunate. I see you, Sink Lar. I want you, your love, your heart, and our young ones."

Synclare nodded and kissed Lo'San. "I see you, too. And I love you."

"We shall fill our home with young ones," Lo'San said, kissing Synclare gently and holding her to him as he realized just how lucky he was to have this female that had not even been appreciated by those who should have loved her.

Chapter 8

Three months later...

Lo'San stood on the Command Deck, watching on the over-sized vid screen as supplies were unloaded in the cargo bay of Command Warship 1. He was every inch the strong, stoic, take no prisoners kind of General he'd always been. His crew was sharp and on point, eager to make themselves a mirror image of the efficiency he projected.

He kept a critical eye on the arrivals of supply containers being loaded to be sure nothing was amiss. There was always the chance that those who didn't care for the Cruestaci could try to sabotage the flagship of their fleet by slipping in a weaponized package of some sort. He nodded to himself slowly as he saw Elite Warrior Re'Vahl stop a container that didn't match their anticipated inventory lists.

Re'Vahl insisted it be returned to the ship making their delivery, much to the chagrin of those who'd delivered it. A ping sounded on the tablet he kept with him when on duty, and on looking at it was pleased to see that Re'Vahl had immediately advised him of the rejected container, as was protocol.

Since becoming more aware of Re'Vahl when he planned to attempt a mating with Synclare, he'd paid more attention to the male. And he'd been quite impressed. He was a trustworthy male — strong of character, brave, honest, hardworking, with a skill set that made him more dangerous than most all of the Elite Warriors. When you added to that a good disposition and integrity, it equaled what Lo'San thought they needed to be on the lookout for — a male that could be promoted and begin training for a position as Lieutenant General. One that could step up and fill one of the places that Elite Commander Kol Ra' Don

Tol had vacated, as a relief officer for those who ran Command Warship 1.

Lo'San watched as Re'Vahl moved across the docking bay, pointing and shouting out orders to the dock workers who just naturally responded to his authoritative nature, though he was not a permanent part of their management. Lo'San pursed his lips as he considered his thoughts. Maybe he was wrong. Maybe Elite Warrior Re'Vahl wasn't to be trained as a sometimes relief officer for his and Zha Quin's post. Maybe he would be better served as being trained as an equal. Sharing in the responsibilities that came with the position on a regular basis.

The communication device strapped to Lo'San's wrist vibrated, letting him know that Synclare was trying to reach him. Lo'San looked down at his wrist and smiled at the image on his communicator. Synclare was standing outside the medical suite, and she'd taken a photo of herself smiling at her communicator with her fingers crossed and the medical suite in the background.

Synclare had explained to him that when she'd been on Earth, it was quite popular for its people to photograph themselves in all manner of activity and send those photos to their friends and family, or post them on what they called social networks. He didn't quite understand the point, but he did know that today was important to Synclare, and even if it wasn't, he always enjoyed looking at photos of his female.

They'd decided they wanted a young one, a child as Synclare called them, right away. She'd been undergoing treatments for the last two weeks in hopes of preparing her to carry and deliver their young. But to date, her hormone levels had not allowed for the processes they required. In short, they needed to harvest one of her ovum, but her blood work indicated that she had not produced any ovum, regardless of the hormone therapy they'd given her to cause her to produce them. Doc was not completely sure of the reason for her body's lack of response. But, he was learning the human body as he went. He was so much more schooled on the anatomy of humans than he had once been, but this was the first human female that he'd attempted fertility treatments on. Lo'San had not explained to Synclare that it should have been a simple one time treatment, and he'd instructed the healer not to tell her either. He didn't want to upset her by telling her it hadn't worked the first three times and that was actually unheard of. He'd encouraged her to keep trying, but was puzzled himself as to the delay.

He typed a quick message to Synclare telling her he loved her, then turned to his tablet, tapping out a message to Re'Vahl to come to the Command Deck later that afternoon when he was finished with logging in the supply receipts, and the rest of his shift on duty. Then he sent another to Zha Quin asking for a meeting with him as soon as he could. Finished with what he felt was important for the time being, he called out to his crew.

"I'll be away from the deck momentarily. I am at all times available. Contact me with anything you feel can't wait the few minutes until I return."

"Yes, General," several of his higher ranking crew answered at once.

His crew was highly adept at their own particular jobs and ran as a well-oiled machine. He was usually there to oversee them, but they could operate without him for short periods of time. He was always only a com away regardless. He threw another glance at the vid-screen and assured that Re'Vahl had things on the docking bay well in hand, then he left the Command Deck with a reminder to his crew. He held his tablet up as he walked through the doors and spoke over his shoulder without looking back, reaffirming they'd know to com him if he was needed. "I'm on standby if needed!"

~~~

Synclare walked into medical a little more nervous than she'd been the first time she'd come in for her treatment. It was a simple process really; she received several injections, and then she went home and waited for her ovum to be produced. The injection was nothing at all to endure, in fact, it was pretty much painless, just a tiny sting. But the aftereffects were horrible. She suffered with nausea, headaches, cramping, her body shivering and cold. She'd always had Lo'San to take her home and tuck her into bed, but this time, she'd insisted he tend to his duties, she could handle it alone. She wanted to be strong for him, not a constantly needy female.

"Synclare," Doc said as she entered his domain. "Welcome. Shall we begin?" he asked.

Synclare took a deep breath. "Yes. I'm ready."

"Do you have more of the medications I prescribed for the aftereffects at home, or need I give you more?" he asked, as he escorted her to one of the examination rooms.

"I have enough for today, but maybe you could send a little more home with me just in case," she suggested, knowing that each of the last three times the effects had gotten progressively worse.

"Of course," Doc answered.

He held her hand as she walked up the set of three, small, metallic steps that enabled her to sit on the examination bed. In order to make her more comfortable, he'd lined the examination table with a pad and a sheet to give it a bit more softness as opposed to the simple table the warriors were accustomed to.

"Now, if you'll lie back, I'll take the samples we need, and then before you go we'll administer your next injection."

Synclare nodded and began to lie back just as someone knocked on the door.

"This room is occupied!" Doc said, raising his voice to convey his irritation.

"Sink Lar?" Lo'San's voice called.

"In here," Synclare called back.

The door opened and Lo'San stepped through smiling broadly at his Sink Lar. He loved her so much it hurt sometimes.

"Aren't you supposed to be on duty?" Synclare asked, secretly thrilled that he'd come to be with her though she'd told him he didn't need to.

"I am on duty," he said, holding up his tablet before setting it on the one chair in the room and walking over to her. He took her hand in his and leaned over to kiss her lips.

"I'm happy you're here," she confessed as Doc raised the supports that allowed for her legs to be elevated while he took the vaginal swab he used, along with blood samples to check for hormonal levels that indicated she was ovulating.

"Always beside you," he said, smiling down at her. Lo'San did his best to ignore the fact that the healer was viewing a part of his female that should not ever be viewed by anyone but him. Despite the fact that he understood the male was a male of medicine and was attempting to help them conceive, he couldn't stop the slight rumble that slipped from his chest.

"I'm merely performing a medical procedure," Doc said immediately in response to Lo'San's clear sign of irritation.

"I am aware, Healer. Forgive my natural tendencies," Lo'San responded, as Doc lowered the supports and returned her legs to the examination table, pulling out the extension of the table to support her legs as they lay relaxed now.

"We need only take a bit of blood for testing, then the injection and you can go," Doc said, explaining what he was doing. He'd gotten into the habit of doing so even with the warriors he treated for whatever their needs were. He'd started doing so at Sirena Vivian's request with the females he treated, and found the warriors liked it as much as they did. It apparently put them at ease to know he was tending them as an individual and not just another body.

Doc took his blood sample, then left the examination room. "Give me one moment," he said, quietly closing the door behind himself. Doc went to his small lab and ran the blood test to be sure Synclare wasn't ready to be harvested. His face scrunched up in frustration as he looked at the hormone count displayed on the clear holovid board just above his workstation. He just didn't understand it. Synclare's hormone levels were all over the place. Each time she came in they were far too high to allow her reproductive cycle to produce ovum for him to harvest.

Shaking his head, he prepared another injection to administer to the hopeful female, and laid the vaginal sample aside to prepare for testing after she'd left his offices and returned comfortably to her own quarters to recover. The treatments were causing her to become brutally ill afterward, despite the fact that he'd reduced the strength of the treatments to allow for her being human. He wondered again if perhaps that was the problem. But he feared if he increased the hormone levels, she would become severely ill and possibly endanger her own health. After preparing the injection, he pasted a smile on his face and returned to the examination room.

Doc paused outside the door and listened to the soft laughter coming from the room. Lo'San was relating some story from his childhood that had her laughing at the antics of Lo'San and his younger brother. He admired Lo'San more than he had before. Lo'San was one of the more analytical rather than emotional males aboard ship, and Doc had often shared meals with him as they debated any particular subject. He'd wondered at the cold, business like nature of Lo'San and how a human female would adapt, when it became apparent he intended to pursue one of the human females, but it had not been necessary. Lo'San had surprised him. The male was proving to be quite supportive and loving with his female.

Doc tapped on the door and opened it, walking in with the injector in hand. "Another injection. Then we'll measure your levels in a few days to determine our next step."

Synclare nodded as she took a deep breath and blew it out slowly through pursed lips.

"Are you ready, my Sink Lar?" Lo'San asked.

Synclare nodded and turned to face Lo'San, giving her backside to Doc.

Doc lifted the edge of the sheet and pressed the cold metal of the injector to the skin just behind Synclare's hip. The soft sound of pneumatically compressed air escaping the injector filled the room, and Synclare caught her breath.

"Alright?" Lo'San asked.

Synclare nodded again.

"There you go. I suggest you go straight home and into bed. I have no doubt you'll be feeling poorly soon," Doc advised.

"I'll get her situated before returning to the Command Deck," Lo'San assured the healer.

"I'll run the additional tests and let you know if there is any change. Otherwise, I'll see you in several days to run hormone levels again." Then he handed several vials to Lo'San. "Here, six to eight drops into anything she wishes to drink will ease the nausea, cramping, and help her sleep."

"Same as before?" Lo'San asked.

"Yes, it is the same medication as before. If her reactions are more severe than they've been, you can add another one or two drops, but not much more. We don't wish to make her sleep for days on end. We just wish to make her reactions to the treatment less severe," Doc explained.

"I understand," Lo'San said, slipping the vials into the pocket of his uniform pants. He helped Synclare down off the exam table as Doc left the room. Then helped her pull her clothes on.

"Come, my love," Lo'San said, guiding her by the hand he held in his out of the room. "Let me get you settled at home, then I'll return to the Command Deck."

"I can get home by myself. I'll be fine, go back to work," Synclare urged.

"I am at work. No one has called. There is no threat. No one needs me at the moment but you. Allow me to settle my female in for a nap, and then I'll go back," Lo'San answered.

"You're stubborn," Synclare said, chuckling softly as they left medical.

"As is my mate," Lo'San countered, grinning at her as she walked beside him.

Synclare took a deep breath and her smile fell slightly.

"Are you well?" he asked.

"Yes. I can feel the cramping beginning, though," she answered.

Lo'San swept her up in his arms, and held her against his chest. "Then I'll carry you."

"Like I can't walk for myself?" she asked.

"No, like I enjoy carrying my female. Relax and allow me a bit of pleasure, hmm?" he asked.

Synclare laughed and did as he asked, relaxing and laying her head against his shoulder as he carried her to the lift that would lead them to the residential floor and to their home.

~~~

Lo'San tucked the comforters around Synclare where she lay in their bed. He'd stripped her, put one of his soft undershirts on her, because it was her favorite thing to sleep in, and put her right into bed. She was putting on a brave face for him, but he could tell she was already feeling unwell.

"I will be right back with a cup of litah and your medication," Lo'San said.

Synclare nodded and leaned back against the mountain of pillows Lo'San had piled behind her. She didn't even try to smile — she was feeling that poorly.

Lo'San came back momentarily and handed her the litah he'd made for her. "Is there anything else you want, my love?" he asked.

Synclare eagerly drank down the litah in larger swallows than usual, knowing the medication that would ease her symptoms was mixed into it. "Could you tell me another story from your childhood? I like hearing about you and your brother and the trouble you got up to," she said, with a soft smile on her face.

"You just find it hard to imagine that I was ever anything but dignified and controlled," he accused.

"Don't forget, I get to see you at your most uncontrolled," she said, raising an eyebrow at him. "And I love that part of you, but I really like hearing about young you as well."

"Very well," Lo'San said, settling in beside her to tell her another of his stories of childhood antics. "I'd forgotten how much I miss my brother," he admitted. "I am very pleased to tell you of our adventures," he said with a smile. As soon as he got comfortable, his tablet beeped. Grumbling he moved to the edge of the bed and reached for it. It was Zha Quin letting him know he was on his way to the Command Deck to meet with him as requested.

"I have to go, Sink Lar. I requested a meeting with Zha Quin and he is on the way to the Command Deck as we speak," Lo'San explained.

"That's fine. I'm already feeling drowsy anyway."

"I'll check in on you as soon as I can. If you need me, either use your wrist communicator, or ask Missy to call for me," Lo'San said.

"I hate to do that, then everyone knows your wife is calling you at work," she said, grimacing.

"I do not care. You are feeling ill. If you need me before I return, either method will get to me immediately."

"Alright. If I need you I'll call. But now, I just want to sleep," she said, tossing a couple of pillows to the foot of the bed and snuggling into those still behind her.

Lo'San kissed her head, tucked the comforter around her once more and left her to sleep through the worst of her reactions to the hormonal treatments.

Chapter 9

"Come here this instant, Ko'San! Do not make me wait!" Ph'eel shouted into the communicator mounted on the wall beside her favorite window seat.

Almost immediately the communicator crackled to life with Ko'San's reply. "I am in the fields, dear one. I shall be there as soon as possible."

"You will be here sooner!" Ph'eel demanded.

There was no reply as Ko'San was already on his way to answer his mate's request.

Several minutes later Ko'San entered the living space of the expansive home he shared with his mate, and her three other husbands. He could hear the sound of Ph'eel's children upstairs playing with their nannies. Not all were his, but all were his wife's, and that made them all his responsibility as well as the responsibility of all of her other husbands. "I am here, dear one. I came at once," he said, walking toward where she sat perched on her window seat, staring at the rather large communicator she held in both hands.

"You should have been here sooner," she complained, before turning the communicator around to face him.

"Of course, dear one," he answered, thrilled that his mate had called for him above her other husbands. They were surely all peeved beyond reasoning as they worked still in the fields of Ph'eel's family's farm.

"Ko'San, we have news of your brother," an older woman's voice announced on the tablet Ph'eel held aloft for him to see.

Ko'San's excitement at being called to his mate's side crashed and burned at his feet as he realized his own mother was the cause of his mate summoning him. "Greetings, Mother."

"Did you hear what I said, Ko'San?" his mother asked.

"Yes, Mother. I did. What news have you?" he asked, obligated to do so.

"He is still aboard that ship," his mother snapped.

"Yes, Mother. He is a General, assigned to that ship. It is under his command," Ko'San answered.

"It is an embarrassment to our people. He does not serve our family, he does not serve our people! Instead he serves a military that is not even associated with our day-to-day welfare," his mother grouched.

"The Cruestaci keep our planet safe, Mother. He serves their military, which in turn is serving us," Ko'San explained. He'd had this same conversation each time his mother remembered how humiliated she was at Lo'San leaving them, and turning his nose up at their entire way of life. He didn't care much what his brother did. He was very thankful Lo'San had left them. It cleared the way for him to be chosen as Ph'eel's mate in his stead. He'd always desired Ph'eel, even as a younger male, and was thrilled when Lo'San had refused her, leaving him to be her next choice, after a suitable period of time, of course.

"I do not wish to hear of your opinions on the matter," his mother snapped. "Ph'eel, I would think you would have taught him better by now," she said, changing the focus of her attention to Ph'eel.

"He is usually much better opinionated," Ph'eel responded.

"Is there more? I am needed in the fields," Ko'San said, irritated that he'd been called to answer yet again for the behavior of his brother. He'd loved his brother once upon a time, and been thankful that he'd refused Ph'eel to follow his own path, but what he hated, and what had become a growing resentment was that Ph'eel, and his mother, always seemed to find a way to make him pay for the sins of his brother. No matter how loyal he was to their family, no matter how he stood at Ph'eel's side, no matter what position she found herself in, he was always reminded that his brother had humiliated her and their family. Then they'd both made it abundantly clear that they were each reminded of Lo'San from time to time when they looked upon him. He couldn't help that he looked almost like a twin of Lo'San.

But the nail in the coffin of his resentment toward his brother had been when Ph'eel had called out Lo'San's name when they were mating. It didn't happen every time, but it was often enough that he no longer believed her explanation that he'd heard her wrong. He knew she'd said Lo'San, not Ko'San and that was the part that made him angriest of all.

"Yes, there is more. He has taken a mate. He thinks to mate with one of the Cruestaci! How can he conceive of such a thing?!" his mother said, as though she was flabbergasted at the mere thought.

"He has been disinherited by our family, Mother. He is no longer on Eschina, and no longer affects our family or anyone living on Eschina. Why does it matter who he mates, or what he does? He is no longer of our people!" Ko'San said, his voice rising with his anger.

"Ko'San! Do not speak to your mother in such a way! It is dreadful behavior that I will not tolerate!" Ph'eel said, rising to her feet.

Ko'San trained his gaze on his mate and simply stood there, waiting to see what he'd be accused of next. It seemed that more and more Ph'eel was holding him responsible for his brother refusing her claim, and his mother blamed him for Lo'San leaving the fold of their family.

"We've decided that it would be to our benefit to visit Lo'San aboard his home. As you've stated, he is in somewhat of a position of power, and we should pay homage to that at least. One never knows when it will be necessary to access his position," his mother said tactfully.

"There is nothing he can do for you, that I can't do!" Ko'San objected.

Ph'eel leaned the tablet against the window sill so that her bond-mother could still be a part of these goings on, and delicately made her way to Ko'San who stood a few feet from her.

"Of course you are correct. I know that you are just as powerful. You are a fine protector and an even better provider. You are my favorite of all my husbands. I simply think that it would be a mistake to not repair any familial lines that have been broken, especially when that family line has a direct link to Sire Zha Quin Tha Tel Mo' Kok of the Cruestaci. Who knows? We may wish to one day ask a favor of them, and as it stands we'd not be heard. His taking a mate is a sign of his growing maturity. Now is the right time to make the first step in repairing our relationship with your brother. These were the points your mother made when she first asked me my thoughts on the matter, and I agree with her. Surely, you can see the benefits, too," Ph'eel said coyly.

"I can understand that much. But I see no reason to visit him. I do not wish to spend time with him," Ko'San stated with an edge in his voice.

"Nor do I, but your mother has requested that we accompany her. I've agreed out of gratitude since she's raised and groomed the perfect match for me... you!" she said, showering him with kisses as she leaned her delicate body against his. "Make me proud, my mate. Escort us, along with your father, to Command Warship 1 so that your mother, and all of us, may make peace with Lo'San and reunite a family long broken," Ph'eel said seductively with a bit of a pout on her beautiful face.

When Ko'San didn't answer, Ph'eel upped her game. "I thought this to be our chance to spend some time alone since it will be your parents and Lo'San visiting most frequently. But, I guess I was wrong in my thought you'd like to be away from here and our mates, to be with me only for a small period of time. I shall ask another of our mates to escort me," she said.

"No! I will take you. No other will have this privilege," he said.

At once Ph'eel's smile turned sly and manipulative as she glanced back at her bond-mother's image on the tablet angled toward them. "I'm so happy to hear that, my Ko'San. Can you manage to be kind to your brother long enough for your mother to repair their relationship?" she asked.

"I can," he answered.

"Very well, we'll make the arrangements. You may return to the fields, but be sure to attend me in my chambers this night. You shall be properly rewarded for your willingness to assist us in our endeavors," Ph'eel said.

Ko'San smiled when Ph'eel presented her cheek for him to kiss. He kissed her, then took the liberty of kissing her again before taking his leave and disappearing from the room.

Ph'eel walked over to the tablet and picked it up, but waited until she saw him striding across the exterior gardens toward the fields before she spoke again. "It is done. We'll be there on the guise of repairing our family. But I'll see to it that Lo'San's female, whoever she is, is disposed of. Once he is brought down by her desertion of him, I'll be there to ease his pains. We will bring him home again, Mother 'San."

"We cannot allow him to mate with any who is not of our species! It will muddy our lines, and cast shame on our family name even more than he already has. I simply cannot abide by it!"

"Do not worry, Mother 'San. I'll take care of it all," Ph'eel said. "Once there, Ko'San will be emotional and in need of my constant affirmations. He will be more than willing to do my bidding regardless of what it may be in order to gain favor with me. We will put an end to whatever mating Lo'San thinks he may have established, and cause Lo'San to return to us both at the same time."

~~~

Zha Quin was striding down the corridor toward the Command Deck when he looked up and saw Lo'San approaching from the opposite direction. "General Lo'San!"

"Sire Zha Quin Tha — thank you for answering my request for a meeting."

"It is no trouble. I've just finished training with Rokai's team. I have time left before I am to report for duty."

"I have noticed an area I feel we need to address," Lo'San said.

"Oh? Very well, should we speak here on deck?" he asked, indicating the doors leading onto the Command Deck, "or should we go to the small conference room?" Quin asked.

"I will be mentioning names, so perhaps the conference room is best," Lo'San agreed.

Both men turned and walked toward the conference room just down from, and across the corridor from the Command Deck. Once inside and seated, Lo'San began his informal presentation.

"Much has happened recently. You have claimed your Ehlealah, Kol has left us for a temporary position on Earth, I've claimed my female, and Ba Re' will inevitably claim his as well. We are short handed in those who are prepared to stand in as Lieutenant Commanders should we need one."

"True, but, we are no longer classified as a war ship. We are now a diplomatic envoy stationed near the universe in which Earth is located. Constant monitoring as though we are on high alert is not necessary," Quin countered.

"I agree. However, we always have one of us on deck," Lo'San said. "Just as we still have all of our battle cruisers on board, equipped and ready for immediate service, and our Elite Warrior Team aboard as well."

Quin grinned. "I see no reason to lower all our defenses."

"Exactly. My point being that we should at least replace Kol's position as a possible relief for our own."

"And I'm assuming you have someone in mind," Quin said.

"Elite Warrior Re'Vahl. I have watched him recently. I've been quite impressed with him. He is all that an Elite Warrior should be, as well as exhibiting leadership qualities. In addition, I find him to be quite good natured and even tempered. I feel he'd be a perfect candidate," Lo'San said.

Quin nodded. "Interesting. I've just finished training with them. He is quick and fleet of foot. I find I enjoy his company as well as his sparring."

"Our lives are changing, Zha Quin. We will have families. We will be called away for some reason or other from time to time. With Kol gone, it means we may not be able to attend our mates, or our families as we'd like. If we take Re'Vahl as his replacement, we are all given a bit of breathing room," Lo'San said.

Quin just looked at Lo'San, and Lo'San realized that Quin was looking at him, but his mind seemed to be somewhere else after Lo'San's last comment. "Zha Quin?" Lo'San asked.

"Yes. Sorry, just thinking about something you said. Please continue."

"I said that if we replace Kol as a Lieutenant Commander aboard this ship, with Re'Vahl, it would give us all a relief when needed."

"You are correct. We should replace Kol's rotation with Re'Vahl, should he be agreeable to the change in status and duty. I think promoting him to Lieutenant Commander would be best. He would not be able to remain as an Elite Warrior and be considered an equal among them, but he could very easily step in anywhere he chose as he will be learning many new responsibilities both when he is shadowing us on the Command Deck and when he is not," Quin said.

Lo'San nodded. "I agree. We can allow Rokai to find a replacement from the Warriors who are waiting for the chance to become an Elite Team member."

"I'll have Rokai contact Kol and find out if he's had his eye on anyone," Quin said.

"Excellent," Lo'San commented.

"I'll speak to Rokai, and Ba Re', and we'll call Re'Vahl in for a meeting this afternoon. No reason to wait," Quin said.

"I'll be ready," Lo'San agreed.

~~~

91

Synclare rolled over in bed as the main com unit in her home began to ping from the living space. She opened her eyes and blinked, trying to focus on what had awakened her. Remembering that she'd been asleep after taking medication to ease her reaction to the fertility treatments, she cleared her voice and spoke to Missy.

"Missy? Who is calling?" she asked.

"Good afternoon, Synclare. There's a call for you, from Eschina," Missy answered.

"I don't know anyone from Eschina," Synclare answered, puzzled, as she allowed her eyes to drift closed again. Then they popped open. "Eschina!" she said, suddenly more alert. "That's where Lo'San is from! It might be news of his family. I have to answer it," she said, throwing back the covers and making her way toward the living space as quickly as she could.

"The pending communication is a vid com. Perhaps you'd like to dress appropriately before answering, Synclare," Missy asked.

Synclare looked down at her body. She still wore only Lo'San's undershirt. "Crap," she exclaimed. "Can you answer the com? Is that even possible?" Synclare asked.

"I can do anything, Synclare. What shall I say to the Eschinians?" Missy asked.

"Tell them I'll be right with them," Synclare said, rushing back into her bedroom and searching for the blue, silken robe that Lo'San had gifted her. She put it on and tied the sash securely before running her fingers through her hair. Standing to glance at her reflection in their mirror, she almost doubled over at another cramp. "This will have to do," she whispered as she grit her teeth through the pain, then slowly made her way into the living space again.

Synclare situated herself on the sofa directly in front of the main com unit and spoke to Missy. "Okay, Missy, please put the vid com through," she said, perching on the edge of the sofa, her back ramrod straight, gazing pleasantly into the com unit as it came to life before her. A matronly woman, with a head full of hair as white as Lo'San's faced her and spoke in a language that Synclare didn't understand. Almost immediately a translation began to play in the background. "I am looking for the mate of General Lo'San."

"I am Synclare. Mate to General Lo'San. How can I help you?" Synclare asked, still smiling and doing her best to not allow her pain to show while she was waiting on the translation of her words to the woman on the vid com.

The woman's face registered disdain before quickly being schooled into a more receptive expression. Had Synclare been at her best, she'd have noticed it. But she was still heavily medicated, and her body was still cramping and causing her to feel dizzy.

"I am Mee'ta," the woman said.

The name meant nothing to Synclare, but before she could ask any questions, the woman cleared everything up for her.

"Mother, to Lo'San."

Synclare's eyes widened. "I am so very happy to make your acquaintance, ma'am."

"I'm sure you are. I shall get directly to the point of my call," the woman said.

"Yes, ma'am," Synclare answered, forcing her face to remain pleasant despite the wave of pain and nausea racing through her.

"I have had news of my son, Lo'San, taking a mate. It has pained me greatly that I am not a part of his happiness. We have been too far apart," Mee'ta said.

"Lo'San has spoken of your family. He greatly misses you," Synclare offered.

"He's said this?" Mee'ta asked.

"Not exactly. But he smiles when he tells me stories of his childhood, and I know him well enough to know that he does miss you all very much. He has said as much about his brother," Synclare added, thinking that would make things more real for Lo'San's mother.

Mee'ta's attention seemed to be focused somewhere off screen before she zeroed in on Synclare again. "I should like to pay my respects to my son's newly mated status, and repair any bonds that have been broken through pride."

"That would be wonderful!" Synclare said, excited for the prospect of Lo'San coming together with his family again.

"Myself, Lo'San's father, Lo'San's brother and his mate and children, will all be arriving for a visit at the soonest available moment," the woman said. Then she quickly added an insincere smile. "With your approval, of course," she amended.

"I think it's a wonderful idea. What can I do to help you with your arrangements?" Synclare asked.

"It must be cleared with those in charge of security, and if possible, I'd like to keep it from Lo'San until we actually arrive. I feel it would be better to surprise him than to keep him anxious at the thought of our arrival."

"You're right. I'll speak to Sire Zha Quin Tha on your behalf," Synclare said. "I'll explain that it's to be a surprise and if he agrees to allow the visit, I'll com you back and we can talk about all the details."

"That won't be necessary. I'll prepare our family for travel. Simply send word of when we are to meet the transport."

Synclare paused for a moment, trying to determine if the woman just didn't want her to com her, or what the situation was. She decided that Mee'ta most likely didn't want to take the chance of Lo'San finding out about their impending visit before their arrival. "Of course. Thank you for reaching out. Lo'San will be so happy to see you all and know that all is right between him and his family."

"Yes, I'm sure he will." The com went blank without further conversation.

Synclare sat on the sofa for a moment feeling like she'd been hung up on, then she realized that Lo'San had this same shortness in all his business dealings and that it was most likely a trait of his people. Another wave of nausea overtook her and she rushed to the bathroom to empty her stomach before returning to her bed to try to sleep a bit longer. In the morning, she'd speak to Zha Quin about the possibility of Lo'San's mother and family visiting.

Chapter 10

"Did you hear that female presuming to believe that she
knows Lo'San better than any, and what he will and won't be
happy with?" Mee'ta asked.

"I did, Mother 'San. Surely he can't be much changed from
the man we knew," Ph'eel said. "I have no doubt that we still
know him better than any female who's met him recently ever
could. You gave him life! I have known him since we were small
young ones! No other could ever know him better."

"Once he is home among us again, he will be reminded of
his bond with us."

"Are you sure we should bring the children? They are such
a distraction," Ph'eel asked, her annoyance clear as she thought
about the fact that her bond-mother wanted to bring her and
Ko'San's children. She didn't care much for them and found that
they took much of the attention from others that should have
been hers.

"Not all of them, only those who are Ko'San's young ones. It
will make our appearance seem more family oriented and true to
script if they are there."

Ph'eel nodded. "You are right. Perhaps I'll bring their nanny
as well so I don't have to fight to keep them in line."

Mee'ta wasn't even listening. She was still thinking about
the beautiful woman with the shining silver hair that she'd just
spoken to.

"She is not Cruestaci! I'm not sure what species she is, but
she is definitely not Cruestaci," Mee'ta said.

"That is fortuitous. The Cruestaci are a strong species. That
she is not Cruestaci will make things much easier for us. I still
believe that we can bring him back to you — to us."

"I want my son home. He is my firstborn and by rights
should be here and attending his Eschina mate and myself, his

mother. He will, of course, be required to issue an official apology to me. A male turning his back on his mother is the utmost example of disrespect."

"I will see to that as well, Mother 'San," Ph'eel said, secretly seething at the sight of the woman that was currently keeping company with the male that was meant to be her first mate.

~~~

Rokai stepped into the exercise facility everyone aboard ship was encouraged to use at their leisure. He looked around at the various people there exercising on the equipment, visiting with one another, running around the track provided for just that, and eventually located the male he was looking for. Standing at the far side of the room where the majority of the active duty warriors preferred to train with a series of heavy weights used for increasing their size and stamina, as opposed to the machines that most of the general population of the ship used. He was training with several other males and they took turns spotting each other with the excessively heavy weights.

Rokai set a path for Re'Vahl. The male's skin color was unusual among the Cruestaci. His skin was bronze. It was a color that was not a common sight, and it set him apart. In fact, Rokai had never met another Cruestaci male, other than Re'Vahl's father and brother, that carried that same trait. It made him easy to pick out in a crowd.

"Re'Vahl," Rokai called out, as he got close enough to be heard from across the room.

Re'Vahl turned toward Rokai. "Rokai," Re'Vahl answered, looking toward him. "Come to train with us?"

"I've been sent to summon you. You are needed in the small conference room across from the Command Deck," Rokai explained.

Re'Vahl realized this was not a friendly visit, so he changed from speaking to his friend, to speaking to his Elite Commander.

"Yes, Elite Commander Rokai ahl. Do I have time to clean up first, sir?" he asked, coming to attention.

"No. Just report to the conference room."

Re'Vahl's eyes narrowed at the information. He knew he'd not done anything to be called to task on, but was still wary to be called to a meeting and not given the opportunity to prepare for it.

"There is no need for concern, Elite Warrior Re'Vahl. Just report to the conference room."

"Yes, sir," Re'Vahl answered. He stepped over to a bench he'd left his shirt on and picked it up, slipping it over his head as he began to walk away, headed toward the exit of the exercise facility.

"Oh, Re'Vahl…" Rokai ahl called out.

Re'Vahl paused and looked back at Rokai ahl.

"Congratulations," Rokai said before grinning and moving to take Re'Vahl's place in the rotation of friends weight training.

Re'Vahl looked at Rokai for only a moment longer before turning and hurrying out of the exercise facility and up to the Command Deck and the small conference room across from it. He knew the only way he'd find out what Rokai meant was to report there.

~~~

"Commander Zha Quin Tha?"

"Yes, Missy," Quin answered.

"Elite Warrior Re'Vahl approaches," Missy answered.

"Thank you, Missy," Quin answered as he, Ba Re', and Lo'San all got to their feet and adopted the Cruestaci military equivalent of standing at attention — all on the same side of the conference table, facing the doors that Re'Vahl would enter through.

A few seconds later and the doors swooshed open granting Re'Vahl access. Re'Vahl came to an immediate stop when he saw the three males awaiting him. They were quite imposing. He inclined his head, and came to attention.

"Elite Warrior Re'Vahl, reporting as requested, Sirs," he said, his eyes trained on the wall behind the three males who faced him.

"Thank you for coming right away, Elite Warrior," Zha Quin said. "I apologize for the lack of notice, but, once decided, we were anxious to speak with you."

"No apology necessary, Sire. I am pleased to be of service," Re'Vahl said.

"Have a seat, Elite Warrior," Lo'San said, gesturing to the chair across the table from them.

"Thank you, General," Re'Vahl answered. He was a bit nervous around General Lo'San, because after all, he'd had designs on General Lo'San's female. Though, at the time she'd not yet been the General's mate.

As soon as he was seated, Ba Re' began speaking. "As we are sure you're aware, Elite Commander Kol Ra' Don Tol has been assigned as Consul on Earth."

"Yes, Sir," Re'Vahl answered.

"And you're also aware that he was one of the Lieutenant Commanders who was in rotation to lead the ship should it be required," Ba Re' said.

"Yes, Sir. I am aware."

"The others are myself, General Lo'San of course, and our Sire," Ba Re' said.

"Yes, Sir," Re'Vahl said.

"We, all of us who share the responsibility of command of this ship, have recently been mated, or are planning to be," Lo'San said.

Re'Vahl gave a single nod.

"We anticipate more of our males following suit. This is a good thing for us and our people, we encourage those in service to our military to claim their mates if they find them. As my Sirena has stated, a highly lethal Cruestaci Warrior is even more dangerous when they have an Ehlealah to fight for," Quin said.

"I am not personally mated, Sire, but I absolutely agree with our Sirena," Re'Vahl said, giving a firm nod.

"Our status as an active war vessel has recently been updated to that of a diplomatic envoy. We are all aware that we keep a warrior force onboard, but those not of our people, are not aware of this fact."

Re'Vahl allowed a slight smile to flicker across his features. "Yes, Sir. We do not stand down, even when on a diplomatic mission."

"Exactly. And because of this, we continue to operate as a Warship, keeping a Commander on the Command Deck at all times."

"This may become a strain in the near future because of the fact that we've all taken mates recently. And as we are not at war, or involved in a conflict of any type, our attention will naturally be split between our duties aboard ship, and our mates and/or families. With Kol being out, it puts a strain on our time. None of us wish to retire to Cruestace, so a natural solution is to find another Warrior that can help us shoulder our duties," Zha Quin explained.

Re'Vahl for the first time allowed his eyes to stray to Sire Zha Quin Tha's, but he did not yet speak.

"Let me be clear, Elite Warrior. We have a ship full of Warriors to choose from, and even more stationed about the other ships currently patrolling different quadrants of the multi-verse, and those guaranteeing the safety of our home planet," Quin said, pausing for effect.

"Yes, Sire," Re'Vahl said, indicating his understanding.

"But we chose you."

Re'Vahl's eyebrows rose.

"We are offering you the position of Lieutenant Commander. Promoting you from your Elite Squad to take your place among us. You will not continue with your other assignments as Ba Re' does. You will be a full time Lieutenant Commander of Command Warship 1. You will train beside myself, General Lo'San, and Lieutenant Commander Ba Re' Non Tol, should you agree to take the promotion," Zha Quin said.

Re'Vahl forgot to keep his eyes pinned to the wall, he was looking Zha Quin in the eye as he listened to him speak.

"It is not only your exemplary record that brought you to our attention. It is your Elite skill set, your natural gift of leadership, and your natural even temper and good nature that make you perfect to rise to the position we offer among our leadership of this ship," Lo'San said.

Re'Vahl sat there, shock evident on his face. "Thank you, Sir," he finally managed.

"Or, you could refuse and return to your position of Elite Warrior. It will not count against your career if you choose to remain with your current team," Ba Re' said.

"No, Sir!" Re'Vahl exclaimed, getting to his feet and pounding his arm crosswise against his chest. "With all due respect and appreciation, Sirs, I will accept the position you offer!" he declared, once again staring at the wall between them.

Zha Quin smiled at Ba Re', then Lo'San. He stood up and leaned toward Re'Vahl. "Then look here, Lieutenant Commander Re'Vahl!"

Re'Vahl snapped his gaze to Zha Quin's.

"You are a Commander in training of Command Warship 1. Stop behaving as an enlisted warrior."

Re'Vahl grinned. "Yes, Sire. Thank you, Sire," he said, unable to stop his smile while he looked Zha Quin in the eye.

"Go to your quarters, gather your things, and take them to General Lo'San's quarters. "They will be yours from now on. They are small, but they are private quarters," Zha Quin ordered.

"Yes, Sire."

"Go to the supply room, and have them issue your new uniforms. You start tomorrow. Lo'San is on duty. You will mirror his schedule this week. Next week, you mirror mine, and then you'll train with Ba Re'," Quin said. We'll continue this schedule until you are fully capable of commanding this ship on your own."

"Yes, Sire. Thank you, Sire," Re'Vahl said, excitedly.

Zha Quin slammed his arm against his own chest in the Cruestaci form of salute, Re'Vahl did the same in answer, and followed suit with both Ba Re' and Lo'San.

"You have today to say your goodbyes to your team, and to prepare yourself for your new position. Do you have any questions?"

"No, Sire. None at all. Thank you for the opportunity, Sirs," Re'Vahl said.

"You've earned it, Lieutenant Commander," Zha Quin said, smiling at the male.

"You are dismissed until you start your new position tomorrow," Lo'San said.

"Thank you, General Lo'San," Re'Vahl said, smiling and giving another little salute.

Re'Vahl turned and left the conference room, and just as the doors slid closed behind him, he let out a shout of celebration.

Zha Quin, Ba Re', and Lo'San all laughed when they heard his shout.

"I'd say he's excited," Ba Re' said.

~~~

The next day Zha Quin sat in the same conference room he had the day before when offering Re'Vahl a promotion to Commander of the Command Warship 1. Only now he was speaking with the mate of his second in command.

"I am not sure this is a good thing, Sink Lar," Zha Quin said, sitting at the head of the conference table in the small meeting room he used for private discussions and small meetings.

"I know that each time Lo'San discusses his family, reminisces about his brother, he gets this wistful look in his eye. He'd even admitted to me that he'd forgotten how much he missed his brother," Synclare explained.

"I am sure he does, yet this is not just his brother," Zha Quin answered.

"I know. But I thought it may be best for them to be reintroduced here, on his familiar territory, his home, rather than a world he chose to leave. At least he'd have the upper hand. If they cross a line, and he decides they are no longer welcome here, he can send them away. In their world, he's kind of stuck until he can get transport out," Synclare said.

"That much is true. And we have become more of a diplomatic envoy versus the war ship we once were," Zha Quin said thoughtfully.

"Exactly. For many reasons, this ship has come to be thought of as an envoy to many looking for repatriation, as well as a start to a new life. If I thought we were truly aboard a ship that is strictly patrolling the multiverse looking for battles to be had, I'd never have considered bringing Lo'San's family aboard. I want to do this for him, so that he can know he's at peace with his family."

Zha Quin listened to Synclare's plea to allow Lo'San's family to visit him, a surprise visit to him aboard ship. He thought about how much it ate away at him when he and Rokai were estranged. And that alone was enough to make him give in to her demands. "Very well, Synclare. I'll approve the visit by his family. However, make it very clear to them, they will be watched closely to be sure they are not out of line in any way. And they must, of course, have to go through all security clearances."

"His mother said it wasn't necessary to confirm with her. It's only necessary that we send them confirmation of a transport date."

"I shall include my conditions for granting their visit in the confirmation we send," Zha Quin said.

"Thank you, Quin. I think it's going to change everything for him. He'll be a much different male when they leave," Synclare said, grinning.

"You are welcome, Sink Lar."

~~~

103

Ph'eel reclined on her lounge pillows and lifted a graceful hand toward the tablet that sat on a table two feet from her. "Answer that," she whined to the servant nearest her.

"Yes, miss," the servant responded, before picking up the tablet and establishing a connection for the incoming communication.

"Why am I speaking to you?" a female's voice snapped.

The servant didn't even have time to answer before Ph'eel was standing beside her and snatched the tablet from her hands. "Give me that!" she ordered.

The servant knew no matter what she said or did, it would always be contradicted, it was the way with her mistress, so she simply handed the tablet over and returned to cleaning the rooms of the expansive home as she always did.

"Mother 'San!" Ph'eel said, looking into the tablet.

"Ready your household, Ph'eel. I have received confirmation from Commander Zha Quin Tha Tel Mo' Kok that our request for a visit has been granted.

"Oh! How exciting," Ph'eel said. "Is he very dominating? Very large and imposing as everyone says?" she asked.

"I did not speak directly to him. I spoke to his Communications Master — some small being called a Vennie, whatever that is. At any rate, they have promised to keep the visit a surprise until we arrive."

"Wonderful! It won't be long until Lo'San is my first husband as he should have been all along," Ph'eel said.

"I've been considering that, Ph'eel. We cannot let them know we have any motive other than a family that misses its eldest son. That includes you paying homage as Ko'San's wife. Should they become suspicious they may very well have us removed from the ship before we're able to bring Lo'San back into our fold. You will have to play your part well."

"He will not be able to resist me," Ph'eel said confidently.

"He will not tolerate you as long as the female he has claimed is at his side. You will play the part of a quiet, loving, supportive wife to Ko'San. You will not give any indication that

104

you still have a desire to make Lo'San part of your home until his female is removed from his side. Am I clear?"

"Yes, Mother 'San. I can do that. It will not be easy, but I can do that."

"And you will be pleasant while doing it."

"Yes, Mother 'San. I will," Ph'eel promised.

Chapter 11

Lo'San, along with Re'Vahl, were on duty late in the day when a returning transport requested docking permission.

"Bring that one in," Lo'San said, standing back to watch Re'Vahl go through the proper protocol.

"Yes, General," Re'Vahl responded. Re'Vahl stood beside Vennie, and oversaw the operation as the Communications Master began the process of bringing the transport in.

Lo'San went about other duties as he just barely kept attention on Re'Vahl, having no doubt that Re'Vahl was completely qualified to oversee the arrival of their returning transport.

He heard Re'Vahl and Vennie as they discussed the weight load the transport carried, the lifeforms aboard, assisted the pilot as he navigated their approach, and assigned him a dock as his smaller transport actually entered the huge, Command Warship 1, and the airlock sealed behind it. And he heard Re'Vahl ask where exactly the transport was returning from.

"Eschina was its last stop, Lieutenant Commander. Several prior stops were made, but its final departure was from Eschina," Vennie answered.

Lo'San turned to look at Vennie when he answered Re'Vahl's question.

"Did you say Eschina?" Lo'San asked.

"Yes, General. The last scheduled stop was on Eschina," Vennie answered.

"Who approved that stop?" Lo'San asked, his temperament clearly on edge as he stalked toward Vennie.

Vennie's tentacled extremities flew over the screen of his computer as he searched out the officer that approved the transport's last mission. "Sire Zha Quin Tha gave mission plan approval, General."

Lo'San stood in place for a moment while he considered all the possibilities, then he spun on his heel and headed toward the doors that would lead him off the Command Deck and into the corridor. "Re'Vahl, Command is yours. Contact me with any issues. I shall return shortly."

"Yes, General!" Re'Vahl answered confidently.

As soon as Lo'San left the Command Deck, Re'Vahl turned back to Vennie. "Communications Master Vennie, get eyes on that transport. Something about it has General Lo'San on alert. Be prepared to call in additional security. In fact, have them on standby."

"Right away, Lieutenant Commander," Vennie answered.

~~~

Synclare waited until the airlocks were in place and the green light above the doors leading out to the docking bay were engaged so she could hurry out to the arriving transport and welcome Lo'San's family. She smiled with anticipation as she watched the green light illuminate and stepped forward to press the sensor on the wall which would open the doors and give her entry.

As she left the comfort of the ship and stepped into the loud, wide open atmosphere in the docking bay, she marveled at the size of it. The ship housed thousands of people, and hundreds of aircraft from standard supply transports, commuter transports, and battle cruisers. It was exactly as it appeared - a mother ship, outfitted for war. "Wow," she said aloud as her gaze flicked here and there taking in all that was to be seen.

Males were working the docks, calling out to one another and laughing as they worked on some of the smaller aircraft, others were busily cleaning the dock itself, some were receiving supplies and inspecting them, others were processing packages and loading them for shipment, and yet others were moving a newly arrived transport into place so that its passengers could disembark on the metal catwalks that gave them access to the inner parts of the ship they'd just arrived on. She didn't miss the warriors stationed strategically around the docking bay, keeping a careful eye on all that came and went for security's sake.

"I hope they're not frightened by the soldiers," Synclare said aloud as she came to a stop just above the transport she knew Lo'San's family was on. She fussed with her clothing just a bit and pasted a smile on her face as she waited nervously for them. She was not aware that a male walked up behind her, his attention focused on her, intent clear in his step.

"Sink Lar!" Lo'San said brusquely as he quickly approached.

Synclare spun on hearing his voice. "Lo'San! What are you doing here? You're not supposed to be here now!"

"Why am I not supposed to be here?" Lo'San asked, his mood obviously guarded.

Synclare didn't want to answer, she'd planned this surprise for him, and here he was ruining it. "Why are you even here? You're not supposed to be here. What made you come down here?" she asked, her grin in place at being found out.

"This is my ship, Sink Lar. Do you believe that a transport from Eschina would arrive without me finding out about it?"

Synclare gave up the idea of a surprise. "I wanted to surprise you. I saw how much you missed your brother, and when your mother comm'd me, I thought it would be a great opportunity to get you all together so you wouldn't have to miss your family anymore. They love you, they want to be in your life."

Lo'San's heart dropped and he shook his head in disbelief. "This is not anything that I'd have ever wanted. You have no idea what you've done, Sink Lar." His voice was tinged with disappointment as he stood there regarding her.

Synclare was shocked by Lo'San's response. "I was trying to help you repair your relationship with your family. I only meant to help you reconnect. I thought this would make you happy."

He stood looking at her, his face masked from any emotion so she wasn't even sure if he was disappointed, or angry, or both.

108

She heard the pneumatic seal on the transport releasing behind her, and he did, too.

Lo'San stared her in the eye for only a second longer before turning and walking away from her, and his family that were preparing to exit the transport.

"Lo'San!" Synclare called, following him a few steps before coming to a stop when he didn't slow his pace, or turn around to look at her.

Then she heard the door open and heard voices. Her stomach was a bundle of nerves, and she was worried about the fact that it seemed she'd hurt her husband, albeit unintentionally, as she pasted a smile on her face again and turned to face his family.

"Where is my son?" a female asked one of the males who attended their transport.

Synclare listened to the translation that immediately followed as the male was getting them unloaded and on their way into Command Warship 1.

"He's on duty. I'm sure he'll make himself available as soon as he can," the warrior answered.

Synclare watched as a matronly woman, with skin a bit lighter than Lo'San's stepped off the transport accompanied by a male who looked like Lo'San would in about 50 years.

"Are you the female my son has claimed?" the woman asked, coming to a stop in front of Synclare.

Synclare again waited for the translation, then responded. "Yes, I am. I am Synclare. Welcome Mee'ta, welcome to Command Warship 1. How was your trip?" Synclare asked, doing her best to seem happy and welcoming.

"Not as smooth as one would have hoped. But we managed," the woman answered. The male standing behind her offered her a slight bow. "This is Lau'San, he is Lo'San's father."

"I'm very pleased to meet you," Synclare said.

The male smiled at her but offered no greeting.

"I cannot believe Lo'San sent such a basic transport for us. Surely he knows we are accustomed to more genteel treatment.

We deserve to be treated as our status indicates!" a young female stated, stomping off the transport and onto the metal catwalk.

"Ph'eel!" Lo'San's mother snapped. "Do not be ungrateful! And remember, Lo'San isn't aware of our visit. His... mate... arranged our transport."

Ph'eel instantly shut her mouth, then looked around until her gaze landed on Synclare. "Are you Lo'San's mate?" she asked incredulously.

"Of course, she is!" Mee'ta answered, speaking for Synclare. "She is perfect for him, do you not think? Tall yet unassuming, slender, quite interesting to look at. I dare say, he picked the perfect mate," Mee'ta said, flashing her version of a smile as she unabashedly examined Synclare as her gaze went from her head to toes.

"Thank you," Synclare said, making a mental note that Mee'ta's smile was cold and calculating enough to remind one of a shark back on Earth.

Ph'eel made her own examination of Synclare before she finally spoke again. "Of course. I forget my place. I am accustomed to never leaving my home and having all my conveniences at my fingertips. Forgive my slip of manners. And may I add my thanks for arranging our visit to our beloved Lo'San? He has been long away from us."

A slight rumble sounded from behind Ph'eel, and another male stepped into view, holding the hand of a younger version of himself.

Synclare's mouth dropped open as she looked in the eyes of a male that was almost an identical twin of Lo'San.

"Yes, they do have quite a similar appearance, do they not?" Mee'ta asked.

"You must be Lo'San's brother! He's spoken about you to me many times. He's missed you greatly," Synclare said, grabbing onto the hope that maybe his brother being here would give Lo'San some happiness about his family's arrival.

Ph'eel smiled when Ko'San didn't reply. "You may speak, Ko'San. She is, after all, family."

"I'm pleased he's missed me," Ko'San said with no emotion at all.

"Perhaps if you could escort us to our lodgings, we can rest a bit and prepare to properly greet my son," Mee'ta said.

"Of course, Mee'ta. Forgive me. If you'll just follow me," Synclare said, turning and leading the way down the catwalk.

"Bring them along quietly," Ph'eel said, which caused Synclare to glance over her shoulder.

Synclare was surprised to see a beautiful girl, with silver skin, decorated with white tattoos, following along behind the family. Her hair was a darker shade of silver than her skin, and her features were delicate, even more so than Ph'eel's. The girl kept her eyes downcast and carried one young boy on her hip while holding the hand of the older child that Ko'San had let go of.

"Hello! I'm Synclare," she said, trying to welcome the girl.

The girl didn't answer, nor did she even acknowledge being spoken to.

"She's the young ones' caregiver, their nanny. She can be housed wherever they are," Ph'eel said as though the female was of no importance at all.

"That's not a problem," Synclare said. "But, I'll need to have her cleared with security."

"That was done before we boarded the transport. Do they not keep you apprised of your anticipated visitors?" Mee'ta asked, sounding slightly amused.

"I suppose not," Synclare answered. Deciding not to respond with a snippy remark, Synclare instead focused on the children . "Your children are beautiful, Ph'eel," Synclare said, glancing back at the children again.

"Thank you. Though they have their father's features, I'm afraid. They do not look a bit like me," Ph'eel answered.

"They are beautiful, nonetheless," Synclare answered, not quite sure what the deal was with this obviously spoiled female. Then she decided to see if she could score some points. They were going to be here for a while and it would be very miserable if they weren't able to forge some type of friendship. It was doubly important as she was obviously Lo'San's sister-in-law. "If they shared in your features as well, they'd surely be too beautiful to look upon!" Synclare said animatedly.

"I do agree!" Ph'eel said, bringing up a delicate hand to lay against her throat, obviously very flattered that Synclare had pointed out her beauty. "Though Ko'San has only been able to give me sons, I do have a daughter at home, from another of my husbands. She looks much like me," Ph'eel said, glancing about the corridor as Synclare escorted them to the quarters they'd be sharing during their stay. "She is my favorite. I have no doubt she at least will provide us with a profitable mating."

Synclare glanced back at Ko'San when Ph'eel had made what Synclare took as a dig at his ability to give her only sons, and was not surprised to see resentment on his face as he glared at Ph'eel from behind.

Keeping her thoughts to herself, she rounded a curve in the corridor and indicated the lift to her left. "This lift will take us up a level. The visitors quarters are there. I've arranged a large set of rooms for you all to stay together, but if you'd prefer two sets of rooms, I can make the change with no problem at all," Synclare explained.

"We'll need three sets of rooms," Ph'eel said quickly.

"Three?" Synclare asked, confused.

"The young ones will be roomed with their nanny," Ph'eel stated coldly. "I need my rest and with young ones near, no one gets rest."

Synclare raised her eyebrows and nodded slowly. "Alright. I can take care of that," she said, slowly. As they exited the lift, Synclare escorted them halfway down the corridor before pausing outside a non-descript door. "These are the original rooms I had assigned to you. There are two bedrooms here, and a living area."

"We'll take these," Mee'ta said. "There is a room for each of us."

Synclare was surprised. Why would a husband and a wife want separate rooms... but, she gave no indication. "If you'll just step over here and allow the scanner to print your hand," Synclare said.

Mee'ta did as she asked, and the scanner logged in her print. "I want to be sure that no one other than my Lau'San and myself have access to these rooms," Mee'ta said.

"I can arrange that," Synclare said.

"Scan complete," the scanner advised.

"Missy?" Synclare asked, raising her voice.

"Yes, Synclare," the ship's computer answered.

"Please ensure that no one other than Mee'ta and her mate can access these rooms. And could you please assign two more sets of rooms, as close to the one I requested for General Lo'San's family as possible?" Synclare asked.

"One moment, Synclare," Missy answered.

Synclare smiled at her mother-in-law and the rest of Lo'San's family as she waited for additional quarters to be assigned, and they watched her completing the arrangements they required. "If you need anything at all, the commissary, or medical, or if you simply wish to take a brief tour of the ship, you need only follow the signs on the walls, or so I'm told, I can't read them," Synclare said.

"You are illiterate?" Mee'ta asked, shock in her voice.

"Oh, no! It's just that none of the signs are in my language. I am very well educated in my own language."

"I suspect you are human," Mee'ta said, "from Earth, yes?"

"Yes. I am," Synclare said.

"I have changed the security on this suite to only General Lo'San's parents. No other will be able to access these quarters," Missy said.

"Thank you, Missy," Synclare answered.

"Two doors down on your right has been assigned to the General's family as well, and is an exact replica of those already reserved by you. And next door to that is the only additional room available at this time. It is smaller with only one bedroom and a small living area," Missy said, interrupting their conversation.

As Synclare listened to Missy advising her which additional quarters were available, she didn't miss Ph'eel making a snide comment about Earth.

"Isn't that the primitive planet the Chairman of the Consortium is from?" Ph'eel hissed on a whisper.

"Bart is indeed from Earth. As is Sirena Vivian of Cruestace. We don't think it all that primitive," Synclare answered, finally deciding that she didn't like Ph'eel at all.

"You actually know Chairman Bartholomew?" Ph'eel asked, looking down her nose at Synclare.

"Yes. He visits our Sirena often. Besides, all humans know one another, you know, since Earth is so small and primitive," Synclare answered, before immediately regretting her sarcasm.

"Ph'eel, that is quite enough," Mee'ta said. Then she turned to Synclare. "Forgive Ph'eel. My beloved daughter in bond is not quite herself. Travel does this to her, and meeting strangers."

"It's fine. Let me show you to the other rooms and I'll be on my way so that you can all recover," Synclare said. "As I'm sure you heard, there are two more suites of rooms available. One is much smaller..."

"That one is fine for the young ones," Ph'eel said.

"I'm not sure there are enough beds for the two boys and their nanny," Synclare said.

"Au'revele can find somewhere to sleep, the floor if nothing else, I'm sure," Ph'eel said dismissively. "If we could hurry, I'd like to rest a bit and prepare myself for my reintroduction to Lo'San."

"Oh, you've met Lo'San?" Synclare asked, not aware of the history that Ph'eel and Lo'San shared.

Ph'eel gave a disdainful huff. "I should say so. Very few know him as well as I."

"Oh. Well, I'm happy you were able to come along as well," Synclare said.

After seeing everyone to their rooms, Synclare returned to the room that had been assigned to the nanny, Au'revele, and the two boys. She stood outside and waited for Missy to announce her presence. Almost without pause the door opened and

Au'revele stood there, eyes downcast, waiting to see what Synclare needed. "May I be of assistance?" she asked quietly.

"I wanted to be sure you have somewhere comfortable to sleep," Synclare said.

Au'revele's eyes peeked up to briefly meet Synclare's before returning to the floor. "I'll be fine, miss," she answered.

"But do you have somewhere other than the floor to sleep?" Synclare insisted.

"I can sleep on the sofa. I'll be fine."

"I can have another bed delivered," Synclare offered.

"No, thank you, miss. That would only bring undue attention. The sofa is very soft and will be more than enough," Au'revele answered.

"Alright then, but if you need anything at all, do not hesitate to let me know. There is no reason for anyone other than you and myself to know you've spoken to me," Synclare said, feeling like the female was most likely not treated very well.

"Thank you, miss. But I'm fine," Au'revele answered.

Synclare nodded, which Au'revele didn't see because she didn't raise her gaze to Synclare's again, and then turned to walk away, having done all she could.

"Miss?" Au'revele asked.

"Yes!" Synclare said, turning back to the female.

"Is there a place for the boys to run and play. It is not fair to keep them inside these rooms for the extent of their visit."

"I'm sure there is. Let me speak to Lo'San about where they can play. I'll let you know," Synclare said.

"Thank you, miss," Au'revele answered.

"I'm Synclare. You don't have to call me 'miss'," Synclare said, trying to let the girl know she was not above her in any way.

"I'm a servant, miss. You are not. Thank you for your assistance with finding an outlet for the young ones' energy," Au'revele said, before stepping back from the doorway and allowing it to close.

Chapter 12

Synclare stepped onto the Command Deck and quickly scanned those busily working for Lo'San. He was not there.

"Synclare, may I be of assistance," Re'Vahl asked.

"I was looking for Lo'San," she said hesitantly.

"He left the deck some time ago. I shall tell him you wish to speak with him," Re'Vahl said politely.

"Thank you, Lieutenant Commander Re'Vahl," Synclare answered as she turned to leave the Command Deck. "Oh, can you tell me if there is a place onboard for children to play?" she asked, turning back to Re'Vahl.

"I suppose they could access the exercise facilities if they wished to run the track. There is also a virtual reality habitat that can be set to mirror many types of surroundings. We've never hosted any younglings before. It is something I can address with Sire Zha Quin Tha if you'd like," Re'Vahl answered.

"That's not necessary. Thank you, though, I appreciate your suggestions." Synclare smiled at Re'Vahl then left Command Deck, walking aimlessly down the corridor, wondering where Lo'San was.

After looking in all the places she hoped to locate Lo'San, and not having any luck, Synclare finally returned to their home. "Lo'San?" she called out hopefully as she stepped inside. There was no answer, wherever he was, he obviously wasn't in their quarters. She walked into the living space and noticed the orange dot blinking on their main com unit, and hurriedly told it to play.

"Play messages!" she said, hoping that the message was from Lo'San.

But it wasn't, it was from Doc. "Synclare, please come to medical at your convenience so that we can perform another blood test to evaluate your hormone levels. I have several ideas of why you have had so much difficulty conceiving. We shall discuss them when you arrive."

Stressed from the meeting with Lo'San's family, and still upset from his response to her attempt to surprise him, Synclare just didn't have it in her to go to medical at the moment. She didn't even bother to erase the message, she just walked out of the living space and into her bedroom. She lay across the bed and let the tears come. Obviously her hormone levels were all over the place, otherwise she wouldn't be crying like this. All she'd endured, all she'd overcome and all it took was her husband, her husband's family, and a message from a doctor to drive her to tears. She allowed herself a few minutes of tears, before pulling herself back together. And getting in the shower to prepare to escort Lo'San's family to dinner in a few hours.

~~~

Lo'San paced in Zha Quin's living space as he asked the same question for the sixth time. "But why did you think it a good idea to allow them to board this ship without first asking me?!" he asked. His irritation was apparent but so was his effort to remain respectful. "This is not a dignitary I must entertain, nor a military envoy anxious to make allies of us. This is personal, Zha Quin! These people are the very reason I left Eschina and requested entry to the Cruestaci military. The very reason I've never, ever looked back!" Lo'San insisted.

Zha Quin sighed as he prepared to answer Lo'San for the sixth time. "Your mate asked that they be allowed to board. She informed me that you spoke fondly of your brother and admitted that you often remembered your formative years with him affectionately."

"My brother, yes. My mother, no! The woman thrives on one thing and one thing only - control of all around her. I will not succumb to her machinations. I will not allow her to sully the life I've built here, with great effort and no small amount of

118

commitment I might add! My female had no right to make this decision without my approval! They will leave. At once!" Lo'San insisted.

"Lo'San, I suggest you calm, and think of several things that are immediately apparent to me," Quin said.

"And they are?" Lo'San asked.

"Firstly, your mate did not contact your family, they contacted her. And even then, I believe she meant only to surprise you with that she thought you'd lost. It was not her intent to cause you pain, or any other unpleasantries."

Begrudgingly Lo'San nodded. "I am aware that she meant no harm."

"Next, they cannot leave until the next connecting transport is available. I cannot dump them on a space station to await a commuter transport from Eschina to arrive to pick them up," Quin said.

"Of course, you can," Lo'San answered.

When Quin simply raised an eyebrow at him, Lo'San shoulders dropped. "Fine. Go on," Lo'San said.

"Third, in light of the fact that you walked away and left your female to deal with it on her own, and the information you've since provided on the nature of your mother, if I were you, I'd be standing in front of my mother making it perfectly clear that my female is to be treated with the utmost respect at all times, or I would see to it that she is removed from this ship at once, and will be left to find her own way to wherever she ends up."

Lo'San stopped pacing and faced Zha Quin. "I left her to deal with them, unaware of what she'd most likely be dealing with," Lo'San said.

"Yes. You did. I've reviewed the incoming communication between your mother and Synclare. Your mother was distant, but respectful. She gave the impression that she was anxious to repair the broken bond between you," Quin said. "I did not approve this visit without a bit of research. And if I may offer yet another opinion... your brother and his mate are here along with his younglings. Perhaps you could give them the benefit of the doubt. Perhaps it's not a manipulative play on their part. Perhaps she does simply wish to reestablish communication with her son."

"That will have to be proven. In the meantime, I think your first idea was the best. I'll pay them a visit to make sure they understand if Sink Lar is mistreated in any way, they will pay for it," Lo'San said, before stalking toward the door. When he was halfway there, he seemed to remember where he was and who he was speaking to. He turned to face Zha Quin. "I meant no disrespect, Zha Quin. None at all. I'm simply taken aback that this has even occurred."

"I am aware, Lo'San. None has been taken. See to your family, and your mate. They will be scheduled on the next transport possible. But it will be several days before the logistics can be worked out."

"Thank you. I'm off to pay them a visit now," Lo'San said, striking his chest with his forearm and leaving Zha Quin's quarters.

As soon as he left, Vivian came out of the bedroom.

Zha Quin turned to look at her.

"That does not sound good," Vivi said.

"No, it does not."

"Why didn't you tell Synclare she'd need to get Lo'San's input before you could approve his family visiting?" Vivi asked.

"I am attempting to be more diplomatic! My own parents constantly tell me this is a skill I must develop. You yourself have said that I lack finesse! I am trying to be sensitive!" Zha Quin said defensively.

"Well, let me just say, that I will no longer lecture you about considering another's feelings. I'm pretty well convinced that you excel at war, battle, and simply telling others exactly what's going to be," Vivian said.

Quin gave a firm nod. "I agree. You can be considerate. I shall be demanding. It is what I know," he said, getting to his feet.

"Agreed — where are you going?" she asked.

"To speak to Vennie about working out the logistics of returning these people to where they came from."

~~~

Lo'San stood outside the door that would place him face to face with family he hadn't seen since he'd grown into manhood. It had been more than thirty years since he'd seen or spoken to any of them. He placed his hand on the sensor which responded by asking him if he wanted entry. He was the General aboard this ship, and as such, had access to all spaces, just as Quin did.

"No, I wish you to announce my presence," Lo'San said.

A few minutes later, the doors opened, and his father stood there, grinning widely. "Lo'San," he said, extending his arms for an embrace.

Lo'San didn't step into the man's embrace. He loved his father, but he didn't have much respect for him. He'd allowed Lo'San's mother to rule his entire life, including driving a wedge between him and his father by refusing to allow his father to have access to Lo'San as long as Lo'San refused to return home and do her bidding.

"Father," Lo'San responded, remaining where he stood.

"Will you not embrace your father in greeting?" Lau'San asked.

"Are you still allowing Mother to make all your decisions?" Lo'San asked.

"You do not give her the credit she is due, Lo'San. We have all we do because of her talent at choosing the right path for all of us," Lau'San said sadly.

"I'm well aware of her plans. Where is she?" Lo'San asked.

"Is that my beloved Lo'San?" Mee'ta's voice called from inside the suite.

"Come inside, Lo'San. Your mother wishes to repair all the damage done between our family," Lau'San said, inviting his son into their assigned quarters.

Lo'San gave a sharp nod. When he went to walk past his father, Lau'San reached out and embraced his shoulders from beside him. Lo'San turned partially and hugged his father back. "I do miss you, Father."

Lau'San grinned widely. "As I miss you. I am very, very proud of your accomplishments, Lo'San. So many admire you and value your opinions. You are much respected."

"Thank you, Father," Lo'San said, not sure how his family knew of all his accomplishments.

"We make sure to keep up with news of your life. We hear a great while after news has happened, but we do hear. Which is why we're here to congratulate you on your mating so long after the mating has actually taken place," Lau'San explained.

"I see. Is that what's brought you. I thought it was because Mother wished to repair our relationships," Lo'San questioned.

"Can I not have more than one reason for asking to be included in my son's life?" Mee'ta asked, coming forward from where she'd been seated in the living space.

"You rarely have a reason that does not involve bettering your own position, Mother. What is the actual reason you are here?" Lo'San demanded.

"Lo'San! How can you think anything other than a mother missing her child?" Mee'ta asked, feigning insult.

"I've been away for more than thirty rotations, Mother. Surely you'd have missed me enough by now to request a visitation."

"Lo'San, I simply didn't think you receptive. You seemed to have embraced your life away from us. Then I received news that you'd taken a mate and thought to myself, perhaps now his heart has softened enough to forgive an old female set in her ways," Mee'ta said.

"She is truthful with you, my son. We have all missed you greatly," Lau'San said.

Lo'San looked around the quarters they'd been assigned, but saw no trace of his brother. "Where is Ko'San?" Lo'San asked.

"He and his mate are in their quarters resting after our long trip," Mee'ta said.

"And his young ones are here, as well?" Lo'San asked.

"Yes, they are. All are anxious to see you," Mee'ta answered.

122

Lo'San stood there for a moment, considering all he'd been told since he'd arrived. Part of him wanted to believe it, but it was very, very difficult to do so. Finally reaching a decision, he looked from his father, to his mother, and turned to give her his full attention. "Let me be clear, Mother. I do not trust your reasons for being here. Had you contacted me rather than my mate, I would have refused your request to come here. My mate, however, is kind and good. She has a loving heart despite all she's endured. She is all that I am concerned with in this entire situation. If you disrespect her in any way, if you upset her in any way, if you make her regret arranging what she thought was a good thing for me, I will evict you from this ship without thought. You will be immediately banished from here and will be on your own as to how or even if you are able to make it back to Eschina," Lo'San threatened.

"Lo'San!" Mee'ta exclaimed.

"Further... arrangements are being made as we speak to plan for a transport to meet ours and return you to Eschina as soon as logistically possible. I do not for one minute believe you arrived here with completely innocent intentions. Do not make my mate regret falling for your claims of missing me." His threats and demands delivered, Lo'San spun on his heel and strode toward the door.

"I am truly hurt by your doubts of my desire to reunite with you, Lo'San. You are my son!" Mee'ta exclaimed, her voice conveying pain, or an attempt to seem pained.

Lo'San paused at the door and looked back at her. "Then prove me wrong, Mother. Prove me wrong. I would welcome it. In the meantime, be on your best behavior. I will be watching to ensure that Sink Lar is not caught up in whatever machinations you have in mind." Lo'San met his father's gaze after inviting his mother to prove him wrong. "I am sincerely happy to see you again, Father. If you can arrange it, I'd like very much the opportunity to spend a bit of time with you alone."

Lo'San looked over toward his mother. "Dinner will be this evening in the commissary. I expect you all to join Sink Lar and myself. We will ALL make her feel less troubled about your presence here. You had no right to drag her into this mess." He didn't say anymore, simply turned and left their quarters.

~~~

Synclare heard the swoosh of the door of the cleansing chamber as it opened, allowing someone entry while she was in the shower. It had to be Lo'San, no one else had access to their quarters.

When he said nothing, she wiped away the fog on the glass-enclosed shower and found him standing there, looking back at her.

"I wish to apologize for my behavior," he said simply, his face showing his guilt over walking away from her so coldly.

"It's okay. I should have asked you if you wanted them to visit," Synclare answered, as she stood there in the shower with hot water cascading down over her back.

"My behavior was not acceptable. No matter the situation, I should never have left you to deal with anything, especially my family, on your own. It will not happen again," Lo'San promised.

"Thank you. I'm sorry, too," Synclare said, quietly. "I only meant to make you happy, not upset you."

"If you wish, we will have dinner with them this evening," Lo'San said.

"Really? I'd like that. I think your mother would like that, too."

"I have just left them. They seem to be interested in establishing communication again," Lo'San said.

"So, maybe I didn't screw up too badly?" Synclare asked.

Lo'San gave her a small smile and shook his head. "It will be fine, Sink Lar. I give you my word."

"Okay."

"You know my people are a matriarchal society," Lo'San said.

"You'd explained that, yes," she said.

"The females of my planet are very manipulative. They vie for the best matches, the best social positions, the most profitable situations. All the power is with the females. They think themselves beyond reproach in their machinations to achieve whatever it is they decide they desire."

"Okay," Synclare said.

"My mother is a master at all of it. When she attempted to better herself by arranging a mating on my behalf, I refused to be one of her pawns, and I left."

"That is when you were claimed, right?" Synclare asked.

"Yes. I'm simply trying to explain to you that nothing any female on my planet does is without premeditation."

Synclare nodded, understanding that he didn't trust even his own mother.

"Just beware. I have been assured that all is as it seems, but remain guarded. Perhaps I will be proven wrong."

"Do you hope to be?" Synclare asked, reaching up a hand to wipe away the steam that was beginning to fog the glass of the shower again, just in front of her face.

"I do," Lo'San admitted. He stood there, watching the suggestion of her naked body through the steamy glass of the shower door. He wanted his mate, felt the need to touch her, taste her, make everything okay by showing her how much he loved her.

"Have you been in the water for very long?" Lo'San asked.

"Just for a little while," she answered.

"I spoke with Re'Vahl just before I entered our quarters. He is on deck at the moment, and doing well. I have a few moments to spare. Perhaps I could join you?" Lo'San suggested.

Synclare smiled seductively and opened the shower door, inviting him in. "That would make me very, very happy."

Lo'San pulled his uniform shirt off and dropped it to the floor as he toed off his boots, and reached for his pants. A rumbling purr sounded in his chest as he stepped barefoot and nude into the shower and Synclare's arms went around him, pulling him closer. "You are all that matters to me, Sink Lar. Only

125

you. As long as I have you, I don't need anything, or anyone else," he whispered. "Do you understand?" he asked.

Synclare nodded. "I do."

Chapter 13

Synclare and Lo'San arrived in the commissary early and chose one of the larger tables that could accommodate Lo'San's family comfortably.

"Shall we choose our meals?" Lo'San asked. "We've been waiting a suitable length of time and they have not arrived."

"Yes, we can do that. Then we won't have to leave the table at all once they arrive," Synclare answered.

It didn't take long before Lo'San had returned to their table, plates full of food and glasses of Synclare's favorite fruity drink before them. They were laughing and whispering to one another when Lo'San's smile fell.

Synclare's laughter died off as she watched his expression turn cold and hard. She followed his gaze and found his family walking toward them across the large room, weaving their way through the tables.

"What's wrong?" she asked quietly, leaning toward him. "I thought you wanted to have dinner with them? You were even the one to arrange it," she pointed out.

"I did not know SHE was here," Lo'San spat.

"Who? Your brother's wife?" Synclare asked, completely confused.

Lo'San turned to look at Synclare. "Sink Lar. She is the female that attempted to claim me as soon as we were of age."

Synclare's mouth fell open in shock. "I didn't realize who she was. I'm sorry," she said at once.

"She is calculating, selfish, and demanding. She makes my mother seem warm and loving."

Synclare glanced at the female clinging to Ko'San's arm as they approached. "Maybe marriage has changed her?"

"I highly doubt it," Lo'San answered.

Lo'San stood as his family approached, and Synclare stood beside him. He made a point of taking her hand in his and linking their fingers tightly together.

"Welcome," Lo'San said, looking back and forth between his father and his brother.

Lo'San's mother stopped once she approached the table and waited for his father to pull her chair out for her. Only she didn't sit right away, she remained standing, looking at Lo'San with her eyebrows raised.

"Please be seated, Mother. I won't be attending you this evening," Lo'San said. His voice sounded even, well-controlled, but Synclare knew he was pressed to his limit by the fact that Ph'eel was here.

Synclare looked up at Lo'San wondering what attending meant.

Lo'San glanced down toward her and gave her a tight smile. "In my mother's culture, the oldest born son tends the mother — greets her with adoration, waits on her every need, and makes her his focus whenever they are in attendance together, even if he is already mated."

"I see," Synclare said.

"My culture? This is also your culture, Lo'San," Mee'ta said.

"No, it is not, Mother. I am Cruestaci by affiliation and oath. Furthermore, my mate is human, and those of her practices that she values are now mine as well," Lo'San said, daring her to contradict him.

"I see," Mee'ta said shortly, allowing her husband to seat her.

Lau'San smiled widely at both Lo'San and Synclare, but didn't speak.

Mee'ta turned her attention to Ko'San and Ph'eel. "Surely you will greet your brother and his beloved mate."

Lo'San moved his gaze to Ko'San. "I am happy to see you, Ko'San. I often think of you and have wished you every happiness."

Ko'San looked at Ph'eel.

Ph'eel pinned Lo'San with an expectant look.

"And you see, Sink Lar, here we have an example of why I left Eschina. Ko'San is not even allowed to speak to me unless the female he mated gives him permission to do so. She expects me to ask permission. So, this will be a very quiet, very quick meal," Lo'San said.

Synclare watched the manipulations taking place between all the members of this family and for the first time in her life admitted that maybe there was a family, more fucked up than she'd ever thought hers had been.

"Sit, my Sink Lar. Let us enjoy our food so that we can be on our way," Lo'San said.

Synclare did exactly what he asked, taking her seat and as she sat, at the exact same time Lo'San did, too. They began to eat their meals, and paid no more attention to Ko'San and Ph'eel still standing beside the table.

"Do you truly think me so unreasonable as to not allow Ko'San to even speak to you?" Ph'eel asked.

Lo'San didn't look up, he simply took another bite of food, and nodded slowly.

"Ko'San, feel free to speak with your brother at will, my first mate. I would never deny you the opportunity to commune with your brother," Ph'eel said.

Ko'San inclined his head, as though acknowledging her kindness, then helped her sit, and got her settled before he sat himself. "I am overjoyed to see you so well, and quite mated, Lo'San." It wasn't a lie. Ko'San was thrilled that Lo'San was mated and no longer available for Ph'eel to attempt to claim. He'd long known he'd been a second choice to Ph'eel's first choice of Lo'San. And she reminded him of the fact that he was not Lo'San regularly.

Lo'San met Ko'San's gaze. "Tell me of yourself, Ko'San. What is it that you do? What is it that you enjoy? What gives you satisfaction?" Lo'San asked, genuinely wanting to know.

"I work on our plantari. I oversee the servants in the field, and help with the harvests. I take great pride in assuring that our produce is the best on Eschina. Our fields yield the most sought after produce," Ko'San said proudly.

"I suppose I am nothing to be proud of?" Ph'eel said, giving Ko'San the side eye.

"Of course, my Ph'eel, you are the most important part of my life. All I do is for you and your happiness. I had no doubt that Lo'San knows your worth. I simply meant to advise him on all I'd added to our plantari with the new techniques we've implemented."

Synclare glanced up at Lo'San.

Lo'San looked down at her and leaned over, kissing her forehead. "Plantari is the equivalent to a plantation of your ancient Earth," he explained.

"Oh. I understand that's quite a responsibility, Ko'San. I'm very impressed with your mastery of agriculture," Synclare said.

Ko'San didn't answer, Ph'eel looked at Synclare.

Lo'San shook his head. "She isn't happy that you spoke to her mate without her permission," Lo'San said, his disdain for Ph'eel clear. Then he burst out laughing when Synclare answered.

"Seems to me, she spoke to my mate without asking me if it was alright, so, I can speak to hers if I choose to."

Ph'eel's eyes would have made Synclare burst into flame if it was possible, but then Ph'eel glanced toward Mee'ta and at once realized that she was not behaving the way Mee'ta had demanded.

Mee'ta began to chortle a bit, and then meeting Synclare's gaze, she offered a wide, welcoming grin. "You are a strong one, Sink Lar. I see now the strength in you. It is no wonder that Lo'San chose you for his mate. He has chosen well."

Synclare smiled at Mee'ta. "Thank you, Mee'ta. I appreciate your words more than you know."

"Please forgive me, Sink Lar. I have never been away from Eschina. I am unfamiliar with the ways of other worlds, and fall back on my upbringing naturally. I meant no offense," Ph'eel said formally. Then she turned to Ko'San. "Ko'San, my dear mate, please, feel free to interact with Lo'San and his wonderful mate at will."

Ko'San gave her a nod of understanding.

"Shall I get your meal for you, Mee'ta?" Lo'San's father asked his mate.

"Yes, please do," Mee'ta answered.

"I shall get yours, Ph'eel," Ko'San said.

"Of course," she answered incredulously, then caught herself and reached out a hand to caress his face. "I would be most thankful."

Ko'San beamed his pleasure at once, before hurrying to get her food.

Once all were seated again, Lo'San looked toward Ko'San again. "I understand you have young ones," he said.

"We do," Ko'San answered. "Two males," he answered.

"We thankfully have a daughter from my second mate," Ph'eel said without even looking up from her food.

Ko'San's smile became strained.

"I had hoped to meet your young ones," Lo'San said, ignoring Ph'eel's comment.

"Ph'eel thought they'd be a distraction. They are taking their meal in their quarters with their nanny," Ko'San answered.

"I would like the opportunity to know them before you return to Eschina," Lo'San said. "If that isn't too distracting," he added.

"We shall make it a point," Ko'San said. "Do you have young ones?" Ko'San asked, knowing that Lo'San didn't, and this was something he'd managed that Lo'San had not been able to.

"Sink Lar and I have been working toward young ones for weeks now. We are hoping to have news soon."

"Are you compatible? Is that why young ones take working with a non Eschinian mate?" Ph'eel asked. And to her credit, she managed to not sound offensive, merely curious.

"As with any mating, there are times that fertility treatments may be beneficial. It will not be long now and there will be so many we will need help tending all our young ones," Lo'San said. He felt Synclare stiffen beside him, and took her hand in his again.

"I wish you beautiful daughters," his mother said.

"And sons," Lau'San added.

131

"Of course," Mee'ta said. Then Mee'ta seemed to realize that Lau'San had not spoken before this.

"Your father would like to spend as much time with you as possible, Lo'San," Mee'ta said a while later. "Tell him, Lau'San."

Lo'San glanced up toward his father and seemed on the verge of making a comment, but his mother stopped him.

"I was sure I'd made it clear you do not need permission to speak while aboard Lo'San's ship, Lau'San. My apologies for my social blunder," Mee'ta said, seeming genuine.

Lo'San shared a silent look with Synclare, and she saw his irritation clearly, though he managed to continue to control himself.

"I would very much enjoy a tour of your ship, Lo'San," Lau'San said enthusiastically.

"I will enjoy showing you, Father. You are welcome to accompany us as well," Lo'San said, speaking to Ko'San.

"Thank you for the invitation. I may, depending on the day and time. I may be occupied with my young ones," Ko'San said politely.

The rest of the meal passed easily, with Lo'San and his father dominating most of the conversation, while Mee'ta made every attempt to engage Synclare, and asked many questions about Earth and their practices. Ph'eel spent the evening leaning heavily on, and practically petting Ko'San who seemed more than happy with all the adoration directed at him.

Once the meal was finished, and there was nothing left to speak of, Lo'San and Synclare escorted his family back to their rooms.

"Thank you for sharing your meal with us, Lo'San," Mee'ta said, offering her cheek for Lo'San to kiss.

Lo'San didn't move toward her, until Synclare squeezed his hand and pushed his arm forward. Giving in to his mate, Lo'San stepped forward and dropped a brief kiss on his mother's cheek that had her all but tearing up in thanks.

From down the corridor they could hear squeals and laughter. Lo'San turned in that direction.

"Forgive the interruption," Ph'eel snapped, beginning to walk toward the room her children shared with their nanny.

"Is that your young ones?" Lo'San asked Ko'San.

"It is. They have not had opportunity to play since arriving. They have much energy," Ko'San said, watching his mate stalk determinedly toward their room.

"Do not chastise them!" Lo'San demanded, hurrying to get ahead of Ph'eel. "They are but young ones and should be able to laugh and play. They have done no harm. Come, Ko'San, introduce me to your young ones," Lo'San said, genuinely excited to meet his nephews.

Ko'San didn't even look at Ph'eel since she'd given him unfettered permission to interact aboard Lo'San's ship. "Come," he said, catching up with Lo'San, anxious to show off to Lo'San what he'd been able to accomplish that Lo'San needed medical intervention to achieve.

"Ph'eel! Allow Ko'San to introduce your young ones. Come, stand with us," Mee'ta said, calling Ph'eel back.

Ph'eel came to a stop at once, irritated that her bond-mother was being so controlling. She glanced back at Mee'ta and when Mee'ta beckoned her to her side, Ph'eel turned and walked back to where Mee'ta stood as Ko'San and Lo'San walked past her toward the room her children were in.

Ko'San reached out and activated the sensor which would open the door to his sons' quarters. When the door slid open, the boys were chasing each other around the room, and came to a sudden stop.

"Is this any way to conduct yourselves?" Ko'San shouted.

"No, it's fine, Ko'San. They are simply playing. Do you not remember when we did the same?" Lo'San said, smiling uncontrollably at the tiny versions of Ko'San staring at him.

Ko'San glanced toward Lo'San, then back at his sons. "This is my brother, Lo'San. This is his ship," he said to the boys.

"The whole ship?" one of them asked. "Why do you need such a big ship?" he asked.

"Hush," the female standing just behind them said gently. "You've not been given permission to speak," she reminded the boys.

"It is fine. They should not have to remain quiet until it is convenient for the adults in their lives," Lo'San said.

"It is not my ship, but I command it on behalf of the Cruestaci," Lo'San explained. "I am very, very happy to meet you both," Lo'San said.

"You look like father," the same little boy said bravely, glancing at his nanny, thinking she'd shush him again.

"Yes, I do. We've always looked very much alike, even when we were young ones like you," Lo'San said. Lo'San turned to look at Synclare. "Sink Lar, come, say hello."

"Excuse me," Synclare said to her mother-in-law and went to Lo'San.

"Did you find a place for us to play?" the boy asked as Synclare approached.

"I was thinking that maybe they could run around the track in the exercise facility. I know they can't be allowed to roam through the weight training and exercise equipment, but they can run," Synclare suggested.

"Of course. Would you like to go for a run? We could have a race!" Lo'San said, obviously thrilled at meeting the children and having the chance to interact with them.

"Yes!" both boys chanted.

"Do you see that?" Mee'ta asked very quietly.

"See what?" Ph'eel asked irritatedly from right beside her.

"That is our key to returning Lo'San to us on Eschina. He adores the young ones. We can encourage a bond with them, and do all we can to make it clear that you could give any number of young ones he may desire. It will be even more convincing since his mate is not able to without assistance."

"I'm tired of having young ones! They take so much away from my personal time," Ph'eel hissed.

"Do you wish to count Lo'San among your mates?" Mee'ta demanded.

"Of course I do! I'm here, am I not?"

"Then you will befriend Sink Lar. As will I. We will welcome her to our family, encourage her in her attempt to provide Lo'San with young ones, and all the while make it clear that you are able to provide him the same at will each time she is away from us," Mee'ta insisted.

"How will we do that without him defending her?" Ph'eel asked.

"Leave it to me," Mee'ta answered with a sinister smile. "I shall take care of it. Then when he is back on Eschina, you will take care of the rest."

Mee'ta and Ph'eel watched as Lo'San continued to visit with the boys, calling them out into the corridor to run back and forth.

"Tomorrow we will go to the exercise facility. We have a large track that we will race upon!" Lo'San promised.

Both boys began jumping and cheering.

After about ten minutes of them running from one end of the corridor to the other, Ko'San finally wrangled them back into their room with their nanny. "Please keep them quiet for the remainder of the night, Au'revele," Ph'eel called out from where she stood with Mee'ta.

Lo'San clearly bristled at Ph'eel's words, and watched both boys immediately quiet down at her demand for them to stop making noise. He took Synclare's hand in his. "Are you ready to go?" he asked her.

"I am," Synclare answered.

"We shall return tomorrow to accompany you and your young ones to our exercise facility," Lo'San said to Ko'San. Then he spoke to Au'revele. "Perhaps you could take the opportunity to see a bit of the ship. You are welcome to explore," Lo'San said kindly.

"She must stay with our sons," Ph'eel interrupted. "It is her sole responsibility!"

Synclare started backing down the corridor still holding tightly to Lo'San's hand. She was trying to get him away from his family before he lost his temper. "I'm getting very tired, Lo'San."

"Let us go, then," he said, allowing her to pull him away. "I shall see you tomorrow, Ko'San."

"Rest well!" Mee'ta called out.

"Perhaps we can tour the ship the following day!" Lau'San called after Lo'San.

Chapter 14

The next day found Synclare, Lo'San, Ko'San, Au'revele, both Ko'San's sons, Lau'San, Mee'ta and Ph'eel in the exercise facility. Both boys jumped and skipped their way through the exercise equipment as they held fast to Au'revele's hands and followed Lo'San and Ko'San as they walked with their father and spoke and laughed remembering their times as young ones themselves. Lo'San was dressed in exercise clothes, as were Lau'San and Ko'San. Lo'San had offered them similar attire and both had readily agreed.

Synclare was dressed in a pair of jeans and a simple teeshirt as opposed to the females of Lo'San's family and even Au'revele who wore long, heavy skirts. Synclare chatted with Mee'ta and Ph'eel as they followed along, doing their best to be good sports at finding themselves in the midst of many a large warrior involved in everything from exercise machinery to weight training.

"There are quite a few already here," Mee'ta commented, pulling her skirts tightly around her as she made sure not to brush against any equipment.

"There are thousands aboard the ship," Synclare explained. There is always someone on duty, and someone else on recreation."

"I see," Mee'ta said. "Are you sure they're safe?"

Synclare laughed. "Absolutely. They look scary, but they're some of the most honorable males you will ever encounter."

"I should hope so," Mee'ta mumbled.

"Is that it? Is that where we're going to race?" the oldest boy cried out excitedly.

"It is!" Lo'San answered, jogging past them and tearing his shirt off over his head to drop on a bench beside the track as they stepped out onto it.

Both boys let go of Au'revele's hands and chased after Lo'San as he took off down the circular track that ran the perimeter of the very large exercise facility. It was raised a couple of feet above the main level where all the equipment and weights were located.

Synclare laughed happily as she watched Lo'San and the boys chasing one another. She was startled to notice Ko'San glaring at Ph'eel when her gaze landed on him. She quickly turned to find Ph'eel watching Lo'San with a hunger in her eyes that was almost embarrassing it was so blatant.

Ko'San continued to glare at Ph'eel until she realized he was watching her, then, he removed his own shirt and turned to run as quickly as he could to catch up with Lo'San, determined to show he was the better athlete.

Ph'eel smiled at Synclare, realizing she'd seen her staring at Lo'San. "It always gives me such great pleasure to watch my young ones at play," she said, glancing toward the boys and Lo'San as they still raced and played on the far side of the track. Ph'eel looked back toward Synclare, trying to play it off as though she was simply watching her sons.

"It is truly a joy," Mee'ta said. "It would be such a tragedy if Lo'San were never given the gift of fatherhood. He is blessed to have a mate that desires young ones as passionately as he does."

Synclare nodded and returned her attention to her mate. She didn't think her mother-in-law meant to, but she'd just made Synclare feel more inadequate than she had in a very long time.

"Aha! I won!" the older boy said, laughing and taunting Lo'San who'd very clearly let him win.

"You are so fast!" Lo'San said. "I just couldn't keep up!"

"I want to race Au'revele! Come on, Au'revele! Race with us!" the younger boy said.

"You may go, Au'revele, if it pleases the young ones," Mee'ta said.

Ph'eel raised her tiny, perfect nose in the air, and agreed. "You may join them," she said haughtily.

Au'revele gripped her skirts in both hands and took off down the track. "I shall not let you win!" she cried as the boys took out after her.

"She seems like a wonderful young woman," Synclare said. "She obviously loves your sons."

"Yes, well, it is her one duty," Ph'eel said.

"Doesn't she get a break, any free time for herself?" Synclare asked.

"She has no need of it. She cares for them day and night. The only thing that would inhibit that is if we found her care neglectful, or if she were ill, then we'd return her to her village. We couldn't risk her illness in our home. Otherwise there is naught to do with the exception of keeping up with our young ones, and that is a full time position."

Shouts of laughter drew their attention again as Au'revele overtook the boys, then let them get ahead again. Au'revele laughed happily as she watched them thinking they'd caught up and were beating her. She loved to see the boys happy.

Her laughter was rich, light and melodic. It drew the attention of several males who were exercising in the facility. But it only caused one of them to lose his grip on the bar he held above his head, layered with weights on either side. The barbell crashed to the floor and made a deafening sound as one deep violet colored male trained his amethyst eyes on the female. His chest heaved as he watched her, her skirts gripped in her hands, as she ran and played with the two small males who called out to her to hurry and catch them.

"Au'revele! Hurry! You can't catch us!"

"I'm coming!" she called back.

And on hearing her voice, the violet male's head canted unconsciously to the side as his lips pulled back in a grimace. He turned in place, watching her progression around the track. It was then that he noticed some of the other males watching her as well. A rumble started as he became outraged at them watching her. Then he seemed to realize what was happening to himself.

"No!" he snarled. "No! No! No!" he shouted, as he stalked toward the exit of the facility.

Several males training with him, looked at each other, then back at him as they watched him go.

Au'revele happened to run down the track at exactly the same time he began to walk beneath it where it arched over the doorway. He paused and watched her go by. Her eyes caught his and she stumbled as she took in the beautiful, fierce male scowling at her. Forcing herself to continue on, she ran past, but kept her eyes on his as long as she could.

He watched her with a growl that increased with each passing second. As soon as she had to look away from him, he threw his head back and released a bellow that made all else go silent. "Nooooo!" he insisted as he slammed his way out of the facility.

They could still hear him snarling and cursing after he'd left the exercise facility and was well on his way down the corridor.

Mee'ta turned toward Synclare with her eyebrows raised in concern. "Who was that?" she asked.

"That was Zahn. He's one of Sirena Vivian's personal guard," Synclare answered.

"Should she be warned that he is near losing control?" Ph'eel asked, clearly alarmed.

Synclare shook her head. "No, I think he's okay," she said, turning to look at Au'revele where she still played with the boys. "Pretty sure, anyway."

~~~

Zahn stalked all the way back to his quarters, cursing and stomping, waving his hands in the air as he spoke the entire way. All he encountered gave him a wide berth, and he didn't even see them, so focused on his rage was he. He walked into the suite he shared with Rel, and stood there, doing his best to retake control of his emotions. He stalked into the cleansing chamber and slapped his hand against the sensor on the wall that would engage the cleansing foam. It was then he noticed the claws at the ends of his fingers were enlarged.

He ground his teeth in frustration and noticed they too were enlarged. Taking a deep breath and letting it out on a deep sigh, he stepped into the small shower-like cleansing unit and closed his eyes as the foam began to coat him as soon as he stood still. He waited while it began to melt away and run down his body. Then a high velocity fan engaged and dried his body before he stepped out of the unit, and hurried back to his room to dress and relieve whoever was guarding his Sirena. He needed to go back on duty. He needed to work. He needed to be sure that he could keep any ridiculous female out of his mind. He didn't want one, didn't need one, and refused to even acknowledge any females, other than those his friends had already claimed, were even onboard Command Warship 1.

"Someone else can have her. I refuse to get caught up on all the nonsense that goes along with a female!" Zahn shouted.

The door whooshed open and Rel stepped into their room. "Someone else can have who?" Rel asked.

"No one. Anyone!" Zahn shouted.

"Why did you leave the exercise facility so angrily? What happened?" Rel pressed.

"I did not leave angrily. I simply left."

"Really? And I suppose it wasn't you shouting, no, no, no, every step of the way?" Rel asked.

"I realized I was late. I'd forgotten to relieve Kail," Zahn lied.

"You were not supposed to relieve Kail. Kail and Asl are guarding our Sirena this day. You and I are on duty tomorrow."

"There has been a change in plan. I did not think to tell you," Zahn insisted as he pulled on his boots.

"Is that so?" Rel asked, doing his best to hold back a grin.

"Yes, that is so!" Zahn snapped.

"Very well. I suppose your behavior has nothing to do with a female running around the track with her two small younglings," Rel teased.

Zahn spun on his heel and faced Rel. "Are they her younglings?" he demanded.

"I did not ask, but, I believe they are her charges," Rel answered.

Zahn looked relieved but then went back into denial.

"I could find out for you," Rel offered. "I could even find out her name if you wish."

"I don't know who you speak of. I do not need to be supplied with any information on anyone," Zahn grouched as he strapped his weapon onto his belt.

"So, you didn't notice a beautiful young female with pale hair the color of moonlight and eyes as green as the seas of our Cruestace?" Rel asked.

"No! I most certainly did not!" Zahn answered. He strode to the door and as soon as it swept open he stepped into the corridor. "I don't wish to discuss this nonsense any longer!" he insisted as the door slid shut.

Rel chuckled, knowing full well what was happening.

The door opened again and Zahn walked back inside. He walked over to his storage locker and snatched his battle helmet from it. The helmet was dark and prevented anyone from seeing his face. "I need this!" he snapped.

"A battle helmet?" Rel asked.

"Yes! It is time we all started dressing more officially while on duty!" Zahn answered, shoving his helmet on his head and leaving their quarters again. "And if I wanted any information on Au'revele, I could find it myself!"

Rel full out laughed when it became apparent that Zahn even knew the female's name already. He heard Zahn snarl as he walked away from their quarters in the direction of Sirena Vivian's quarters.

Zahn walked stubbornly down the corridor, fully dressed — including his battle helmet — on his way to relieve Kail from his shift watching over Sirena Vivian. He knew Kail had no clue he was about to be relieved, but that was not the point. He needed to stay busy, stay focused. He reached up and patted the helmet, making sure that it was securely on his head. He knew it

142

wouldn't stop him from seeing Au'revele if she happened across his path again, but it would stop her from recognizing him, and that in itself was half the battle, he told himself.

~~~

"Will we be much longer here?" Mee'ta asked after almost an hour of watching the males of her family all playing like the children they once were.

Lo'San ducked away from the hand of one of his nephews as it reached out to tag him and looked toward his mother.

"You know? I think we'll all go to the commissary and have a snack. We can have some litah and visit," Synclare suggested.

"Sink Lar..." Lo'San said, planning to dissuade her.

"That would be most enjoyable, my daughter in bond," Mee'ta said.

"Yes, please, let us go there," Ph'eel added.

"We'll go to the commissary while you're here. It will be nice," Synclare said, walking toward Lo'San as he began to walk toward her. Once they were within reach of each other, Lo'San pulled her into his arms and kissed her. "I love you, Sink Lar," he said, looking into her eyes.

Synclare smiled at him and kissed him again. "We'll be fine. I love you, too," she said. "Have fun. You know how to find me if you need me," she said.

"And you me," he said a little too forcefully while throwing a glance toward his mother and Ph'eel.

"It'll be fine," Synclare insisted.

Mee'ta and Ph'eel very happily accompanied Synclare away from the exercise facility and thankfully entered the commissary a short time later.

"So," Synclare said as they took their seats at Synclare's favorite table, "tell me all about Lo'San as a child. What was he like?" she asked.

143

"Lo'San was a wonderful young one. He was kind and attentive. He was happy and always attempting to make others laugh," Mee'ta said.

"He was very protective of those he loved," Ph'eel said.

"You grew up with him…" Synclare said.

"Yes, we were the best of friends. It was always assumed that he'd accept my claim when we were old enough," Ph'eel said. "Everyone thought so."

"We did, yes. You were the perfect pair," Mee'ta said, wistfully. "So perfect for one another."

Synclare just gave the hint of a polite smile, yet said nothing.

"Oh, but the gods knew what we didn't," Mee'ta said. "You were out here, and so much better matched for Lo'San on his adventures through the life he's chosen for himself!"

Synclare did smile then. "Thank you, Mee'ta, that means so much to me."

"Mother 'San," Mee'ta said. "Call me Mother 'San. I am your bond-mother after all."

"Oh my goodness!" Synclare said, fanning herself. "You're going to make me cry. Thank you so much. I've never had a close family. You just don't know how much it means to me to be accepted into yours."

"Tears! Oh! No tears, Sink Lar," Mee'ta said, getting up and going around the table to hug Synclare from behind. "You have us now. We are family evermore!" Mee'ta said. Mee'ta's words did not match the sinister look she shared with Ph'eel who sat smirking when Synclare turned in her seat to hug Mee'ta. If anyone had been paying attention, they'd have known right away from that look alone, the two females were up to no good.

"Mother 'San is right, Sink Lar. I've long wished for a sister. As my mother only had me, it falls to you, as Lo'San's mate to become my bond-sister. And I couldn't be more pleased."

"Thank you, Ph'eel. I was worried we wouldn't get along once Lo'San told me that you'd once tried to claim him."

"Oh, Sink Lar. That was so, so long ago. And I've given my heart to Ko'San now. All has happened as it should have."

144

Synclare smiled as Mother 'San patted her shoulder and went back to her seat. "You have both made me so happy," she admitted, smiling at both Mother 'San and Ph'eel.

"And you us, my bond-daughter. Perhaps we can have another visit such as this tomorrow," Mee'ta said.

"Oh, I'm sorry, but I can't," Synclare said. Then she thought about it for a moment. "Well, I guess I could, but it would have to be earlier in the day."

"Why is that?" Mee'ta asked.

"I've got an appointment with our healer tomorrow afternoon," Synclare answered.

"Is this about helping you give Lo'San young ones?" Mee'ta asked.

"It is, yes. He wishes to meet with me, then we'll schedule the next treatment," Synclare explained.

"I certainly wish you well. It would be so unfair for Lo'San to not be able to have young ones. And doubly unfair if you are unable to provide him with them," Mee'ta said regretfully.

Synclare looked down at the cup held in her hands. Mee'ta's words were like a knife through her heart. She'd already thought of that herself. She didn't understand why she hadn't been able to produce ovum yet. According to all she'd heard and read, it should not have been that much of a problem to entice her body to produce ovum through the fertility treatments she'd endured. But then again, they shouldn't have made her as sick as they did, either.

"The treatments make me very ill. It takes days before I'm able to get up and function again," Synclare confided.

"Oh my! That is such a sacrifice," Ph'eel exclaimed.

"It is, but children are important to us both," Synclare said.

"I'm sure Lo'San will learn to be happy if you cannot give him young ones. He did, after all, choose you. I have no doubt he is devoted regardless," Mee'ta said. "He'll become accustomed to the idea of no young ones if it's at all necessary."

"We're not giving up. We're doing all we can," Synclare assured them.

"I am sure you are, my bond-daughter."

Chapter 15

Lo'San entered his and Synclare's quarters quietly. He'd covered the afternoon and most of the night shift on the Command Deck, then spent some time with his brother's family, and was sure Synclare was sleeping. He took his clothes off and slid into bed beside her, pulling her into his arms.

"Missed you," she mumbled.

"You should be sleeping," he answered.

"Did you have to work both shifts?" she asked, knowing he was later than anticipated.

"I spent some time with Ko'San, Ph'eel and their sons when I got off duty," Lo'San explained.

"I'm glad you're enjoying your time with them," she said, turning over so he'd spoon her from behind.

"I had forgotten how much I missed the feeling of home. It is a unique thing when those who knew you as a child see you and still care for you as an adult. It has given me a sense of pride."

Synclare opened her eyes and stared into the darkness. His comment made her feel that it was the opinions of those recently reentering his life that mattered more than hers. Shaking her head at her insecurities, she settled back down and closed her eyes for sleep.

"What do you shake your head about?" he asked.

"Nothing," Synclare answered.

"Ph'eel told me that she and my mother had a wonderful visit with you. She says the three of you spent the remainder of the day together and have grown quite close."

"Your mother has taken to calling me her bond-daughter."

"I am very happy you've found common ground, and even happier that my family has accepted you, my Sink Lar. I didn't realize how much it would mean to me," Lo'San confided.

Synclare shivered a bit when Lo'San pressed a kiss to her shoulder. "Thank you for bringing them here. Thank you for giving me the opportunity to have them prove me wrong. It would seem they truly only want me back in their lives, and they in mine. I would not have known this if not for you," Lo'San said, the appreciation clear in his voice.

Synclare teared up a bit. She felt so many things she wasn't quite sure which was making her so emotional. She blinked her eyes furiously, then closed them against the tears that threatened.

"Sink Lar?" Lo'San asked, propping himself up on his forearm as he looked down on her from behind. "Why do you cry? Has someone harmed you?"

Synclare shook her head again. "I'm just emotional lately. If I can't tell you why I cried, then it's not worth even speaking of," she said, her voice shaky.

"If you cry at all it is worth speaking of!" Lo'San said passionately.

"Just... let it go. I'll be fine. Get some sleep. We both have long days tomorrow."

Lo'San eventually settled in behind her, holding her as close as he could.

Just before she drifted off to sleep, she heard him softly speaking to her. "I do not like your tears, my mate. They hurt my heart. No more tears," he said, kissing her shoulder again, then the back of her neck.

Synclare didn't reply, so Lo'San just snuggled her closer, and fell asleep with her in his arms.

~~~

Synclare woke the next morning alone. She lay in her bed, looking around the bedroom. She knew that Lo'San had most likely left her sleeping out of consideration, but she still would have liked to be able to see him for a few moments before he

148

reported for duty. He'd been spending every available moment with his family, and squeezing in any hours he could to repay those covering his shifts when his family was most available.

Sighing dispassionately, she kicked the covers to the foot of the bed and sat up. The thought of getting up and dressed seemed like a monumental task, but it had to be done. She had to get up and ready to face the day, then go to the commissary to meet Mee'ta and Ph'eel for a brunch visit, before her afternoon appointment with Doc. Synclare shuffled into the galley in search of litah, or better yet, coffee, to get her going, but as she searched her small pantry, she remembered she'd used the last of it and since her in-laws' arrival had not had an opportunity to replenish her supplies.

Grumbling she headed to the cleansing chamber. "Quick shower then coffee at the commissary," she said aloud. Then a little bit of her grumpiness crumbled when she noticed a small handwritten note on the counter top beside the sink. She and Lo'San left each other little handwritten love notes. She'd started to do it just so he'd know she'd been thinking about him each time he came across one, and he'd responded by doing the same. His were almost elementary in the block handwriting he used when writing in the English language, and sometimes the words were out of order, but the fact that he even understood the emotional value, and made the effort to leave notes for her meant the world. She'd treasured and kept every single one of them. She looked down at the one she'd just found and smiled. "You are my happiness," he'd written and drawn little hearts around the words. Synclare smoothed her fingers over the words and left the cleansing chamber to add it to the ones she kept with her nightgowns in her dresser drawer. She placed her hand over her heart and smiled as she returned to the cleansing chamber. Though she felt a little lighter, she still needed coffee — badly.

~~~

Vivian and Kitty sat at her usual table in the back corner of the commissary enjoying their breakfast. Out of habit she watched the door each time anyone came in. She liked to greet everyone personally if they happened to glance her way. It made them feel 'seen' by her, and to her, it made all the difference in the world to know you mattered, especially to those you felt didn't even know your name. She watched as Synclare walked through the doors, her eyes glued to the station just before the serving line that offered all forms of drinks.

Vivian smiled to herself when Synclare poured herself a cup of coffee, added a splash of cream, and sipped heartily from the cup. Synclare topped it off, turned to walk away, then faced the drink station again. She appeared to be examining the large, silver decanters of drinks, and satisfied with whatever she'd found, lifted one of them and carried it with her as she walked toward the vicinity where she usually sat, looking for an available table. The commissary was filled almost to capacity and there weren't a lot of spaces available this morning.

"Synclare!" Vivian called.

Synclare raised her gaze and finally noticed Vivian sitting with Kitty.

"Come join me," Vivian invited.

Synclare nodded and made her way over. She pulled out a chair opposite Vivian and plopped down in it, then settled her entire decanter of coffee on the table in front of her.

"You good?" Vivian asked.

Synclare nodded. "Yeah. I'm just so... I don't know. I'm on the verge of tears all the time. I'm exhausted. No matter what I do I feel like it's not enough. My emotions are just all over the place," Synclare confided.

"Anything I can do?" Vivian asked.

Synclare shook her head.

"I've got strong shoulders if you want to unload," Vivian offered with a smile. "Is it Lo'San's family?"

"You know, I thought it might have been, and I'm sure the stress of getting to where we are now hasn't helped, but we really seem to have found some common ground. His mother is even calling me her bond-daughter."

"That's wonderful!" Vivian exclaimed.

"It is," Synclare agreed, gulping her coffee and reaching for the decanter to serve herself more.

"How are the treatments going?" Vivian ventured.

Synclare shrugged her shoulders. "They make me so sick I almost wish I'd just go ahead and die until the pain stops. But if it can help us have children, I'll do it every damn day," Synclare said.

"Is Lo'San supportive?" Vivian asked.

"Oh, yes! He's wonderful. Even when I tell him he doesn't have to attend the treatments, he shows up every single time. And when the pain gets so intense I can't even think, he prepares my medication and makes sure I take it so I can sleep through most of the pain." Synclare sat there drinking her coffee and let her thoughts tumble out of her mouth. "I wonder sometimes if my past is catching up with me."

"What do you mean?" Vivian asked.

"It's no secret. I've not hidden it from anyone. I put more chemicals into my body than anyone has a right to. And I can't help but wonder if maybe I poisoned my body. Maybe I've not produced the ovum Doc needs to harvest to provide Lo'San and me with children, because I damaged myself somehow. Maybe this is my punishment for living my life as I did on Earth," Synclare said. "That added to my age and the fact that I'm just about past child bearing age doesn't look good for us."

"Synclare, that's not the case. You are not the only woman who's ever dabbled in recreational drug use. Using drugs when you're young doesn't preclude your having children later in life. And you weren't doing it because you wanted to party, you were dealing with the loneliness and the fact that everyone in your life wanted nothing but your money! I think that earns you a pass. And the age thing... these healers are phenomenal with the things they can do. Just give it a bit longer and it'll be fine."

"Dabbled?" Synclare asked. "I used them to forget who I was, I used them to be able to sleep at night, and I used them to wake up in the morning. I can't remember a day that I made it the whole twenty-four hours sober. Now, of course, I was the perfect debutante socialite — no one ever knew. And it is what it is, I can't go back and undo it. But, I can't help wondering if that's why I'm not responding to the fertility treatment. That and the fact that my body just won't produce what it can no longer make."

"Synclare..." Vivian said, preparing to try to talk some sense into her.

"It's fine, Vivian. I'm sorry for unloading on you. I'm sure I'm just feeling sorry for myself. I have another appointment today and I'm not looking forward to delivering myself to Doc knowing I'll be suffering until at least tomorrow. Seems like the side effects are getting stronger with each treatment I undergo, which means the medication he gives me to counteract the pain and the nausea are stronger each time as well."

"And the hormones could explain the emotional unbalance, and the fatigue, too. Don't take all this on you. You're going through a lot right now, and meeting new family, and adjusting to being newly mated. I'm sure it will all be fine," Vivian encouraged.

Synclare nodded and drank her coffee. "You're probably right." Synclare's gaze wandered over to the large guards standing on either side of Vivian. One was Rel, the other was fully uniformed and helmeted. "Expecting trouble, or got a new guard?" Synclare asked.

Vivian's brows scrunched down and she turned to follow Synclare's gaze. "Oh, yeah, no. That's Zahn. For some reason he now insists on wearing his battle helmet, you know, like he wasn't scary enough already now he's got no visible face!" Vivian said, feigning excitement.

"I am simply attempting to be more focused on my duties, Sirena," Zahn responded patiently.

"And that needs a battle helmet?" Vivian asked.

"It can," he answered.

"Or maybe you just don't want to be seen," Rel mumbled.

Zahn used his thumb to lift the front of the helmet and glared at Rel. "You feel the need to add to the conversation?" he demanded.

Rel slowly shook his head as he stared straight ahead with a smirk. "Not me," he answered.

Zahn allowed his eyes to scan the commissary quickly before dropping his helmet back in place.

Vivian watched them, surprise on her face as they picked at each other. She turned back to Synclare as she spoke. "Never a dull moment around here, I'll tell you that." She realized that Synclare was watching Zahn with a slight smile on her face. "You know something I don't?" she asked.

Synclare pulled her attention from Zahn and looked at Vivian. "Maybe. I think I'm going to go for a run. Exercise always gives me more energy. Want to come?"

"Yeah, I think I will. Kitty loves to run and I haven't taken him in a while. Come on, Kitty," Vivian said, getting to her feet.

Synclare and Vivian with Kitty in tow, left the commissary with Vivian's guards following at a respectful distance. What they didn't notice was Ph'eel and Mee'ta sitting only four tables away having their breakfast, and sharing a sinister smile as they watched the two women leave.

"Did you hear all I did?" Ph'eel leaned toward Mee'ta and asked in a hushed voice.

"I did. And I have an idea," Mee'ta responded.

~~~

After a quick couple of laps around the track, Vivian and Synclare were huffing and trying to catch their breath while Kitty batted around a large medicine ball. Zahn and Rel stood near the track, yet far enough away from Vivian to give her the sense of some privacy, and kept a wary eye as Vivian and Synclare cooled down after their run.

153

Synclare was dragging a towel over the back of her neck when the voices of two excited children caught her attention. Synclare turned toward the door of the facility and broke out in a huge smile when she saw Au'revele and both of Ko'San's sons coming their way.

"Watch this," she said quietly to Vivian.

"What?" Vivian asked, looking around.

Synclare indicated Zahn with a nudge of her chin and lifted an arm to wave at Au'revele. "Au'revele! How are you today?" she called out.

Almost immediately Zahn's chest began to rumble.

Synclare shared a look with Vivian that said 'see?'.

"Miss Sink Lar, we are quite well. I trust you are well, too," Au'revele replied but didn't quite meet Synclare's gaze.

"Just finished our jog for the morning," Synclare answered.

"The boys have become quite used to a bit of playtime before breakfast," Au'revele explained. "Thank you for arranging permission for them to play here."

"It's nothing. Just took pointing out that they wanted to come to it, and it was approved right away," Synclare said. Then she looked over toward Vivian. "Au'revele, may I introduce you to Sirena Vivian of Cruestace? Vivian, this is Au'revele. She is the nanny to Ko'San and Ph'eel's sons."

Horror crossed Au'revele's face, and she immediately dropped into an uncomfortable combination of a curtsy and a bow. "Forgive my insolence, Sirena. I had no idea who you were," she rushed out on a whisper.

Zahn took half a step forward, his rumbling a definite distraction. Vivian glanced toward him. "Really, dude? You want to frighten everybody here, today? Get yourself under control." Then she turned her attention back to Au'revele. "Au'revele? Am I right?" she asked.

Au'revele dipped her head in a quick nod as she kept her eyes pinned on the floor.

"You have a beautiful name. And I'm very happy to meet you. But I can't properly meet you unless you look me in the eye," Vivian said, her voice happy and encouraging.

154

"Oh, Sirena, I couldn't..." Au'revele replied.

"Of course, you can. Because I'm telling you, you can," Vivian said.

Slowly, and very hesitantly, Au'revele lifted her gaze to Vivian's.

Vivian smiled brightly. "There you are! Hello, Au'revele," Vivian said.

Au'revele smiled shakily. "Hello, Sirena."

"Do you bring the boys here everyday?" Vivian asked.

"Yes, Sirena," Au'revele answered.

"And you run and play with them?" Vivian asked.

"Yes, Sirena," Au'revele answered.

"Why don't you dress for it? It can't be convenient to run in all those yards of skirts," Vivian said.

"I am not allowed to dress in any other fashion, Sirena. I'm only a servant..." Au'revele said, as though that explained everything.

Vivian wasn't quite sure she understood the part of having to wear a heavy, plain, drab colored dress, but she did know one thing. This girl was not just a servant. She was someone's daughter, someone's sister, someone's someone very special, and Vivian didn't like to see her so obviously afraid to be herself.

"Au'revele, look at me again, please," Vivian asked.

Au'revele gradually lifted her eyes to meet Vivian's again. "You are not just a servant. You matter, just as everyone on this ship matters. Do not ever think that you don't. Do you understand?" Vivian asked.

"Au'revele, hurry up! We want to pet the shraler!" the oldest boy shouted.

"No!" Au'revele shouted and darted toward the boys where they were on their way to Kitty.

"It's fine, Au'revele! Kitty won't hurt them," Vivian called out, moving at the same time to get nearer to Kitty.

Before they could reach the boys and Kitty, the youngest boy reached up and tapped Kitty on the nose. Kitty's face wrinkled up as he pulled his head back and regarded the tiny person in front of him. Then he lifted a huge paw and tapped the boy on the nose so hard the boy fell over backward. Then Kitty walked over to the boy and leaned his huge head down to press his nose to the boy's. The boy laughed and reached out taking hold of Kitty's ears, and Kitty licked a huge swath of wetness up the side of the boy's face.

"He likes me!" the boy yelled.

"Kitty! Get off the child!" Vivian ordered.

"It's okay. I like him! Can I have him?!" the boy asked.

"No, I'm afraid he's staying right here with me. He thinks I'm his Mommy," Vivian answered, pulling Kitty back so the boy could get to his feet.

"He's big," the older boy commented.

"Yes, he is," Vivian agreed.

"I'm so sorry, Sirena. They didn't know he was your pet," Au'revele said.

"Nothing to apologize for. I'm going to let you and your charges play, and I'm going to get something to drink, and get cleaned up."

Zahn's chest rumbled again, and Vivian threw him a glance. "And maybe switch out a guard or two," she added.

"I need to go as well. I need to get some supplies to restock my galley, and I have a brunch date with Mee'ta and Ph'eel, then I have an appointment later in the day," Synclare said.

Au'revele's face reflected immediate fear.

"What's wrong?" Synclare asked.

"If they knew I'd spoken to..." she began, but stopped short of finishing her sentence.

"No worries, Au'revele. I spoke to you first and you had to answer me. And for the record I find it pretty damned sad that they even control who you can and can't speak to," Vivian said.

"They even have to give Ko'San and Lau'San permission to speak. It's not a lifestyle I care to be a part of," Synclare admitted. "I'm so thankful that Lo'San chose to live his life here rather than there."

"Control happy much?" Vivian asked, strolling toward the exit doors, with Synclare at her side.

156

Vivian threw a glance over her shoulder and found Rel right behind them, and Zahn following along as well, but his attention was back on Au'revele as she chased the two little boys that were her responsibility.

"Zahn and Au'revele?" Vivian mouthed, her eyes wide.

Synclare raised her eyebrows and gave a can-you-believe-it expression. "Girl... do you see the resistance to what is obvious to everyone else?" she asked.

"He's the most stubborn I think I've encountered yet," Vivian answered.

"He's obviously obsessed with her," Synclare said.

"He has made it painfully clear each time one of his warrior brothers has found their Ehlealah, that a female of any kind, Ehlealah or not, is not something he's interested in even considering," Vivian said.

"Hmpf, you know that saying... The bigger they are the harder they fall? I think he's going to fall harder than all the rest," Synclare said with a chuckle.

Chapter 16

Synclare smiled as she took the seat between Ph'eel and Mee'ta that Mee'ta indicated.

"Tell me, bond-daughter, how has your day been?" Mee'ta asked.

"Very good," Synclare answered.

"This is good. It is important to go to your treatment with a complete lack of stress," Mee'ta said.

Synclare nodded politely. "I try. As stress free as I can be."

"Why does it cause you stress? I understand it is a simple procedure," Mee'ta said

"Mother 'San, if you recall, Sink Lar stated that the treatments make her ill and cause her a great amount of pain. Surely it is difficult to proceed knowing these will be the results each and every time," Ph'eel said.

"Oh, of course. Forgive my inattentiveness. How may I help, I wish to be of comfort to you, my bond-daughter."

"It's not necessary. Lo'San always puts me in bed and gives me the pain medication that Doc prescribes. He sits with me until I fall asleep before going back to work. It's about all that can be done," Synclare said.

"I know! I shall tell Lo'San that we'll stay with you while he works and you struggle through the suffering that will no doubt come," Mee'ta said.

"Oh, that's not necessary," Synclare said.

"But it is! I would do the same for Ph'eel, just as I would my own daughter had I had one. You two are the daughters of my heart now. You understand how much it means to me, I'm sure," Mee'ta said, clasping her hands to her heart and forcing a sheen to her eyes that enforced her impassioned plea.

"I don't want you to go to any trouble, Mother 'San," Synclare said.

"And I don't wish you to go through this alone. As long as I am near, you will have me to care for you," Mee'ta said.

"And me, too," Ph'eel added.

"I don't know what to say," Synclare admitted.

"Just say that you will allow us to care for you. Lo'San does his best I'm sure, but he is not female, there is no way he can actually understand all that you go through," Mee'ta insisted.

"Alright then, I'll tell Lo'San. I can't guarantee that he'll agree, but I will try," Synclare promised.

~~~

Synclare sat across from Doc as he went over the details of her chart and all the treatments she'd undergone. She held a cotton ball to the crook of her elbow where he'd just taken a small blood sample.

"I must be honest, Synclare. I am very concerned that you've not yet responded to treatment. With Cruestaci women, the response is almost instantaneous. Even with women of other species, I'm not aware of more than one week between the onset of treatments and the harvesting of a healthy ovum for fertilization."

Synclare sat speechless across from Doc. She'd been under the impression that it was routine to have to endure many treatments before finally being successful. When she recovered enough to speak, her shock was evident in the tears she attempted to hide. "Are you telling me that my course of treatment is not standard? I should have been finished with all this and pregnant by now?" she asked.

"You must understand, Synclare. I have never treated one of your race. All I know of your people, I have learned while working with the females brought aboard. Your response to our treatment could very well be normal for your race," Doc explained.

Synclare let his words roll around in her head. "And the pain that always plagues me afterward?" she asked.

"I have not seen it before," he admitted.

"What if we called in human physicians and got their input?" she asked.

"We could, but, they are completely unfamiliar with our medical practices and success in fertility improvement in our own people. We would be speaking two different languages — in more than one way. But, if you wish, we can try."

Synclare shook her head. She understood what he meant. The human doctors didn't know the procedures he was trying to do to the human body to encourage fertility, any more than he knew the human body and the responses that it would have to the Cruestaci procedures. They couldn't help each other. "No. Let's just try a little longer before I give up."

"I will not give up, Synclare. I will continue my research and perhaps with any luck at all, I will find the piece we are missing to enable you to have younglings," Doc promised.

Synclare nodded. "Thank you," she answered. She stood when Doc did and followed him out of his office and into the examination room next door. While Doc turned his back and prepared the injection, as well the instruments to swab her, Synclare stripped down and donned the disposable gown waiting for her. She climbed up on the table and when he turned to her, she raised her hand to swipe at the tears that streamed silently down her face.

"Do not give up hope, Synclare," Doc encouraged.

"I haven't. I'm just surprised to find out that what I'm experiencing is not the norm." She swiped at another tear and huffed a laugh. "You'd think with all these damn emotions I'm fighting lately, I'd already be pregnant!"

Doc extended the stirrups for her feet and she allowed him to place her where he needed her. He took a swab, then gently returned her feet to the table and extended the table end to allow her to rest comfortably. "Ready for your injection?" he asked.

"I'm here!" Lo'San said, as he opened the door and rushed inside the room.

"Lo'San," Synclare said tearily, reaching for him.

"I am sorry I'm late. But I made it," he said, going to Synclare's side and holding her hand in his.

"All is well. You made it in time," Doc said. "Now, if you could turn to your side, Synclare..."

Synclare turned and Lo'San pulled the gown aside so that Doc could give her the injection. Once that was finished, Doc stood there looking down at Synclare.

"What is it?" Synclare asked.

"Just something you said. I have some more research to do, and if you will allow me to take another sample, I would like to perform another test."

"Whatever you think might help," Synclare answered.

Doc made quick work of taking another blood sample, capped it and put it safely in his lab, then returned to them with more vials of pain and nausea medicine.

"These will help with the side effects as usual. Do be careful with the dosage. This is very strong and could possibly have adverse effects," Doc said.

"Of course," Lo'San answered.

Synclare whimpered a bit and squeezed Lo'San's hand.

"Already, Sink Lar?" he asked, surprised that her body was already responding to the injection she was given. It usually took a bit longer before it hit her.

"You should see her home. I will perform the additional testing and contact you if necessary. Do not be surprised if I do not contact you right away. I may take the opportunity to reach out to Earth's physicians and ask a few questions. I wonder if I have not been remiss in my assumption that they could provide no information simply because of their unfamiliarity with our fertility procedures."

"Thank you for all your efforts," Synclare said.

Doc left them so that she could get dressed, and he hurried to his lab. He had a new theory that he just couldn't believe he'd not considered before.

~~~

Not even halfway to their quarters Lo'San had to pick up
Synclare and carry her in his arms. The pain set in so quickly and
so severely that she couldn't stand any longer, much less walk.

"This is not worth young ones, Sink Lar. I cannot bear to
watch you suffer like this any longer," Lo'San said.

"It's not that bad," she insisted.

"You cannot walk, the pain is so intense," Lo'San pointed
out.

"But it will pass. And then, we'll have a little you running
around," Synclare said, smiling through the grimace on her face
as she attempted to ride out the pain.

Lo'San stepped off the lift and turned toward their
quarters. The moment he did he was surprised to find his
mother and Ph'eel waiting outside their door. "This is not a good
time," he barked.

"No, it's okay. They wanted to help me after the
appointment today. I told them that I'd speak to you about it, but
you got there late and then...," her explanation faded as a wave of
nausea hit her.

"I'm not leaving you like this," Lo'San said, holding her
closely to his chest as he slapped his hand against the sensor
beside their door.

"You're on duty," she said quietly. "And your mother can
take care of me if I need anything," Synclare insisted.

"Sink Lar..." he started, as he walked inside and his mother
and sister-in-law waited for his decision politely outside their
door, watching him hold Synclare as though she would break she
was so fragile.

"I have grown very fond of my bond-daughter, Lo'San. My
heart aches for her attempts to provide you with a young one.
Her dedication to your happiness has won me over. Please allow
me to help in her care," Mee'ta said.

162

"I admire her as well," Ph'eel said. "If she needs you, I will come for you at once."

"I'm not leaving until she is resting easy," Lo'San said adamantly.

"Please, whatever you want to do is fine. I just really need to take my medicine," Synclare said, urging him to hurry up with whatever decision he'd make.

"Very well, enter," he said to the two women waiting for his decision, before spinning and carrying his mate toward their bedroom.

He laid Synclare on their bed and removed her clothing, then pulled another of his soft undershirts over her head and dressed her in it. Then he tucked her under the covers and kissed her. "I'll be right back," he promised.

Synclare rolled over to her side and held her stomach where she cramped so intensely, and allowed herself to fall into uncontrollable sobs. She knew somewhere deep inside that she was letting go of the dream of having children. She just couldn't go through this anymore. Not only was it becoming physically prohibitive, but Lo'San had just told her he couldn't endure watching her suffer anymore. His words were, 'it wasn't worth young ones'.

Lo'San hurried out of his bedroom and went to the galley, where he pulled out all he needed to prepare a cup of litah for Synclare. Once done, he withdrew one of the vials of medicine from his pocket and carefully measured out the dosage before mixing it into the litah.

"Is that the medication she needs?" Mee'ta asked.

"It is. You must be very precise when measuring. Too much can cause her harm," Lo'San said. He placed the vial on the counter top, then picked up the cup of litah and stepped around his mother. "I'll show you exactly how much to give her, and how long you must wait to give her more, before I go."

"Very well, my son," Mee'ta answered, her eyes full of concern.

163

Synclare lay sniffling and trying to catch her breath when Lo'San returned with her litah.

"Here, Sink Lar. Drink this," he said, kneeling beside the bed as she lifted herself to lean against the pillows behind her.

"Thank you," she answered, as she brought the hot, sweet liquid to her lips. She detected a slight bitterness from the medication laced through it, but all that did was give her hope that she'd soon be asleep. She drank the litah down as quickly as she could, then handed the cup back to Lo'San. Settling back against the pillows again, she couldn't help but need to ask Lo'San why he'd kept the truth from her. She watched as he rose to his feet to return the cup to the galley, and couldn't help the words as they fell from her lips.

"You weren't honest with me. Why did you hide the truth from me?" she asked.

Lo'San turned to face Synclare, confused by her question. "I don't understand. What truth did I hold back?"

"Lo'San. I'm not a fool. I know you probably did it to protect me, but don't you think I should have known?" she asked.

"I didn't think it important. I still think it's not important. It is true that I once loved her and hoped for a life with her, but I no longer love her. It was a long time ago. She refused to forgo all other mates. I left because I couldn't share her — it was better to be alone than to have to share Ph'eel. I could not be a part of that world any longer. What I once felt for Ph'eel doesn't matter now. We are mated and that is forever. It cannot be undone," Lo'San said, thinking she meant what he once felt for Ph'eel.

Synclare sat in their bed, her mouth hanging open in shock. He'd never told her that he was in love with Ph'eel, and that she refused to have only him for a mate. He told her that he'd been claimed and refused to accept the claim.

"I thought you said you left home because you refused to accept her claim," Synclare managed to get out.

"I did."

"You didn't say it was because she refused to have only you for a mate," Synclare added. "You let me believe that you just didn't want to live that life."

"I did not want to live the only life available to me with her. She is cold and calculating," Lo'San insisted.

"And refused to be exclusive with you. And now your brother is mated to her, and looks resentfully at the both of you each time Ph'eel is kind to you," Synclare said, closing her eyes when the medicine she'd taken began to make her loopy.

"Sink Lar," Lo'San said, shoving the cup toward a dresser as he returned to her side and took a seat beside her. "It is all in the past. I am not the male I was then. I am a mated male. The things I wanted then do not apply now."

Synclare turned her back to him and held onto her pillow. "I was asking why you didn't tell me that I should have responded to the fertility treatments by now. I didn't mean Ph'eel and any feelings you had for her."

"I didn't wish to cause you unhappiness. And I was hopeful that the treatments would be successful."

"Why did you think that I was asking about Ph'eel?" Synclare asked.

"That is what I first thought of when you said I'd withheld the truth," Lo'San admitted.

"It must have been heavy on your heart," she commented.

"Sink Lar, I was a different male then. It matters no longer."

She gritted her teeth fighting a wave of nausea, and Lo'San reached out to smooth her hair away from her face.

"I can't watch you suffer like this again. We are finished with the treatments," he said.

"I want children, wanted to give you a family," she said.

"Those things are no longer important, Sink Lar. You must release that desire. I see now that we should have just remained as we were," Lo'San said.

Synclare's heart broke a little, and she lifted a hand to push his away from her. "Go away. I'm fine."

"You are not fine!" he insisted.

"I will be. And I have your mother to care for me if I need until I'm better, and if I need the Healer, I'm perfectly capable of asking Missy to call for him. You don't have to worry about me any longer. I won't be undergoing any additional treatments."

165

"Thank you for understanding, Sink Lar," Lo'San said.

Synclare didn't answer, she couldn't even form words she was hurting so badly, both emotionally and physically. Lo'San had just told her they should have never mated, they should have just remained friends. She wasn't sure what hurt more, her body, or her soul. She felt the effects of the medication beckoning her to sleep, and just allowed herself to let go of consciousness.

Lo'San sat there until she was breathing evenly, then he leaned over her, kissed her face. And rested his head against hers. "As long as you're at my side, Sink Lar, I do not need young ones. I only need you. Rest, my mate. When you awake, we will plan the rest of our lives with many adventures to fill our days."

Lo'San left the bedroom with no idea that he and Synclare had just had two totally different conversations.

He thought he was encouraging her to stop torturing her body, thinking that he needed young ones to be happy. He was trying to tell her that they should have never tried to force something that didn't happen without medical assistance, they should have just remained as they were and let things happen naturally or not on the child front.

She thought he was saying that they should have remained friends as they'd been before mating. She thought that he was admitting that his feelings for Ph'eel were close to the surface and they — herself and Lo'San — should have just remained as they were so that he'd be free to claim Ph'eel now.

The last thought Synclare had before the drugs knocked her out was that at least with Ph'eel, he'd be able to see his family regularly, and Ph'eel could give him the children she never could.

Lo'San walked out of his bedroom and back into the living space.

"How is she?" Mee'ta asked, standing as he entered.

"She is suffering, and she is heartbroken. I've told her that our treatments are finished. I cannot watch her suffer any longer. I love her too much to put her through this," Lo'San said.

"I'm so sorry, my son. I had wished for young ones in your life," Mee'ta said.

Lo'San thought about it for a moment and smiled sadly. "I don't need them. I thought I did, but all I need is Sink Lar. Our lives will be full of love for one another. It is all we need," he said, ending with a peaceful smile.

"I'm very happy to know that you are at ease with this. And if you feel you wish to be near young ones, Ph'eel and Ko'San will surely have more they will welcome your influence upon," Mee'ta said.

"Yes! I am extremely fertile and anxious to have many more. Ko'San's sons have become attached to you, as I'm sure any other young ones I may have will as well."

"They are fond of Sink Lar as well," Mee'ta added.

"Oh, yes! Very fond," Ph'eel said.

"Thank you both for understanding, and for being here with us. I am grateful for your kindness to my Sink Lar."

"We love her as well as we love you," Mee'ta said.

Chapter 17

A short while later Lo'San was lying beside Synclare when Missy roused him.

"General Lo'San?"

"Yes, Missy," Lo'San answered.

"You are needed on the Command Deck, sir," Missy informed him.

"I'll be right there, Missy," Lo'San answered, gently leaving the bed and dropping a kiss on Synclare's head before he left.

"Lo'San!" Ph'eel said a bit too happily when he came back into the living space.

"I have to return to the Command Deck. Can you stay with Sink Lar until I return?" he asked his mother, not responding to Ph'eel's greeting.

"It is why I am here, Lo'San. Go, tend your duties, we will be here watching over your mate," Mee'ta encouraged.

"Thank you, Mother. Come, let me show you the proper dosage for her medication should she wake and need more," Lo'San said, walking toward the galley with his mother right behind him.

~~~

Ph'eel stood just inside the storage locker that held all of Synclare's and Lo'San's clothes. She wore a condescending smirk as she shoved all Synclare's clothing to one side, as far away from Lo'San's as she could get it. "She doesn't even have clothing appropriate to Lo'San's status. She cannot possibly represent him properly!"

168

"I suppose for an alien, she is doing the best she can," Mee'ta answered.

"It almost sounds like you have accepted her," Ph'eel said, looking toward Mee'ta with a horrified expression.

Mee'ta met Ph'eel's gaze and held it for a moment before laughing riotously. Ph'eel matched her laughter. Once they'd both recovered, and were fanning themselves to recover from the exertion the laughter required, Ph'eel continued on her search of the bedroom Synclare and Lo'San shared. She wandered over to a dresser and pulled open drawer after drawer until she happened upon one that contained Synclare's satin nightgowns, and the love notes that she'd kept from Lo'San.

"What is this?" she asked, picking up the stack of notes that consisted of different sized scraps of paper to full sheets.

"Some kind of letter, I think," Mee'ta said.

"Why bother with such an antiquated form of communication when one can much more easily have a vid com sent?" Ph'eel asked.

"Perhaps they did not wish to have the content made a matter of public record," Mee'ta suggested.

"What could it possibly say that needed to be kept confidential?" Ph'eel asked, still thumbing through the notes.

"Do you have your tablet with you? Scan them. See if our technology can translate the messages," Mee'ta said.

"Of course," Ph'eel said. "I shall be right back!" she exclaimed, dropping the notes to the bed and hurrying through Synclare and Lo'San's home on her way to the rooms she had been assigned while aboard the ship.

Mee'ta gathered the notes and returned them to the drawer, then went to the storage unit and closed the doors to make it appear untouched, should Synclare awake or Lo'San return unexpectedly.

Eventually Ph'eel returned, her tablet in hand. "I have it!" she cried out, waving it over her head as she hurried back into the bedroom. "Where are they?" she asked.

"I put them back in the drawer," Mee'ta answered.

Ph'eel removed the notes from the drawer and spread them out on the foot of the very bed Synclare slept in. Ph'eel scanned the notes and told her tablet to translate them, then returned them to the drawer again. "There's a credit band in here, as well," Ph'eel said.

"It must be Sink Lar's. I've noticed that Lo'San wears his," Mee'ta said, standing to investigate. She lifted the band and tried to turn it on. When it didn't work, she carried it over to the bed and used Synclare's finger print to activate the band. Mee'ta sat on the edge of the bed and used Synclare's finger to press the buttons on the side of the band and go through all the settings.

"She has fifteen thousand credits in her name," Mee'ta said, still scrolling.

"It isn't much," Ph'eel said.

"She doesn't need much, she lives here with Lo'San," Mee'ta said. A few seconds later Mee'ta's eyebrows raised when she was able to access Lo'San's account. "Lo'San has well over a million credits in his personal account."

"He has done very, very well for himself," Ph'eel said.

"Come, let's replace this, and leave her to rest for now. I have much to consider," Mee'ta said.

It was sometime later, after they'd already retired to the living space, that Synclare awoke, and could be heard moving around in the bedroom.

Mee'ta glanced at Ph'eel. "Give me strength," she muttered before rising and returning reluctantly to the bedroom. "Sink Lar? Are you awake?" Mee'ta called out. "Oh, goodness! I see that you are. Can I assist you, my bond-daughter?"

"Lo'San?" Synclare asked.

"He was called back to the Command Deck. I told him that I would stay with you. What can I get for you?" Mee'ta asked.

"Cold cloth," Synclare answered.

"Of course. Do you need more medication?" Mee'ta asked.

Synclare shook her head. "It is time?" she asked.

Mee'ta made a big show of checking the time. "No, Sink Lar. I'm sorry I offered, it is not yet time. I'll return momentarily with a cold cloth. You rest."

Synclare settled back against her pillows and her still sedated eyes closed almost immediately.

Mee'ta strolled back into the living space.

"I have the translations!" Ph'eel said excitedly, leaning over her tablet.

"What do they say?" Mee'ta asked, coming to sit beside her.

Ph'eel scrolled through the translated messages, her brow furrowing with each one. "They are declarations of love!" Ph'eel spat.

"It is unfortunate that Lo'San is so attached to a female that does nothing to better his position," Mee'ta said.

"It truly is," Ph'eel said, swiping the screen of her tablet to turn off the screen as she sat back and crossed her arms over her chest disgustedly.

The com unit began to tweet — its signal that an incoming com was waiting to be answered.

"Should we answer that?" Ph'eel asked.

Just then the com unit answered the call, and the females were able to hear it as it was recorded.

"Synclare! I have news! After your session this morning and our conversation during the same, I had an idea and contacted Consul Kol Ra' Don Tol at Earth Base 28. He put me in touch with healers who work under his supervision and they provided me base lines for certain hormonal and enzyme levels as they apply to human females. We'll be working in conjunction in the future and I'm extremely excited at the concept.... Forgive me, you care not about these things. The reason for my com is, I ran tests according to their guidelines. I know why you've not ovulated as expected. I know why your body has reacted so violently to all the fertility treatments. I am a fool for not considering it before. You are already with youngling, Synclare! Your body has been fighting off all the attempts we made to force you into ovulation because you've already conceived. It's protecting your youngling! Come to my office the moment you get this com,

Synclare. And do not take any more of the medication to ease your symptoms!"

The com ended and the unit chimed three times, indication that it had been recorded.

Ph'eel and Mee'ta sat, watching each other wide eyed.

"What do we do?" Ph'eel asked.

"Give me a bit of time. I have to think this through," Mee'ta answered, her mind already working on a plan.

~~~

Mee'ta moved a chair into the bedroom and sat beside the bed as Synclare slept. She'd deleted the com left by the ship's healer, sent Ph'eel back to her family to be seen out and about with Ko'San, brought the cold cloth that Synclare had asked for when she'd momentarily awakened and dutifully administered exactly the correct dosage of medication when it was supposed to be administered. And now she waited for Lo'San to return.

Sure enough, as soon as his duties were seen to, Lo'San returned home, striding into his home and directly into the bedroom without pause.

"Mother?" he asked as he approached Synclare and smoothed his hand across her brow as she slept. "Has she awakened?"

"She did. She wanted a cool cloth, which I brought, and then she slept until it was time for her medication. I woke her and gave it to her, and she's been asleep ever since," Mee'ta assured him.

"Has she been ill?" Lo'San asked.

"She's been in pain, but nothing more. Once I administered her second dose, she seemed to ease a bit and has rested better."

"Thank you, Mother. I am indebted to you for watching over her. I have hated having to leave Sink Lar alone after each treatment. I cannot explain how much I appreciate you being here with her today," Lo'San said, taking Synclare's hand in his as he took the seat his mother had vacated.

"Nonsense," Mee'ta said. "I'm so happy to be of service."

"Have you eaten?" he asked his mother, as her hovering caught his attention.

"No, I have not. But I am well. What can I do for you?" she asked.

"Nothing. I meant only to come home and hold Sink Lar while she recovers," Lo'San answered.

"I shall rest in the living space in case I can be of assistance," Mee'ta said.

"No, go on back to Father. I'm sure he worries about you. If I need assistance, I'll call for you," Lo'San said.

"Are you sure, my son?" Mee'ta asked.

"Absolutely. Go, and thank you, again, Mother."

"Very well. I shall check with you in the morning, if I don't hear from you this night," Mee'ta said. She made a big show of leaning over Synclare and kissing her forehead, before standing and pulling Lo'San down so she could kiss him as well, then quietly left their home.

Lo'San felt grateful that his mother had been there for him. And began to strip out of his clothes to slip into bed beside Synclare. But, at the last moment, he felt the need to go into the galley to check the medication and how much was left. Lifting the bottle, he was relieved to find that exactly the amount he'd instructed his mother to use was gone, no more — no less. Smiling to himself that things were finally seeming to repair themselves, and how Synclare had been the catalyst for it all, he returned to the bedroom and got into bed beside her. He pulled her gently into his arms and kissed her hair, inhaling the calming scent of his mate. "You have truly blessed me, Sink Lar," he whispered. "All in my life is better because of you."

The next morning, he woke early, and found that he was alone. Then he heard it, the sound of Synclare in their cleansing chamber, emptying the contents of her stomach. He jumped to his feet and rushed to her side. Entering the cleansing chamber,

173

he placed his hands on her shoulders. "Sink Lar, why didn't you wake me?" he gently scolded.

Synclare didn't answer, she couldn't. The dry heaves that had taken over her body stole all the strength she had. After they eventually stopped, she sank down onto the metallic floor and lay there, thankfully letting the coldness of the floor cool her sweaty skin. Her body trembled as she felt a cold, damp cloth being pressed against her face and neck. She opened her eyes to find Lo'San hovering above her.

"Can I take you back to our bed?" he asked, looking down at her with pity in his eyes.

Synclare shook her head and closed her eyes again. Her stomach clenched and she grimaced as she curled up into the fetal position.

"Sink Lar, what can I get for you?" Lo'San asked.

Synclare shook her head, remembering his words that they should have just stayed as they were. "Just want to sleep," she finally whispered.

"Alright," he answered, scooping her up in his arms and carrying her back to the bedroom. He tucked her back in bed and walked out of the bedroom, only to return moments later with another dose of her medication.

Synclare accepted the medication gratefully, and turned her back on him, knowing it would only be moments before it took effect and she'd be out again.

"I shall stay with you," Lo'San said.

Synclare shook her head again. "It's not necessary. I know you have responsibilities. I'll be fine," she answered.

"I have to be sure you're well," he insisted.

"I am well. I'll be recovered shortly and you won't have to even consider it again. We'll be just like we were before."

"I am not on duty this day. I am staying with you," Lo'San insisted.

"Go spend time with your family. All you will do here is watch me sleep, and neither of us needs that," Synclare said, her voice gruff and raspy from being sick to her stomach and the pain she endured.

"Do not argue with me, Sink Lar!" Lo'San insisted.

"Do whatever you want," she murmured as the medication finally took effect, quickly pulling her into a drugged sleep. "Whatever you want is fine."

~~~

"I was thinking that today would be the best day for you and Lo'San to spend together," Mee'ta said over a breakfast in their quarters.

"Do you?" Lau'San asked, perking up a bit.

"I do. He is not on duty this day, and we have all been occupying his every free moment. Today should be just you and your oldest son, Lau'San. In fact, after we finish our meal, I shall accompany you to his home, offer to watch over our bond-daughter, and give you both the gift of an entire day without the distraction of the rest of us," Mee'ta answered.

"I would be very happy to have such a day, but if his Sink Lar is ill, he will surely prefer to stay with her, as is to be expected," Lau'San said.

"I stayed with her yesterday and most of last evening. I am sure he will be comfortable with me caring for her. After all, we only have a limited time remaining before we will be leaving the ship. It is best to take advantage of our days while we can," Mee'ta said.

Lau'San thought about it. "We can ask," he said, hoping for any time with his son. "But if he prefers to stay with Sink Lar, we will not push him."

"Of course," Mee'ta said, sipping her litah and planning in the back of her mind.

Smiling as he took his last bite of food, he pushed his empty plate away and stood. "I'll prepare for the day. Will you be long?" Lau'San asked.

"Only a moment or two. Go ahead and get dressed."

"Very well, Mee'ta. Thank you for considering today for Lo'San and me."

"Of course, Lau'San. What kind of mate, or mother would I be if I didn't place your needs above my own whenever possible?"

~~~

Lo'San sat in his living space, going over the events of the last two days in his mind. Something just seemed off. He wasn't sure what it was, but he knew it had to do with Sink Lar. He was worried about her, and feeling a little disconnected from her, if truth be told.

A chime let him know someone was waiting outside his door, and frustratedly he rose to answer it. Standing before his door he was surprised to find his mother and father smiling warmly at him. "Have I forgotten an arranged meeting?" he asked.

"No, Lo'San. But, I thought that since you are not on duty this day, and you and your father have yet to spend any time together without all the rest of us being in attendance, that you could spend the day with him," Mee'ta said sweetly.

"Sink Lar..." he started.

"I will sit with Sink Lar just as I did yesterday. She will be fine. Our days here are limited, you know. I would feel ever so disappointed if I didn't help to give you and your father some time to spend alone," Mee'ta said. "I have been selfish with your time. It was very thoughtless of me."

"Shall we take a tour of the Command Deck, then you can show me your training facility, and then perhaps engineering. I've always wondered at the inner workings of a ship this size!" Lau'San said excitedly.

Lo'San thought about it. "I look forward to spending the day with you, Father, but perhaps we can spend a few hours together tomorrow..."

"You are on duty tomorrow and you would have only a few hours at best. You should take advantage of the day. Sink Lar is sleeping, is she not? She will not even know that you are not beside her. I will tend her just as carefully as yesterday," Mee'ta assured him.

"Perhaps we could go to the simulation room and play a lively game of Ru'geel!" Lau'San said.

Lo'San grinned, remembering the rough game his father used to play with him and Ko'San when they were children. The object was to scale a jagged cliff face, locate a hidden likeness of the once feared Ru'geel — a violent raptor inhabiting their home planet of Eschina. It was a game based on ancient tradition of a demonstration by the males of how they could provide for the females, if they were chosen. The ancient game was originally played just before the gala during which the females would offer their claims on the available males.

Now, though, it was simply a reminder of a time long gone, which was often played for fun by fathers and their sons to teach them of their history.

"I would very much enjoy a game of Ru'geel," Lo'San said. "Our simulators have been programmed to our cliffs at home," Lo'San explained.

"Go, then. I'll sit with your Sink Lar. Enjoy your day with your father," Mee'ta encouraged.

"Very well, but, you must promise to call for me the moment she wakes. I wish to speak with her, to let her know that I am even more committed than she knows," Lo'San said.

"I understand, my son. It is sometimes difficult to feel seen by your bonded if they suffer. All will be well when she awakes," Mee'ta said. "She will not mind you being away from home. It was Sink Lar after all that has been instrumental in our reunion. She would not want to interfere with your time with your father."

"We can wait for another day," Lau'San suggested.

"No, Mother is right. I am not on duty this day. Sink Lar is resting. It is the perfect time. Allow me a few moments to change and we go straightaway," Lo'San said, excited to spend the day with Lau'San.

Chapter 18

Mee'ta had been alone with Synclare for less than an hour when the chime outside the door sounded to signal someone was awaiting admittance.

Mee'ta walked over and released the hold on the door so it could sweep open.

"I've brought my tablet, just as you advised, Mother 'San," Ph'eel said, standing with Ko'San directly behind her and holding out the tablet for Mee'ta to take from her.

"Excellent. Enter. We have much to do," Mee'ta responded.

"You have not explained to me what we are doing," Ph'eel complained.

"We are returning Sink Lar to her planet Earth. We will make it seem as though Lo'San has done so to all those who encounter her, and we will make it seem as though Sink Lar has done so to Lo'San. He will be broken, and return to our family for solace. Our home will once again be as it should have been. Your home will increase by his presence, and all will be well in our world," Mee'ta said, proudly.

"How will we achieve such a thing?!" Ph'eel asked, clapping her hands giddily.

"Ko'San will pretend to be Lo'San. He will take her off this ship and deposit her with the Consortium."

"I will not! I will not become second to him! You do not need him in our home!" Ko'San nearly shouted. "I have spent my life being reminded that I am not Lo'San. Finally, I have my own mate, my own children, and now you force me to step back and allow him to rule over all that I have? I refuse!" he insisted with a snarl.

Mee'ta and Ph'eel shared a shocked look and Mee'ta gestured toward Ko'San.

Ph'eel's manipulative mind sprang into motion and she stepped closer to Ko'San, pressing her body against his and stroking his arm and chest with her long, delicate fingers. "Ko'San, you misunderstand, my love. Lo'San will join our family as a fourth husband. You will become first. You will have the advantage over him and all my husbands. Your simple act will prove your dedication to me, and I will adjust all to make you first among our family. You will determine exactly what the responsibilities and contributions to our household are for all my husbands. They will all bow to you, including Lo'San."

"And as you have always remained loyal to us, and you're assisting us in returning your brother to his rightful place in our family, you will now be the preferred son," Mee'ta said. "You will take the honorary place he once held."

Ko'San wanted nothing more than to be able to command more respect than Lo'San did. He resented Lo'San for all he'd attained while Ko'San had remained only a third husband to a female that regularly reminded him that he was not Lo'San.

"What do you want me to do?" he asked.

"You will dress in his uniform, order a transport to take you both off to the Consortium's satellite station, and leave her there," Mee'ta said.

"You want me to intentionally take Lo'San's mate to the Consortium's station? Do you think they won't realize I'm not Lo'San?"

"It is not the Consortium's Space Station, it is one of the smaller satellite stations between here and Earth. Surely Lo'San has not been there. They've only likely seen him on holovid. They will never know you are not him."

"Sink Lar will never cooperate," Ko'San objected, not wanting to put himself willingly into such a precarious position.

"She will not need to. She will be unconscious, drugged beyond any ability to even be aware she is not in her own bed. I will create messages for both Lo'San and for Sink Lar," Mee'ta said.

"For what?" Ko'San asked, thoroughly confused.

"Lo'San's will say that after spending time with his family, and after many attempts to provide him with a young one, it is clear to her that she does not belong with him. She has realized she's made a mistake and is going back to her own people. His will say that after spending time with us, and Ph'eel, he has come to realize just exactly what he'd be giving up by mating outside his own race. Furthermore, Ph'eel can and will provide him with the young ones he so craves, while at the same time giving him daily access to his family."

"How will you create those messages. You cannot mimic their voices," Ko'San asked.

"I don't need to mimic their voices. I merely need to mimic their handwritten words. It will be simple enough to do," Mee'ta said.

"How?" Ko'San asked.

"We've translated several messages they've written to one another. It's a simple matter of creating the message we want and translating it to the language they write in. Then we copy those messages and leave each where its intended recipient can find it," Mee'ta explained.

"He will never believe it," Ko'San said.

"He will. I am loading more than half his credits onto her credit band. It will look as though she's left him and taken half his wealth to keep herself afloat. It will appear to her that he sent her away but did send her with the means to care for herself. It makes the entire situation more believable," Mee'ta said.

"I'm so excited!" Ph'eel squealed, following Mee'ta to the table to watch as she began to create her messages.

"Why? Because you will now have Lo'San?" Ko'San snapped.

"No, my favored first husband. Because you will finally have the recognition you've always deserved. And because with Lo'San home, your mother will no longer be unhappy. All will be restored, and I'm proud that it's you who's now the most respected in your mother's home, and ours," Ph'eel said coyly.

Ko'San stood a little taller, but watched her suspiciously.

"You know, I thought I was going to have to order you to assist your mother, but I see now that you are so loyal, so selfless in putting her and me first, that you are the first husband I've desired all along. Forgive me for not seeing it before," Ph'eel said, dropping her head and feigning shame.

Ko'San smiled wide, his chest filling with pride. "I am pleased to be all you need, my Ph'eel. You shall not ever be reminded of the slight of my position. I am proud to serve you in all you need."

"Am I forgiven?" she asked with a pout.

"You are forgiven," he said magnanimously.

"Go get him outfitted in one of Lo'San's uniforms," Mee'ta said, as she tore a piece of paper in half and began to practice the symbols that Ph'eel's laptop provided in response to her request to translate the sentences she'd typed in.

"Wait!" Ko'San objected as Ph'eel tried to lead him into the bedroom where Synclare slept. "Won't she wake?"

"I've already given her another dose of medication. She will not wake. And just to be sure that she won't wake on the trip, I'll give her another dose before you leave, and you will do the same before you drop her off," Mee'ta said.

"Won't that kill her?" Ph'eel asked.

"Does it concern you that she may no longer breathe?" Mee'ta asked. "What do you want? Lo'San back in your bed, or searching for his errant mate, should he decide to go after her? She may live to see her planet again, and she may not. Either way it is of no concern to us."

"Lo'San in my bed, of course! It is all I've wanted for years!" Ph'eel answered without thinking.

Ko'San watched his mate, then turned and looked back at his mother who was busily copying information from Ph'eel's tablet. It just didn't feel right to him. Neither was behaving as though they simply wanted Lo'San back home, and neither was behaving as though they now recognized him as first husband.

Ph'eel glanced up at Ko'San and realized what she'd said. "As long as it pleases my first husband, of course," she amended, flashing Ko'San a seductive smile.

Ko'San didn't respond, he just followed along when she grabbed his hand and led him into the bedroom.

~~~

The doors granting entry to the docking bay swung wide as Ko'San approached them with Synclare in his arms. He wore his battle helmet, and had the face shield raised so that his face could be seen.

"General!" several males on duty who recognized him said, snapping to attention as he approached.

"Which of these transports is ready for use?" Ko'San asked.

"Farthest on the port side, General. Same as usual, can I assist you with anything?" the warrior asked.

"Yes. Get me a pilot at once. I'll be waiting aboard the transport," Ko'San answered.

The warrior lifted his communicator and swiped across a few screens. "I have no flight plan filed for you, General."

"Whatever pilot you send to fly it will file the flight plan," Ko'San snapped.

"It can only be flown by the pilot assigned to it, sir," the warrior said, his brow creasing in confusion.

"I know that. Bring him to duty now!" Ko'San demanded.

"He's on duty, General. In the lounge there, waiting to be needed, as are the pilots of the other two transports ready and waiting," the warrior said, not sure why General Lo'San wasn't remembering this was standard protocol. There were always three transports left available for immediate use, and those pilots assigned to those transports were in the lounge, a small glass-enclosed room particularly for them to kill time in until or unless they were needed, until they were relieved and another pilot took their place. The warrior lifted his arm and pointed to several males laughing and talking in a small room across from them clearly able to be seen from the flight deck.

"Then send the right one to the transport," Ko'San ordered.

183

"Yes, sir," the warrior answered, knowing that Lo'San was acting out of character, but deciding at last that he was after all General Lo'San and with his family aboard, he obviously had a lot on his mind. "May I help with your mate, General?" the warrior offered.

"No. She is sleeping and I do not wish to awaken her."

"Very well. I'll send your pilot," the warrior said, giving a salute across his chest and hurrying off toward the lounge.

Ko'San made his way to the transport the warrior had indicated and got on board without further delay. He chose a seat in the very rear of the small transport and laid Synclare on the bench along one side of the cabin. He looked down at Synclare, feeling a small pang of regret at what they were about to do. She was wrapped in a blanket from her bed, and her head was covered. She was breathing so shallowly that Ko'San couldn't detect it. He pressed his fingers against her throat, feeling for a pulse and was somewhat relieved when he felt it.

Startled when a voice spoke from right beside him, he jumped and shouted. "What do you want?" he demanded.

"Where will I be taking you, General?" the pilot asked, stepping back from General Lo'San when he obviously startled him.

Ko'San glanced up at the man who'd just stepped back from him. "Forgive my outburst. I am somewhat on edge of late."

"I understand, sir. Where am I taking you so that I can file the flight plan?" the pilot asked.

"Unified Consortium Defense Satellite Station," he said simply.

"Yes, sir. Right away," the pilot answered, moving up to the pilot's seat without further delay, and beginning the preflight checklist.

Ko'San sat in the back of the transport, his right leg pounding out a constant rhythm as it bounced a thousand times a minute, as he waited for the transport to finally take off.

"General?" the pilot asked.

"Yes," Ko'San answered.

"I'm being asked to confirm your presence onboard, sir. If you could please step forward so that the Command Deck can confirm and grant take off."

"Why? That's not necessary. Just do what I say," Ko'San insisted.

"Sir, Lieutenant Commander Re'Vahl, and Communications Master Vennie have requested confirmation that you are aboard this transport since they've no record of your planned expedition from the ship," the pilot said.

Ko'San's stomach dropped, but he stood and walked forward to the pilot's seat. The pilot indicated a translucent vid spanning the windshield, and Ko'San looked into the small area that seemed to reflect two males shown in white and gray as opposed to their true appearance. They were as translucent as the readouts and numbers that were ticking around the rest of the display.

A small male with tentacles peered back at him.

"General Lo'San, we are approving a flight plan to the Unified Consortium Defense Satellite Station as per your request."

"Thank you," Ko'San said.

"Identity confirmed, flight plan granted," the tentacled male said as another male still watched him.

"Cleared for takeoff, General. Please return to your seat and strap yourself and your mate in," the pilot advised.

"Done," Ko'San answered, stalking back to his seat.

~~~

Re'Vahl stood beside Vennie's chair and watched the small, green, tentacled alien as he confirmed Lo'San was aboard the transport.

"I'm surprised he didn't make us aware of his plans," Re'Vahl said. "He was here with his father this morning, surely he would have said something."

"Do you wish to question General Lo'San? I've already confirmed with my own eyes that he is aboard that transport," Vennie said. "You saw him, too."

"No, I suppose that is all we need. Still, he's very precise in everything he does. Would he not have advised us of his plans to leave the ship?" Re'Vahl asked.

"He is off duty for the day. Perhaps he wishes to spend some time with his female among some of her own kind. You heard his pilot tell him to strap himself and his mate in. There are several humans aboard the Consortium's satellite station. Perhaps she is acquainted with them and misses her own kind."

"Very well. Please log in the use of Transport 3V4 by General Lo'San," Re'Vahl said. Re'Vahl turned and watched the tiny dot that was the transport shown on the main vid screen as it left Command Warship 1's docking bay, and their ship's tracking devices picked it up and followed its progress in the direction of the Consortium's satellite station.

"Still don't feel comfortable with this," Re'Vahl said, his instincts telling him something was off with the way Lo'San had left the ship.

"I do not know what you require to be at ease with our General deciding to take a transport for a short while, Lieutenant Commander Re'Vahl. I can hail the transport and you can ask General Lo'San yourself why he didn't get our approval before leaving," Vennie said.

Re'Vahl straightened his back and raised his chin. "No. It is not my place to question General Lo'San on his decision to take his female off Command Warship 1."

"My thoughts exactly. General Lo'San is not a male to question," Vennie answered.

~~~

The simulator was a large room dedicated to whatever pastime any warrior requested. The home worlds of most of those aboard Command Warship 1 had been programmed in and could be accessed at will. If one was not aware they were in a simulator, they would actually believe they were on their home world. The simulator could provide the appearance, sounds, smells, and feel of any world it had been programmed to simulate. One only had to choose the program they wanted, and allow it a few minutes to revise the structure of the simulated world, then enter it. It could provide unbelievable structures, bodies of water, fields, skies of any color, and the sounds to accompany each.

Lo'San often went there just to be surrounded by the feel of his home world, but today, he actually had someone to play the game he'd entered into the simulator's data base long ago. He'd stopped playing it alone — it wasn't much of a challenge without someone to play against. Today, though, Lo'San was not holding back. He'd already raced to the top of the cliffs after climbing a rock wall to reach the Ru'geel's nesting area, and was now on his way back. He'd only climbed halfway down the rock wall that simulated the cliffs of Eschina. He turned and dropped the rest of the way to the ground, then ran wading through an expanse of water before eventually charging up the gentle rise of the hill deemed neutral territory and planting his sword in the highest rise there.

"Again!" Lau'San shouted, laughing good-naturedly as he followed Lo'San up the hill only a few moments later. "You win again!"

"I was taught by the best!" Lo'San said, laughing and smiling himself.

"The Cruestaci are a very adept people," Lau'San said, nodding for affirmation.

"I meant you, Father. You taught me long before I ever trained with the Cruestaci. I would never have achieved all I have had you not prepared me in my youth for greater things than even I ever imagined," Lo'San said.

Lau'San nodded and hugged his son. "I am so pleased with your life choices, Lo'San. No matter our customs, I cannot help but be proud of the path you've forged. It is something I'd have never had the strength to do. But you, you have never faltered. You saw another way, a better way for yourself, and you never stopped."

"Thank you, Father. That means more to me than you will ever know."

"Now," Lau'San said, patting Lo'San on the shoulder. "Another game? We've been playing all day, and I have yet to win one!"

"And you won't win one!" Lo'San shouted, as he took off at a full run for the cliff they'd just climbed down.

Chapter 19

Ko'San stepped off the transport after it docked on the United Consortium Defense Satellite Station. He glanced around and made his way toward an older male who stepped toward him just slightly and beckoned for his attention. The male was dressed in a deep purple colored uniform with a loose white robe flowing from his shoulders. The robe indicated that this was an ambassador, not a military male. Which made Ko'San relax a bit. He felt surely Lo'San would have had more interaction with the military class than the diplomatic class.

"General Lo'San! Welcome," the male called out. "I am Ambassador Karel. How may I be of service?" he asked, his gaze obviously lingering on Synclare in Ko'San's arms. "Have your men freed yet more females?"

"Not exactly. This is, or was, my female. She has made the decision to return to her home planet, and I've given my word to comply with her wishes. She often becomes distraught over travel, so she's been sedated for the trip. I want secure quarters for her to rest in, and request that she be returned to her planet — Earth — on the first available transport."

"Of course, we can arrange that, General, but I wonder why you didn't make arrangements with Consul Kol Ra' Don Tol to have her returned directly to Earth. He is of your crew originally, is he not?"

"I cannot be away from Command Warship 1 for the length of time it would take to return her to Earth, and it is not safe to have her sedated for that length of time. I am instead entrusting her to you and your forces until she is returned safely home," Ko'San said, not exactly sure who the ambassador was speaking of.

"I understand. Of course, you cannot be away from Command Warship 1 for so long. Come. I will show you her quarters so you can be assured she is safe."

Ko'San followed the male through the corridors, keeping his eyes straight ahead and making no eye contact with anyone as he carried Synclare securely in his arms. When the ambassador stopped outside a door, Ko'San stopped, too. "This is one of the rooms we've assigned to several of the females you and your warriors have freed over the last several years. Those on either side are empty as all the other females have returned to their home worlds, so she will have plenty of quiet time. We will, of course, assign security as well. They will remain here in the corridor."

"Thank you."

The ambassador moved his hand over the sensor and the door opened, granting them access.

Ko'San carried her into the room, glancing around to see a bed, a storage unit for clothing, and a door that led to a cleansing chamber.

"It is not large, but it is very safe," the ambassador commented.

"It will do," Ko'San said. He laid Synclare on the bed and stepped back, looking down at her. "May I have a moment?" Ko'San asked.

"Of course, General," the ambassador said, leaving the quarters that had been given to Synclare without delay.

Ko'San looked down at the unconscious female his brother had chosen to mate. He stuck his hand into the pocket of his trousers and withdrew the vial holding several more doses of the medication she'd been given. His mother had instructed him to administer another dose before they left Lo'San's home, and yet another upon arrival on the Consortium's station. She knew it would kill Synclare, but insisted it be done anyway. Ko'San simply couldn't do it. He'd not given her the dose before leaving her and Lo'San's home, and as he stepped closer to the bed, and looked down at the helpless female, he knew he wasn't going to give her the second dose now either. He didn't want to kill her.

She'd done nothing to earn the fate his mother had outlined for her. She was simply a means to an end, and he couldn't find it in himself to end her life needlessly. He set the vial on the small stand beside the bed, and withdrew the note from his pocket his mother had given him to leave with her. He placed it beside the vial, began to step away, then turned back and pulled the blankets from beneath her body, and covered her. He checked to be sure the credit band with half of Lo'San's credits transferred to it was securely fastened around her wrist, then exited the room.

"Thank you for your assistance," Ko'San said, as the door to what was now Synclare's room closed behind him.

Two males in battle gear appeared at the far end of the corridor and strode purposefully toward them.

Ko'San's stomach did flips wondering if they had realized he wasn't Lo'San.

"These are the males assigned to guard your mate, General," the ambassador said.

"I see," Ko'San answered. Then he looked at the ambassador. "She is my mate no longer. I can only honor her wishes to return her to her home."

"Of course, General. Will you stay to see her awake?" the ambassador asked.

"No, I must return to my ship. I have left her medication should she need it, and she has more than enough credits for use however she may wish. She should want for nothing. This is her desire so my presence is not required," Ko'San said.

"I understand. I'll see you to your transport," the ambassador said.

As he and Ko'San began their walk back to the docking bay, Ko'San looked back one more time to see the guards take up their positions across from Synclare's doorway. At least he knew she'd be safe until she could be returned home.

Ko'San boarded the transport and ordered his pilot to return them to Command Warship 1.

"But, General, your mate?" the pilot asked.

"She's asked to be returned to her home world. I have complied with her wishes as any honorable male would do," Ko'San said solemnly.

The pilot seemed to be taken aback for a moment before slamming his arm across his chest in salute. "I am most sorry to hear of your loss, General. I'll get us back home right away."

Ko'San gave a nod and started past the pilot toward the back of the transport. He could have felt many things at this point in time — satisfaction, achievement, happiness, even relief. He'd followed his mate's and his mother's directive - for the most part anyway — and secured his place as first husband and most favored son. He'd no longer be compared to the brother who'd haunted his every move since reaching adulthood. Instead, that brother would be dependent on his generosity as first husband. He had everything he'd ever wanted spread out before him. Why then, was it that he felt like the lowest life form in the galaxy?

~~~

After transport 3V4 was fully docked and secured, the doors on its airlock released and the pilot rose to exit the small ship. "May I be of additional service?" he asked, when Ko'San continued to sit where he was and stare into the air before him.

Ko'San blinked then focused on the pilot. "I did not hear your question," he said.

"May I be of additional service, General? We are back on Command Warship 1, and you've not attempted to disembark yet."

Ko'San looked around the ship and glanced behind the pilot to the open door of the transport. "No, thank you. You may go. I will follow."

The pilot gave their salute — a forearm and fist over the chest — and left the transport.

Ko'San slowly rose from his seat and without looking anyone in the eye, quickly and quietly made his way to the quarters he and Ph'eel had been assigned when they arrived. He suddenly felt sick to his stomach and didn't wish to speak with anyone.

As he walked through the door and into the living quarters he shared with Ph'eel, Ph'eel jumped to her feet. "Is it done?!" she asked excitedly.

He looked at Ph'eel, finding himself disgusted by her very pretty, very dainty, very perfect appearance for the first time in his life. "It is," he answered, moving to walk past her and into the cleansing chamber.

"Is she dead?" Ph'eel asked giddily.

Ko'San stopped and turned to look at Ph'eel. He knew his place, had been raised to believe that his female was the only thing in life that mattered other than honoring his own mother, but at this moment all he wanted to do was get out of her sight. He didn't answer, he simply turned and went into the cleansing chamber, the door sliding shut behind him. He stood in front of the large mirror that reflected his image. He looked at himself wearing Lo'San's uniform. He looked into his own eyes, until he could bear it no longer. "What the hells have you done?" he whispered.

Then he heard Ph'eel's voice as she spoke to his mother on a vid com on her personal tablet. "All is well!" she proclaimed, laughing happily.

"Excellent. Remember, no one was here tonight but myself. I'm going to sleep now, you should do the same. Tomorrow will be very trying for us all," Mee'ta answered.

~~~

Lo'San and Lau'San walked out of the simulator room smiling, talking, and patting each other on the back. It had been a long, long time since they'd been able to bond as they had today. They'd spent hours with Lo'San giving Lau'San a personal tour of the ship, then finished up the evening, and most of the night engaged in games in the simulator room.

"I'm starving! A meal?" Lau'San asked.

"Yes!" Lo'San answered, before looking down at the wrist communicator he wore. His brow creased when he realized how much time had passed, and that Synclare had not attempted to contact him once during that time. "I'd not been aware of how long we've been away. It is late into the night. Surely Sink Lar would have missed me by now," he said.

"I'm sure your mother has things well in hand. If either she or Sink Lar were needing either of us, she'd have contacted us. They are most likely both soundly sleeping by now," Lau'San said.

Lo'San thought about it. Synclare had needed a bit more medication than usual and if she'd awoken and still been in pain, his mother would have tended to her, so she most likely was sleeping just as his father had stated.

"You're most likely right, and I don't wish to wake her just to assure myself I'm not needed. If she needed me, I'd know," Lo'San said. "Very well, let's share a meal, then return to my quarters," Lo'San said.

"Excellent," Lau'San answered.

It was a couple of hours later and well past 2:00A.M. when Lo'San and Lau'San finally returned to Lo'San's home. Knowing that everyone was sleeping, and they were not missed at all, they took their time eating, and reminiscing of the past. As the door swooshed open to grant them access to Lo'San's quarters, they both quietly stepped into the darkened living space.

"Missy, lights to half power, please," he asked quietly.

At once the lights cast a soft glow over his sleeping mother on the sofa.

Lau'San walked over to her. "See? Just as we suspected — sound asleep," Lau'San said before gently touching Mee'ta. "Mee'ta, wake. It is time to return to our quarters," Lau'San said quietly.

Mee'ta began to wake slowly, slightly disoriented as she looked around. Then her eyes found Lau'San and she smiled. "Oh, Lau'San! I must have fallen asleep," she said.

"It is very late, Mee'ta. My apologies for the inconvenience, but Lo'San and I were having such a great time I just didn't want it to end," Lau'San said as he leaned over her to help her stand.

"It's nothing. No need to explain, I'm happy that you were able to spend some time with your son," Mee'ta answered.

"Thank you for watching over Sink Lar, Mother. Did she wake often?" Lo'San asked.

"Just the one time. She's not awakened again that I'm aware of. Perhaps I should have napped beside her..." Mee'ta said.

"No, she'd have called out if she needed. Thank you again for watching over my mate," Lo'San said, walking toward his bedroom.

"We'll be going, Lo'San," Lau'San called out.

"I'll see you tomorrow, Father. I have duty, but will arrange a few hours for meals with you all," Lo'San said.

"We will look forward to it," Lau'San said as he guided Mee'ta toward the door to exit Lo'San's quarters.

Lo'San walked into his bedroom and undressed in the dark.

He got into bed and turned toward Synclare's side of the bed, reached out to pull her into his arms, and realized she wasn't there. "Missy, lights on!" he said urgently.

The bright lights of the bedroom immediately responded, and Lo'San looked around the room. He rose from the bed and before he even walked out of the bedroom was already calling Synclare's name. "Sink Lar?!"

There was no answer.

"Sink Lar!" Lo'San called out more insistently. He went to the cleansing chamber, but on finding it empty, turned and sprinted back down the corridor to their second bedroom. "Sink Lar?" he asked, stepping into the room as the door slid open. "Lights up!" he ordered.

The lights shined brightly in the room, but it, too, was empty.

"Sink Lar!" he shouted, rushing back into the living space, then the galley before hurrying into the bedroom again. He grabbed his pants, laid carefully across a chair and yanked them back on, then his shirt before shoving his feet into his boots and grabbing his wrist communicator from the top of the dresser, intent on finding Synclare. His first plan of action was the medical clinic. Perhaps she'd begun to feel worse and left his mother sleeping when she'd left their home.

Lo'San ran to the lift, then paced inside the lift until it finally opened on the level that featured the medical clinic. He ran to the clinic, not even slowing as he barged into the reception area, startling the medical assistant on duty. "Where is my mate?!" he barked out.

"I'm sorry?" she asked.

"My mate! Sink Lar, she is not in our home. What room is she in? Is she very ill?" Lo'San demanded.

"General Lo'San, there is no one here this night but me. Your mate is not here," she assured him.

"Who was on duty before you? Maybe she's here and you were not advised," he insisted, beginning to walk down the corridor opening and closing doors to examination and hospital rooms.

"Sir, if anyone was here, I'd know. It is protocol to hand over all information on any patients in attendance when we change shifts. In addition, I'd have her vitals showing up here on these monitors if she were here. There is no one in medical tonight, sir," the medical assistant explained.

Lo'San stopped opening doors, and turned to face her. His mind raced trying to figure out where Sink Lar was, and why she didn't tell him. He remembered the wrist com and swiped his fingertips over it, bringing it to life. "Com Sink Lar," he ordered the small wrist unit.

The wrist communicator gave a series of beeps before it disconnected the connection he'd tried to initiate.

"Com Sink Lar!" he ordered.

Again the communicator attempted to do as he asked, before beeping and disconnecting the attempted com again.

196

"This makes no sense," he growled. Then he turned his attention on the medical assistant. "Check your records, has she been here before you came on duty?" he asked.

The female began to scroll through information that ran across one of the screens sitting in front of her. "She was here yesterday morning, but she's not been back," she explained.

"There is nothing else in there?" he demanded.

The female scrolled a bit more, then turned to look at him. "No sir. That's the last time she was here. There is a note that the Healer Master attempted to contact her, but according to this, she's not yet responded to his message. She's simply not here, sir. Perhaps she is with friends."

Lo'San turned and ran from the medical clinic. He rushed toward the lift and while the lift was taking him to the Command Deck, where he knew Zha Quin was currently on duty, he spoke to Missy again. "Missy, find Sink Lar!"

"I'll search for her, General," Missy answered.

The lift doors opened and Lo'San sprinted out of the lift, barely pausing as the doors to the Command Deck almost didn't open in time for him to squeeze through them as he burst onto the Command Deck. "Is Sink Lar with your Ehlealah?" Lo'San demanded.

Ba Re' looked up as Lo'San asked if his female was with Elisha. "Of course not. Elisha is fast asleep. Why would you think she's with my Elisha?" Ba Re' asked.

"General Lo'San?" Missy interrupted, ever the polite AI system.

"What?!" Lo'San barked out.

"I've completed a sweep of the ship, sir. Your mate, the human Synclare, is not aboard, sir."

Lo'San's heart dropped. His chest began to heave, he was practically hyperventilating.

"What do you mean, she's not aboard this ship?!" Ba Re' demanded of Missy.

"I've swept the ship for her identifying vitals, Lieutenant Commander. She is simply not onboard," Missy answered.

"That can't be right! Search again!" Ba Re' ordered.

"One moment," Missy answered.

Lo'San and Ba Re' stared at each other while the seconds ticked past like hours, until Missy finally collected the information they needed.

"The human Synclare, is not on this ship," Missy said once more.

"It can't be right!" Lo'San growled.

"When did you last see her?" Ba Re' asked.

"Early this morning. I spent the day with my father, my mother stayed with Sink Lar. She was sleeping as we'd just finished our last fertility treatment. They make her ill, she took her medicine and slept the day away," Lo'San explained. "I haven't seen her in so many hours," he said, his voice betraying his worry. "I should have stayed with her," he said, swiping his hands down his face nervously.

"Maybe she went to medical but was not checked in," Be Re' said.

"I've been there. She's not there, hasn't been there," Lo'San said, his voice going deeper with each passing moment.

"The computer has been misled before," Ba Re' said, trying to ease his mind. "I can run a check on Missy's systems."

"I'm going to check with Rokai," Lo'San said, spinning on his heel and rushing away.

"Why Rokai?" Ba Re' asked.

"Maybe she's with Rosie," Lo'San answered.

"I'll start the analysis on the system now. I'll let you know what I find," Ba Re' called after him. "But how well do you trust your family?"

Chapter 20

Rokai was sleeping when a pounding outside his quarters woke him up.

"The hell is that?" Rosie asked, sitting up in bed.

"Someone wishing to be shot," Rokai grumbled.

"I call first shot," Rosie answered.

Rokai got out of bed and went to his door completely naked. As he swiped the sensor for the door to open, he shouted 'What do you want?' as loud as he could.

Lo'San was standing on the other side of his threshhold as the door opened. "Is Sink Lar with you?" he asked.

"What?" Rokai said, a little more calmly.

"Is she here?" Lo'San demanded.

"No!"

Lo'San turned and ran back down the corridor.

"Where are you going?" Rokai stepped into the corridor and shouted.

"She's missing!" Lo'San yelled back without turning back to him.

"Son of bitches!" Rokai cursed, going back inside his quarters to put clothes on and go after Lo'San.

"What's wrong?" Rosie asked, as she met him halfway between their bedroom and their living space.

"Lo'San has already screwed everything up. Synclare is missing. I'm going to help him look."

"Unbelievable. You need me to come help?" Rosie asked.

"No, my Rosalita. Go back to sleep. I'll return shortly.

~~~

Lo'San was standing outside his parents' assigned quarters, pounding on the door when Rokai caught up to him. "Open this door!" Lo'San demanded.

Lo'San looked at Rokai as Rokai stepped up beside him.

"I thought you had access to all quarters," Rokai asked.

"I do," Lo'San said.

"Then open the damn door!" Rokai complained.

Lo'San looked back at the door and swiped his hand over the sensor, then the two of them stepped into the quiet interior of the living area of his parents' temporary quarters. "Mother!" Lo'San shouted.

Sounds could be heard from the bedrooms before Lau'San rushed into the living space. "Lo'San! What is the meaning of this?" he asked.

"Where is my mate?" Lo'San demanded.

Mee'ta entered the living space, tying the sash of her robe around her waist. "Lo'San, what has happened?" she asked, coming to a stop when she saw Rokai standing beside Lo'San.

"You tell me! What have you done with my mate!" he demanded.

"I have done nothing but give her the medication you left for her. Is she ill? Was it too much? I followed your directions explicitly!" Mee'ta insisted.

"Where is she?" Lo'San repeated, his voice deep and deadly now. The spines on his shoulders were beginning to break through his clothing as they grew in size and the darker spots of rough skin on his temples, cheeks and forehead were beginning to expand with his anger.

"She's sleeping, my son. Or she was, the last time I saw her. Is she not in your home?" Mee'ta asked.

"She is not. The ship's computer has stated that she is not on board this ship," Lo'San growled. He stepped closer to his mother and looked down at her intimidatingly. "If I find you've harmed my Sink Lar, or are behind her disappearance in any way, you will be sorry I was ever born," he threatened.

Mee'ta shored up her courage in the face of a threat by her own son. "When you find your mate alive and well, I will be here waiting for your apology!" she said haughtily.

Lo'San turned and stormed out of his parents' quarters, leaving Rokai to face his mother and father.

"You better hope she's safe, or I'll help him hide the bodies," Rokai promised with a smile.

Mee'ta hissed in a shocked gasp as her hand flew up to cover her throat. "I would never harm that dear child. She is on board somewhere, I have no doubt!"

"If she's not, I'll be back," Rokai said, before turning and leaving their quarters. "Missy! Where is Lo'San?" he asked.

"General Lo'San appears to be returning to his quarters, Elite Commander Rokai ahl," Missy answered at once.

As Rokai set a path for Lo'San's quarters, he realized that Missy was able to tell him exactly where Lo'San seemed to be heading, yet she couldn't find Synclare. "Fuck," Rokai cursed as he hurried to catch up with Lo'San.

As soon as Lo'San and his very scary friend had left their quarters, Lau'San turned to Mee'ta. "What have you done?" he asked, shaking his head and looking at her as though she was a stranger.

"Nothing! And who are you to question me?!" she answered defensively. "I take it as a personal attack that you, my first husband, thinks it acceptable to question me! You are a part of my household, not the other way around. Do not forget your place, Lau'San!" Mee'ta snapped.

Lau'San stood there looking at her, the sinking feeling in his gut telling him all he needed to know. His mate was somehow involved with Sink Lar's disappearance. "If they find a way to prove you responsible, you will have much more to deal with than taking offense at my questions. I hope for your sake, and mine, that I am wrong," he said quietly, before walking out of their quarters.

"Where are you going?! Get back in here this moment!" Mee'ta demanded.

Lau'San stopped walking and looked back at her. "I'm going to help my son search for his mate. You would think as his mother you'd be doing the same."

Mee'ta stood where she was with her mouth hanging open as she looked at the place her first mate had just been when he spoke to her so disrespectfully. Then she realized that he was right. She needed to at least make the effort to seem concerned. Hurrying after her first mate, she schooled her features from an expression of irritation to one of concern and even managed to produce a few tears as she made her way to her son's quarters to give the impression she was as worried about his worthless mate as he was.

~~~

Synclare stretched her legs out below her and her arms above her as she began to wake. She rolled onto her back and took a deep breath. She took stock of her body and realized that the pain was gone. She'd managed to get through yet another fertility treatment. Then the nausea hit and she got to her feet, planning to run toward the cleansing chamber, but instead tripped over a piece of furniture. She tumbled to the floor, she called out to the ship's computer. "Missy, lights!"

Picking herself up off the floor, still surrounded in darkness, Synclare became even more and more confused when she realized there was no soft floor covering beneath her. The floor was cold, hard metal.

"Lights on!" Synclare said again.

The lights in the room she was in responded and Synclare's breath caught. She was in a room she'd never seen before. And the nausea hit her again — hard this time. She slapped her hand over her mouth and spun left, then right looking for a cleansing chamber, a garbage pail, anything. Her eyes fell on another door and rushing into that room, she found herself in a cleansing chamber. Falling to her knees in the cleansing unit, she vomited until she was weak and shaky from the exertion. Then the tears came as the confusion about where she was and why she wasn't in her rooms returned. Had Lo'San had her removed from their quarters since he no longer wished to be mated to her?

Synclare pulled herself up off the floor and used the walls of the small cleansing room and sleeping quarters to steady herself as she went back into the bedroom. Her gaze bounced around the room as she looked for anything that looked vaguely familiar. Then she saw it — a vial of the medication she'd been prescribed by Doc to battle the side effects of the fertility treatments, and beside it a piece of paper.

Synclare took a seat on the bed she'd awoken in with the paper grasped in her hand. The first thing she noticed when she unfolded it was that it was the same block style lettering that Lo'San used when writing her love notes. Her hand trembled as she read the words, but before she got to the end of the letter, her mind was spinning.

~Sink Lar,

You were correct in your efforts to reunite myself and my family. Spending time with them has made me realize the importance of them in my life and the emptiness caused by their absence. I have made arrangements to rejoin my people. I am fortunate Ph'eel considers me worth adding to her household after my insults to my people, and fortunate that she has promised me many young ones on my return. I am sure you can see that our mating was a mistake as well. After learning of your past, it is of no surprise that your body cannot provide me with young ones — it has been poisoned through your own actions. I am sure you understand my position. I have made arrangements for your return to your home, and provided you with more than half my credits so you will be able to provide for yourself. I wish you well in your endeavors.

Lo'San.~

Synclare sat on the bed, her mind reeling. She remembered Lo'San saying they should have just remained as they were, but she never dreamed he'd have her removed from the ship and returned to Earth without even asking what she wanted. The tears began to stream down her face and she crumpled the paper in her hand, balling it up and throwing it against the wall as she sobbed through her tears.

Eventually she looked around the room again, still not knowing where she was. "Can't be on Earth already," she said. She knew she'd not slept for three days, and that's how long the journey from where Command Warship 1 was orbiting to reach Earth took. "I'm still on the ship, at least," she said, swiping at her eyes and standing up. "Gonna find Vivi. I'm not going home. He'll just have to deal with it," she said aloud. "Missy? Where is Vivi? Please tell her I want to speak with her. Tell her I need to speak with her!" Synclare said, choking back another sob as she walked toward the door of the room she'd been moved to.

The door slid open, and Synclare stepped through it before freezing in place. Two males in deep purple uniforms she recognized as being from the Unified Consortium Defense Force stood at attention as she stepped into the corridor. She looked up and down the corridor before looking back at the males.

"This is not Command Warship 1, is it?" she asked.

One of the males shook his head, but didn't speak.

"Who are you?" she asked, the tears beginning to overtake her again. One of the males stepped toward her and out of fear, she shuffled back toward the room she'd just walked out of.

"You are safe here," one of the males said, reaching out toward her. "Do not fret, female. We are assigned to protect you. No one will harm you," he promised in accented English.

"Where is here?" she asked, still standing away from them, though she thought she already knew the answer.

"You are aboard the satellite station of The Unified Consortium Defense. You've been granted asylum and protection until you can be returned home to your world. You are not in danger."

"How did I get here?" she asked, as tears spilled from her eyes.

The males shared a glance, then looked at her once more. "Cruestaci General Lo'San arrived with you during the night."

Synclare let a soft sob escape as she began to cry uncontrollably again. He'd just brought her here while she was unconscious, and dumped her here.

"Does Vivian know?" she asked.

"Who is Vivi-an?" one of the guards asked.

"Sirena Vivian Tel Mo' Kok of Cruestace. Does she know I'm here?" Synclare asked.

"I know not, female. Only General Lo'San of the Cruestaci has been here, but fear not. We will protect you," the other male answered.

"I want to go home," she muttered to herself, as the uncontrollable tears began again and she squeezed her eyes closed.

"Ambassador Karel has reached out to Consul Kol Ra' Don Tol of Earth. I trust it won't be long," the first guard said.

"I don't want to go to Earth! I want to go back to Command Warship 1!"

The guards looked at one another again, then back at Synclare. "General Lo'San left you here at your request. He clearly stated to Ambassador Karel that you wished to dissolve your bond with him and return to Earth," the first guard said.

"He lied! I want to go back to Command Warship 1. Right now!" Synclare insisted.

The first guard took a communicator off his belt and swiped its screen a few times before pausing, and speaking in a language she didn't understand. He received an answer almost immediately, in the same language he'd spoken in, and nodded to himself before reattaching it to his belt. He looked at his fellow guard, then at Synclare. "We'll escort you to Ambassador Karel's offices. You can speak with him and together unravel this confusion."

Synclare nodded, and began walking down the corridor in the direction the first guard indicated. She paused in her stride only once when she heard one of her guards whisper to the other. "Why would she want to return to a male who has humiliated her and discarded her so callously?"

"I thought General Lo'San a respectable male. He is a fool. Many of our males would welcome her in bonding."

Synclare thought about their words as she walked down the long corridor with them at her back. They were right. Why would she fight to return to a male who'd thrown her away, personally taking her off the ship while she slept?

"Turn to your right, female," the first guard instructed from behind her as she approached an intersecting corridor.

Synclare took the right he instructed then realized they'd spoken to her about Ambassador Karel, whoever that was, but not Chairman Bartholomew. "Where is Chairman Bartholomew? He is a friend of mine, can I speak to him?"

"He is not assigned to this station. His offices are aboard the Unified Consortium Space Station," the first guard answered.

"Isn't that where I am?" she asked.

"You are aboard a satellite station of the Unified Consortium Defense," he answered. "We have only one Ambassador assigned here. That Ambassador is Ambassador Karel."

"Can Bart be reached?" she asked.

"I'm sure he can, Ambassador Karel can assist you as necessary," the guard answered.

Moments later and several lift rides later, Synclare stood in front of a desk with a small male, wearing a deep purple uniform, just like the ones her guards were wearing, but with his, this male wore a long white robe. Bart also wore this uniform and robe combination and Synclare recognized it as identifying the male as an Ambassador of the Consortium.

"Ahh, I see you have awakened," the male said. "How may I be of service?" he asked, coming around the desk to greet Synclare.

"I... I don't want to go back to Earth. I have nothing there, no one is waiting for me there," she said.

The little man's face registered confusion. "I thought General Lo'San advised that you wished to return to your home planet. We've been working to secure your papers that you might return there," he explained.

Synclare shook her head. "I did not end my bond with General Lo'San. I did not ask to be returned to Earth. I do not want to go back there," she said, the anger she was feeling beginning to outweigh the heartbreak.

"Oh! I'm so sorry, my dear. Clearly I must have misunderstood," he said, trying to help her save face.

"No, I'm sure you understood perfectly well. General Lo'San lied to you. I did not ask to be returned to Earth," she said emphatically.

Shocked speechless, Ambassador Karel searched for the right thing to say, diplomacy was always important in his career, but diplomacy was difficult to find in this particular situation. "I'm not quite sure what to say," he finally admitted.

"Me either," Synclare said quietly as she hugged her arms around herself and looked around the room.

"May I ask, did you ask General Lo'San to sedate you because you fear travel?" the Ambassador asked.

Synclare snapped her gaze to Ambassador Karel. "No! No I did not. I was medicated because I was ill. I was ill because I underwent medical treatments he was well aware of. He's discarded me because I can't give him children."

The little man stepped forward and took one of her hands in both of his. "I'm so sorry, dear. There is no excuse for that behavior. Rest assured that we will work to get you to any location you prefer. Where do you wish to be?"

Synclare's brows furrowed and the tears started again. "I don't know," she answered.

"You stated you wish to return to Command Warship 1," the quieter of her two guards offered.

Synclare shook her head. "You were right. I can't be there. I don't know where to go," she admitted.

"There is no rush, dear. You are welcome to stay here until you decide," Ambassador Karel offered.

~~~

Rokai rushed into Lo'San's quarters through the still open door. "Lo'San!" he called out.

"I'm here," Lo'San said quietly from his bedroom.

Rokai walked toward the bedroom, and on entering found Lo'San standing beside the bed with a note in his hand.

"What is it?" Rokai asked.

Gradually, Lo'San's gaze left the paper in his hand and met Rokai's. "She has left me."

"What?" Rokai asked. "She would not have left you. She was trying to have little, silver, squalling humans with you!"

Lo'San held out the note to Rokai. Rokai took it from him and began to read the words printed there. "This makes no sense, Lo'San. Did you tell her you wished to return to your family and mate with this Ph'eel?" he asked.

"No, I did not! I told her that as long as she was at my side it would be all I'd need! I never said I'd return to my planet. I never said I wanted Ph'eel."

"Somewhere, she got the idea that you do. And she's decided that you would rather have younglings with this female from your planet, than stay with her," Rokai said.

Lo'San sat down on the bed and Rokai handed him the note again.

Lo'San read it again from the beginning to end.

"This can't be right, Lo'San. I do not understand it; it makes no sense. Your female loves you. She would not have left," Rokai said. "Rosie and I both saw it with our own eyes. And she waited long for you to claim her! She would not leave you."

"Unless she was made to believe that I would be happier without her. She would leave me if she thought it was what I wanted."

"I find even that hard to believe," Rokai answered.

"It's here in the letter. 'I know Ph'eel can give you what I can't. I've taken some of your credits to be able to provide for myself — I hope you don't mind. I wish you every happiness'," Lo'San said angrily.

"Lo'San! I've come to help you search for Sink Lar!" Lau'San said, hurrying into the bedroom having entered through the still open door.

"She's gone," Lo'San answered, handing the note to his father.

Lau'San looked down at the letter in his hand and saw nothing but scribbles and loops. "I can't read this, my son. It's not in a language we write on Eschina."

"We're here! We wish to help!" Mee'ta said, joining them with Ph'eel at her side.

Lau'San shared a look with Lo'San, then Rokai, then he handed the letter to Mee'ta.

Mee'ta looked down at the letter. "Oh, my. I'm so sorry, Lo'San. Why she'd ever think she was making you happier by leaving you is a question I'm afraid we'll never have the answer to."

Lo'San stood from the bed and faced his mother. "How do you know what the letter says, Mother?" he asked.

"Mee'ta…" Lau'San said sadly.

"It's easy enough. I've been studying the Earth language since learning your female was of Earth," Mee'ta explained, realizing she'd tipped her hand by knowing what the note said.

"How did you know what language of Earth to study?" Rokai asked. "There are many!"

"I do not like your tone," Mee'ta said, daring in her arrogance to stand up to Rokai.

"I do not like you!" Rokai countered, taking a step toward her. "You will answer the question. Now!" Rokai insisted.

Mee'ta's mind scrambled as she grasped at answers, then she smiled when it hit her. "After I spoke to Sink Lar via vid com I simply asked our communicator to provide me lessons in her home language. I find it difficult to understand when spoken, but much easier when written."

Rokai watched her through suspicious eyes as he had to admit the possibility existed that she was telling the truth.

Chapter 21

Lo'San walked over to his mother and snatched the letter from her hands. He glared at her, then walked over to the storage unit where Synclare had kept her credit band. He rifled around the drawer for a moment, then slammed it shut.

"Her credit band is gone," he commented.

"At least you know wherever she is, she is not without means," Mee'ta said.

"Did she have her own credits?" Ph'eel asked.

"Yes," Lo'San answered.

"Hopefully she left your credits untouched, then," Ph'eel answered.

"The letter she left says she took some of his credits," Mee'ta said.

"Without permission? How presumptuous!" Ph'eel exclaimed.

Lo'San turned to Ph'eel, looking at her with the resentment he felt at the fact that she was even here. "Do you think I give a damn about credits?" he snapped. "She can have every credit I'll ever possess as long she is at my side!"

"Well, of course," Ph'eel amended. "I didn't mean it in a derogatory manner," Ph'eel said.

"Everything you say is meant in a derogatory manner," Lau'San commented. "Tell me how I can help, my son," Lau'San added, turning to Lo'San.

"I have no idea where she could be. Missy says she's not here, but surely she is. She could not have possibly made it off the ship without my knowledge," Lo'San said, speaking his thoughts aloud.

"I believe she may have," Rokai said.

"We shall know shortly. Ba Re' is running a systems check," Lo'San said.

"I don't need a systems check," Rokai answered. "I asked Missy where you were when you left your family's quarters. Missy told me exactly where you were."

"How?" Lo'San asked. "Who would have taken her from this ship knowing they'd answer for it? Where could she have gone?" Lo'San asked, his voice conveying the defeat he clearly felt.

"I'm here for you, Lo'San," Ph'eel said, stepping toward Lo'San. "No matter the outcome, I will be here to help you through it, just like when we were children," she said, reaching out to touch Lo'San as she approached.

Lo'San growled and moved away from her intended touch.

Rokai stepped in front of Ph'eel to stop her progression. "He doesn't need your help," Rokai said, his voice dripping with disdain.

Ph'eel stood frozen in place, terrified by the male she'd offended. "I only meant to..."

"I know what you meant!" Rokai yelled. "We all do! Leave us, Now!" Rokai demanded.

Ph'eel screeched and ran from the room.

"There is no reason to frighten my bond-daughter!" Mee'ta snapped. "Lo'San, surely you will not tolerate his treatment of Ph'eel."

"I do not care about Ph'eel in the slightest," Lo'San mumbled, lost in his thoughts.

Rokai turned toward Lo'San who wasn't even paying attention to what was happening as his mind ticked off ways he may be able to find Sink Lar.

"Missy is not experiencing system failures. She is on line and operating as she should," Rokai said confidently.

Lo'San met Rokai's gaze, beginning to see beyond the shock of learning that Synclare was gone. "Missy?"

"Yes, General," Missy responded.

"Where is Sink Lar?" he asked again.

"She is not aboard the ship, General," Missy answered.

"Where exactly is she?" Rokai asked.

Missy didn't answer for several moments as she searched her data banks for the answer. "I do not have that information, Elite Commander Rokai ahl."

Lo'San snarled, and threw the letter to the floor. Then his head tilted to the side ever so slightly as he realized the question they should have been asking. "How did she leave the ship, Missy?"

Again Missy searched her data bases before answering. "She left aboard Transport 3V4, General."

"Who piloted the transport?" Lo'San demanded.

"Pilot Kr's'haw is assigned to Transport 3V4, General."

Lo'San said nothing more, simply started for the door of his quarters.

Rokai stooped over and grabbed the letter, then fell into step beside him, and Lau'San right behind them.

"Lau'San!" Mee'ta called out.

"I'm going to help my son," he answered.

"You've done enough," Mee'ta snapped.

"No, Mee'ta. But you have. I suggest you prepare yourself for whatever comes from this."

"I have had no hand in Sink Lar's disappearance!" Mee'ta claimed indignantly.

Lau'San shook his head. "I don't know how, or what you've managed to do, but I have no doubt that you are involved. I'm going to help my son. You do whatever you wish."

~~~

Ph'eel arrived back in her quarters out of breath and outraged.

"This is not a place I wish to be any longer!" she screeched. "I will not stand for the treatment a female of my status receives aboard this ship!" she insisted, stalking around the bedroom she found Ko'San in.

213

Ko'San sat on the edge of the bed with his head in his hands as he stared at the floor. He gave no reply.

"Did you hear me? You must take a stance! No worthy male would allow his female to be disrespected in the manner I have been!" Ph'eel demanded.

Ko'San sighed and raised his head, looking over at Ph'eel. "What is it you find unacceptable this time?" he asked tiredly.

"This time? This time! You know I am a patient female! I do not complain unnecessarily! How dare you insinuate that I am a difficult female?!"

"Of course you're not difficult," Ko'San said sarcastically.

"No, I am not! And you should watch your tone," she insisted.

"Of course," he said dispassionately.

"You will go to Commander Tel Mo' Kok and you will lodge a formal complaint!" Ph'eel insisted.

"Over what?" Ko'San asked.

"Over the fact that I've been insulted. Lo'San has only just found out that his mate has left him, and I sought to offer him comfort. That criminal... the one the Cruestaci have claimed as their second prince, he threatened me! He chased me away from Lo'San! He had no right!" Ph'eel screeched again. "Everyone knows I should be standing with Lo'San as he recovers from his mate leaving him! It is my place!"

"She did not leave him. She was taken away from him, without her consent," Ko'San shouted.

Ph'eel took a step back when he shouted at her. Her males did not speak to her in such a manner, else they risked being banished from her home, and from all proper society on Eschina. Gathering her courage, she raised her delicate pointed chin and looked down her nose at him. "You will not speak to me this way. I do not deserve, nor will I tolerate this treatment."

Ko'San shook his head, and pressed his lips together tightly as he considered the amount of loathing he had for himself since allowing himself to become complicit in the kidnapping of his brother's mate. "No, you don't deserve treatment of this nature."

"Exactly," Ph'eel agreed.

"You deserve much worse," Ko'San said as he stood, and stalked from the room.

"Wait! Where are you going?!" Ph'eel demanded. "Come back here this moment!" she called out, running after him.

"I'm going to find Lo'San. I'm going to tell him all that you and Mother have orchestrated," he answered as he approached the door that would lead him into the exterior corridor.

"You can't! You were the one to take her from the ship, you were the one to give her the fatal dose! You'll be prosecuted! We all will be! Think what you do!" Ph'eel exclaimed, rushing toward Ko'San. "We have much to be thankful for. Our young ones need us. We will return home and all will be as it should be. We do not need Lo'San in our household," Ph'eel said nervously, offering any argument she could to stop Ko'San from telling Lo'San what they'd done. "He'll never know," she insisted.

"I'll know, Ph'eel. And I cannot live with myself knowing what I've done. Let the pieces fall where they may, I'm going to Lo'San," Ko'San said, turning away from her.

Ph'eel grasped his forearms, gripping him as tightly as she could. "No! I will not allow it!"

"Unhand me, female!" Ko'San said, shoving her away from him. "Find some dignity and prepare to answer for your crimes."

"I will banish you!" she screamed.

"Please. I would consider it an honor to be released from you and your manipulations. I will take my young ones and seek an appreciative female — should I survive Lo'San's wrath." Ko'San walked out of their quarters and the door slid closed behind him.

He went directly to the lift that would take him to Lo'San's home, and simply shook his head disgustedly when he heard Ph'eel's scream of frustration from down the corridor as she threw her tempter tantrum at not having him bow to her wishes.

~~~

Lo'San and Rokai burst onto the landing deck and began searching for Pilot Kr's'haw. "Warrior!" General Lo'San shouted to the first male he saw.

"Sir!" the warrior answered, coming to attention.

"Where is Pilot Kr's'haw?" Lo'San demanded.

"He is off duty, General. We have several pilots in the lounge awaiting a call to duty. I'm sure one of them can serve your needs."

"I need Pilot Kr's'haw," Lo'San growled, turning to leave the landing deck.

As Rokai and Lo'San stepped back into the corridor, they met Lau'San coming toward them. "Any luck?" Lau'San asked.

"The pilot is off duty. We are going to find him now," Rokai said, as Lau'San fell into step with them.

Taking the lift back up to the residential levels, they stepped off the lift as Lo'San spoke to Missy. "Which quarters are Pilot Kr's'haw's?"

"They are third down on the aft side, General," Missy answered.

Lo'San didn't even waste time requesting entry, he simply scanned his hand across the sensor and when the door opened, he stepped into the room holding two beds and two storage cabinets — it was typical for unmated warriors of enlisted rank to share quarters. "Pilot Kr's'haw?!" he called out as they searched his quarters.

Rokai walked over to the cleansing chamber and peeked his head inside. "He is not here. No one is."

"Where is Pilot Kr's'haw, Missy?" Lo'San asked.

"He is in the commissary, General," Missy answered.

"Why did you not tell me that?!" Lo'San bellowed.

"You didn't ask where he was, you asked where his quarters were, General," Missy answered.

Lo'San growled as he left Pilot Kr's'haw's quarters, headed toward the commissary.

On entering the commissary, Lo'San simply raised his voice and demanded Pilot Kr's'haw come to him. "Pilot Kr's'haw" he shouted. "Front and center, Now!"

A male seated with several friends halfway across the room stood. "I am here," the male said, as he began to walk toward General Lo'San.

"Where is my mate?" Lo'San snarled, advancing on the male.

"I presume she is exactly where you left her. Aboard the United Consortium Defense Satellite Station," Pilot Kr's'haw answered.

Lo'San stuttered to a stop. "What did you say?" he asked.

"I said, I presume she's exactly where you left her."

"I did not leave her anywhere but our quarters," Lo'San insisted. "What nonsense do you speak of?"

"You had me transport the both of you to the Consortium Satellite Station yesterday. Only you returned," Pilot Kr's'haw declared.

"I did no such thing!" Lo'San shouted.

"I did," a voice from behind Lo'San, Rokai and Lau'San said calmly.

Lo'San turned at the admission and his face became a mask of rage. "What have you done?" he bellowed, advancing on Ko'San.

Ko'San stood his ground, not even flinching as Lo'San clearly planned to attack.

"Lo'San!" Lau'San shouted, stepping between his sons before Lo'San actually got close enough to get his hands on Ko'San. "Let him speak before you take out your vengeance."

"I'll kill him," Lo'San snarled, as the spines on his shoulders enlarged and his natural armor began to cover his skin.

"And I'll deserve it, accept it even, but first you should know exactly who executed this entire manipulation," Ko'San said calmly.

Lo'San was breathing heavily, just barely holding himself back as he allowed his father to stand between him and his brother.

"I've come in search of you for selfish reasons, my brother. I wish to ease my soul of the crushing guilt I cannot escape. If you wish to kill me after you know the truth, so be it. I would certainly do the same were the circumstances reversed," Ko'San said.

"Ko'San!" their mother's voice called out. "What have you done? How could you kill such a gentle, trusting female?" Mee'ta rushed out as she and Ph'eel hurried into the commissary and quickly took stock of what was happening.

"Ko'San! I forbid you to speak any further. Your admission of guilt is enough!" Ph'eel said.

Ko'San looked over toward his mother and his mate. "Contrary to your orders, Mother, I've not killed her. I could not find it in my heart to harm the female. She's had no part in any of this other than to try to unite us all."

Mee'ta's expression fell and became one of fury.

"That's right, I disobeyed your orders, you wretched female," Ko'San said.

"Stop speaking!" Ph'eel screeched at the top of her lungs.

"You stop speaking!" Ko'San raged at Ph'eel. "I'm done with you and all that you represent!" Then Ko'San turned back to Lo'San. "Our mother drugged your mate, then ordered me to dress in your uniform and take her off this ship. She knew we look so much alike, no one would question me. And she was right, it worked. But once I looked down at your female, sleeping helplessly in my arms, I could not make myself administer the additional doses Mother and Ph'eel ordered be administered. Your female is not dead. She is safe and under the guard of the Unified Consortium Defense. She awaits return to her home world," Ko'San said.

"You will never return to my household!" Ph'eel screamed. "Your false accusations will be proven."

Lo'San stood with his father's hands still against his chest as he listened to his brother's explanation.

"If she found herself aboard a strange ship, she would have reached out to me," Lo'San said, still unsure if his brother had harmed her or not.

Ko'San shook his head. "Our Mother wrote letters. One for you from her, and one for her from you. She had Ph'eel's tablet create messages based on the handwritten letters Ph'eel found

218

in your storage unit. Mother recreated those messages to appear as they were written by each of you. She also transferred your credits to your female's credit band to further the appearance that she left you."

Lo'San glared at his mother, she glared back.

"Who will you believe — a jealous brother who's lived his adult life compared to you, or your own Mother, Lo'San?" Mee'ta asked.

"What did her letter say?" Lo'San asked, his voice a constant growl.

"I know not!" Mee'ta answered defiantly.

"Ko'San?" Lo'San growled.

"That you had decided you could not live a life without your family and young ones of your own. Ph'eel had agreed to give you a place in her household and all the young ones you wished for. And it explained that you'd loaded her band with credits so that she wouldn't need for anything," Ko'San said.

"That's ludicrous! I would never do such a thing, and I'd never harm that poor, innocent female...." Mee'ta began babbling incessantly in defense of herself.

"Silence!" Rokai bellowed, causing everyone in close proximity to wince at the decibel level of his shout. Then he turned his attention to Lo'San. "What do you wish to do?"

Lo'San didn't hesitate. "Take them into custody. They are to be held without possibility of release until I return, then I'll decide exactly what's to be done with them," he ordered.

Several nearby warriors responded to Lo'San's orders. As Mee'ta, and Ph'eel screamed and cried, proclaiming their innocence, Ko'San very calmly allowed the warriors to take him into custody. When one of them placed a hand on Lau'San's shoulder and made to turn him so that he could be remanded as well, Lo'San stopped him.

"Leave my father free. He was with me all day," Lo'San said.

"Are you sure he was not party to it, meant to keep you preoccupied while Synclare was spirited away?" Rokai asked.

Lo'San glanced at Rokai, then his father.

"I had no idea of their plans, Lo'San. Had I, I'd have warned you. I'd have prevented their actions any way I could," Lau'San said sincerely.

"Shut your mouth! Why do you and Ko'San think you have the freedom to speak at will? Stop speaking!" Mee'ta ordered almost hysterically.

"My father is not involved," Lo'San said.

"Take them to the holding cells below deck. Do not allow them any conveniences not provided for any other prisoner. The preliminary charges are kidnapping," Rokai said.

"And theft," Lo'San growled.

"And attempted murder," Ko'San added from where he was being held by two warriors. "Do not forget they instructed me to give her two additional doses of her medication in a plan to kill her!"

"Silence!" Ph'eel screamed.

"No! You be silent! I renounce you! I am no longer a part of your household and as is law, my young ones will be forbidden in your home as well!" Ko'San yelled at Ph'eel.

"Everyone be silent!" General Lo'San ordered. "Take them away!"

All of his family except for his father was dragged from the commissary as everyone in attendance looked on. Lo'San had another quick thought and stepped into the corridor to call after them. "Place Ko'San in his own cell!"

"Thank you!" Ko'San's voice could be heard yelling back to Lo'San.

"That was kind of you," Rokai said, coming to stand beside Lo'San and watch as Lo'San's mother, brother and sister-in-law were taken away.

"He was ordered to kill Sink Lar — he did not," Lo'San said.

Rokai shrugged. "Very well. What now?"

"Where is Sire Zha Quin Tha?" Lo'San asked.

"He is indisposed," Rokai answered.

Lo'San looked over at Rokai. "What does that mean?"

"It means he's given orders that he is not to be disturbed. He is tending our Sirena today."

Lo'San spun on his heel and set out for the flight deck. "Missy!" he snapped.

"Yes, General," Missy answered.

"Prepare a transport! I'm going to get my mate!"

"No!" Rokai shouted as he ran along beside Lo'San. "We should take a battle cruiser! Better yet, let's take two!" Then Rokai spoke to Missy. "Missy! Order my team to assemble on the flight deck at once!"

"Right away Elite Commander Rokai ahl," Missy responded.

~~~

Zha Quin lay on the sofa in his and Vivi's quarters with her sleeping atop him. He'd spent the day at her side, just being the mate he'd promised to be when he claimed her as his Ehlealah. Their main vidcom unit began pinging startling her as she napped on top of him. He snuggled her close, murmuring to her quietly to lull her back to sleep. She'd had a hard day and he wanted nothing to upset her any further.

"Missy," he said as quietly as he could and still be heard.

"Yes, Commander," Missy answered.

"Disable the main com. We are not to be disturbed at all!" Quin said.

"Disabled," Missy answered and the pinging stopped at once.

Vivi settled down and her breathing evened out as she began to fall back into a deep sleep. Then the communicator he wore on his wrist began to sound.

On a snarl he lifted his arm and ripped it from his wrist, then pressed anything he could find to turn the damned thing off. Doing his best to calm his irritation, he almost lost it when the communicator Vivi wore began to sound.

"Why does no one obey me?!" Quin snapped.

"What's wrong?" Vivian asked sleepily, beginning to lift herself off him.

"No, stay where you are, Ehlealah," Quin said gently, pulling her back down onto his chest. "Missy! Block all communications to myself and Sirena Vivi!" Quin ordered.

Vivian snuggled down into his arms as he removed her communicator from her wrist, and tossed it to the floor along with his.

"Who's trying to get us?" she asked.

"I do not know. It does not matter. I have not given you an uninterrupted day since you boarded this ship. It is time I did so," Quin said, smoothing a hand back and forth over her back.

"It's okay. I understand," she said on a yawn.

"You should not have to understand. If all others can take time for their females, I can certainly do the same. Especially today," he said.

"With Re'Vahl's promotion, you'll have more time," she said.

"Yes, I will," he agreed.

"Maybe I should have waited until he's fully trained," Vivian suggested.

"Nonsense. You should never have to wait for anything you wish. If I can grant it, it's yours."

"Thank you, Quin," Vivian mumbled sleepily.

Missy spoke, interrupting them again. "Commander, you are needed on the Command Deck immediately."

"I am not reporting to the Command Deck. I told you I am not to be interrupted today — numerous times!"

"I was ordered to override that order, Commander," Missy replied.

"By who?" Quin demanded.

"By Sovereign Zha Tahl Tel Mo' Kok," Missy responded.

Quin lifted Vivian from his chest, and settled her on the sofa. "I'll be but a moment, Ehlealah." He walked over to the main com unit and flicked it on. At once he was greeted by the angry face of Chairman Bartholomew, his father - Sovereign Zha Tahl Tel Mo' Kok, and his mother — Sovereigna Eula Tel Mo' Kok.

"What is happening?" Zha Quin demanded on seeing their demeanor.

"You tell us!" Bart demanded.

"I don't understand," Zha Quin answered.

"Explain to me why two Cruestaci battle cruisers docked on the United Consortium Defense satellite station, despite the fact they were denied permission to dock!" Bart demanded.

Chapter 22

The soldiers of the Unified Consortium Defense held their weapons trained on the twin battle cruisers that had docked — against orders — and now sat secured on the pads they'd chosen at will. They heard the airlocks release on both cruisers, they stood watching, waiting, wanting anything but a battle with Cruestaci warriors, but not afraid to do whatever was necessary to defend the Consortium they'd sworn to protect.

~~~

The communicator in General Lo'San's battle cruiser crackled. "They do not look happy to see us," Rokai's voice said clearly from his transport.

General Lo'San shook his head and heaved a sigh. "I do not care," he grumbled in answer.

"Who's stepping out first to see if they fire?" Rokai asked.

"I am," Lo'San said, unstrapping his safety harness and standing to make his way to the exit.

"I am!" Rokai argued. "Lo'San!" Rokai said, his voice raised in volume when Lo'San didn't answer. "Lo'San! We step out together!"

"No. I'll go first, then you follow — respectfully," Lo'San said.

"I have a plan..." Rokai insisted.

"I don't need a plan. I'm finding my female and we're leaving," Lo'San said.

"I don't believe they'll let you take her without a fight! Allow me to speak..."

"I will handle this, Rokai!" General Lo'San grumbled, cutting off whatever Rokai was planning to say.

Rokai didn't say anymore, he simply grumbled under his breath about stubborn Generals and their lack of imagination when dealing with dignitaries, as he made his way to the exit of his cruiser and stood in wait with half of his Elite force behind him. The other half was onboard the other cruiser with General Lo'San.

~~~

The soldiers of the Consortium kept their weapons trained on the exit door of the first battle cruiser as it slowly raised to reveal its occupants. Once fully open, most of them recognized General Lo'San.

"I wish no battle! I am here only for my mate," Lo'San said.

"With two battle cruisers?" an Ambassador said as he stepped from behind the small wall of military males.

"Upper level officers of the Cruestaci do not travel without forces," Lo'San said simply, as he heard the exit door on Rokai's cruiser lifting.

"You seemed to have no trouble coming with only your pilot little more than twenty-four Earth hours ago," the male pointed out.

"I did not come to this station twenty-four Earth hours ago," Lo'San said.

"I spoke to you myself! I know who I spoke with!" the Ambassador insisted.

"Do you, though?" Rokai asked from the exit of his battle cruiser. "Do you? General Lo'San has not left Cruestaci Warship 1. He has been present and accounted for at all times."

"Then explain your arrival to relieve yourself of your female," the Ambassador said. "I suppose you are going to try to tell me that you've been the victim of an impostor... someone has stolen your uniform, pretended to be you, stolen your female away from you, and deposited her here!" the Ambassador snarked.

"That is exactly what I'm telling you," Lo'San said.

The Ambassador shook his head in disbelief. "Get back on your cruisers and leave this station at once. The female in question does not wish to interact with you. She's requested shelter and our protection. We've granted it. Leave us."

"No! I am not leaving without my mate!" Lo'San snarled and set foot on the catwalk leading from his cruiser to the dock floor of the station.

All weapons were readied, high-pitched whines could be heard at the same time dozens of clicking sounds rattled the air.

"The only reason we've not responded with force, General, is that we were ordered to deny permission to dock. If you insisted, we were to receive you, explain the situation, and ask you to leave willingly. That is exactly what we are doing. It is out of respect for your Sovereign and Sovereigna that this consideration is being given. Chairman Bartholomew is with them now and assures me that you bear no ill will toward the Consortium. Should we have reason to regret our actions, we are prepared to protect this station as necessary."

"Your point?" Lo'San asked, frozen mid-step.

"Do not push me, General. You have entered a neutral governing territory with hostile intent. We would be well within our rights to blast you and your cruisers from our station."

"Hostile? You think this is hostile?" Lo'San growled. "I can show you the difference between insistence and hostility."

"Do you threaten us, General Lo'San?" the Ambassador asked.

"He does not!" Rokai said insistently. "What is your name?" he called out from the doorway of his own cruiser.

"I am Ambassador Karel," the male answered.

"Ambassador Karel, of course. Once you represented yourself with the steadfast strength I've just witnessed, I had no doubt that you must surely be Ambassador Karel. I have heard much of your prowess and capability," Rokai said.

Lo'San turned his head and looked at Rokai like he'd lost his mind. He knew full well Rokai had never heard of this male.

"And you are?" Karel asked.

"I am Prince Rokai ahl Tel Mo' Kok of the Cruestaci. Reformed scoundrel and honored Elite Force Commander of the Elite Forces aboard Command Warship 1," Rokai said, performing a little bow. "I am pleased to finally make your acquaintance."

The Ambassador didn't seem to know how to respond, which gave Rokai the opportunity to continue.

"My brother, Sire Zha Quin Tha Tel Mo' Kok and my parents, Sovereign Zha Tahl Tel Mo' Kok, and Sovereigna Eula Tel Mo' Kok, have been much pleased with your rise through the levels of diplomacy. Bart has told us of you, and we share a belief that you will be a great asset to the peoples of all worlds in your role as Ambassador."

"Well, I... I am humbled to learn that my name has carried forth and made me familiar," Ambassador Karel finally said.

"As are we!" Rokai said, striding confidently down the catwalk. "May I call you Karel? Your formal title makes us seem as strangers. Please, call me Rokai, Prince Rokai," he said, extending his arms and holding them palm up in a presentation of himself to the universe, as he continued on his path down the catwalk to the floor of the landing dock.

"Is there a place that we may discuss what has become a mess of a situation, Karel?" Rokai asked.

"I have not been given permission to allow your forces onto this station, Prince Rokai," Ambassador Karel said, watching Rokai's Elite team begin to follow him down to the floor level.

"Oh, do not mind them. They simply must accompany me wherever I go. Do you have any idea how irritating it is to have men you fight beside, stand just outside the cleansing chamber when you clean your body? It is a perk of this royal life I've not come to enjoy."

Karel didn't answer, he kept his eyes nervously on the Elite Team of Cruestaci Warriors now striding to stand just behind Rokai.

227

"Allow me to explain briefly, and might I say, I'm somewhat surprised that you must request permission from Bart — is this not your station?"

"He is Chairman Bartholomew, the Chairman of the Consortium. It is customary to defer to him in all things out of the ordinary," Ambassador Karel explained defensively.

"Yes, but, why should a man such as you need direction? I digress... let me tell you of our situation, Karel. General Lo'San has been long estranged from his family. One member of that family is Ko'San — his brother. They could easily pass for the same male. Ko'San has long wished ill on Lo'San, and upon the reconciliation of the family, took the opportunity to kidnap Lo'San's new mate, and spirit her away. Now surely you can understand the intense need of General Lo'San to find and reclaim her at once. If it were your mate, would you allow her to believe that you'd simply tired of her? I think not, you're a better male than that," Rokai said confidently. "You'd move the entirety of the multi-verse in order to find and reclaim her. I know you would, you are a male of great character!" Rokai said confidently.

"Of course I would. Which is why I cannot just hand her over to you."

Rokai shook his head and raised both eyebrows, an almost comical look of surprise on his face. "I'm sorry, I don't understand."

"While I hear your words, Prince Rokai, and if true, sympathize with them, I will need more than your explanation as proof," Ambassador Karel explained.

Rokai's eyebrow rose even higher as he straightened to his full height and held a hand against his chest as though wounded. "Are you accusing me of telling untruths?" he asked, his voice rising indignantly.

Karel, whose gaze had been trained on Lo'San, immediately gave Rokai his full attention. "Not at all, Prince Rokai. I simply need evidence of your explanation. Even once that evidence is no doubt supplied to me, I can not simply turn the female over to you. She's been promised safety, and she does not wish to see anyone representative of the Cruestaci. She has been betrayed and wants no part of anyone that has dishonored her!"

"She's only been misled by an impostor pretending to be me!" Lo'San shouted from right beside Rokai where he'd quickly moved to stand while Rokai distracted Karel. "She's not been betrayed, she's been kidnapped!" Lo'San insisted.

Rokai seized on that. "Kidnapped indeed! And I believe that as you are refusing to grant General Lo'San access to his kidnapped mate, you could possibly be accused of being complicit in her kidnapping. Oh my," he said, his finger tapping his chin as he allowed his eyes to travel across the forty or so soldiers assembled to convince them to leave the station, "I wonder how many of you could be held in offense for hindering a member of the royal family of Cruestace and the commanding General of their military from access to his kidnapped mate."

"No one is hindering access! We are simply complying with her wishes!" Karel insisted.

"If you are sure you are not holding her against her will, what have you to hide? You should allow me to speak to her. If she still refuses to leave this station I will not force her, but be prepared to house me long term — I will not leave without her," Lo'San said. "And, if she informs me that you are indeed holding her against her will, your keeping this station safe from the Cruestaci will not be an issue for you any longer - you won't live to see me destroy it."

"I am certainly not involved with any crime, especially not one of holding females against their will. Prince Rokai has already stated that I am known for my diplomacy!" Karel said defensively. "I have not committed any crime!"

"Oh, of course, yet here we stand on an official Cruestaci mission, attempting to save a female, a member of the Cruestaci people by claim, and you greet us with military force."

Ambassador Karel sputtered. "You didn't... there are battle cruisers! We hailed you and asked your reasons for arrival, no one responded! We warned you away! Yet you docked anyway!"

"I did not hear anyone hail our cruisers, did you General?" Rokai asked.

"Yes, I certainly did. But why would I speak to those holding my female against her will," Lo'San rumbled. "Why give them warning of their impending battles when I could just as easily land, rescue her and leave them behind in the rubble of their chosen fate."

"We do not hold her against her will! We protect her!" Karel insisted. "And now you threaten us!"

"General Lo'San is reacting to the fact that he's not yet been assured of the safety of his female. For all we know she may be enduring horrible abuse as you stand here detaining us," Rokai answered.

"She is safe, secure and well protected!" Ambassador Karel insisted.

"Prove it," Rokai said simply.

~~~

Synclare sat in Ambassador Karel's offices, chewing on her nails nervously as she waited, watching on security vids as Karel and his soldiers faced off with Rokai, his Elite Forces, and Lo'San. Lo'San, she missed him so much, but her heart hurt just thinking of his name. The com unit behind her pinged nonstop, and she turned to look at it. "Shut up!" she hissed at the unit.

The com unit stopped pinging for only a moment before it started up again.

Clenching her teeth, she turned away from the irritating constant ping of the unit and focused on the black and white image of Lo'San as he seemed to argue with Ambassador Karel. He looked tired, and he wasn't wearing his uniform. He wore the same clothes he wore when he trained with his warriors, but, not his uniform. That was peculiar. She watched as Karel seemed to shout at them in response, and Rokai stood to his full height indignantly. Then her eyes rounded in shock as Karel spun on his heel and moved toward the interior of the space station with Lo'San, Rokai, and Rokai's Elite Forces following closely.

Synclare jumped to her feet and ran out of the office, stopping only long enough to determine where she'd best run to hide. She didn't want to see Lo'San — she couldn't face him. She was so devastated with his dismissal of her, and her heart was shattered. The last thing she wanted was to even be in the same room with him. She didn't know the station as well as she did Command Warship 1 and had no idea of the best places to lose herself. So she just ran, turned down a corridor that seemed to be leading away from the docking bay, and rushed away.

"Where are we going?" one of her guards asked.

"Away. I don't care where, just away," she answered.

"Away from..." he said.

"I don't wish to see them," she answered. "I don't know where to hide!" Synclare said, beginning to get upset again.

"Come," he said, indicating a different direction.

Synclare stood where she was, considering his suggestion.

"Come, return to your quarters and face him. Do not allow him to see you weak and afraid."

"I am not weak and afraid!" Synclare insisted.

Her guard pinned her with a questioning look. "Then do not behave as though you are."

Synclare wanted to punch him, but he was right. "I'm not going to my quarters. I'm going back to Karel's office. I'll face him there."

"It matters not where you face him, just that you do, with strength and calm," the soldier said.

Synclare took a deep breath and nodded. "You're right." She walked back the direction she came and when she passed between her two guards they fell into step on either side of her. Every step grew heavier and heavier, and her heart pounded in her chest as she got closer and closer to the office she'd eventually face off with Lo'San in. She had no idea why he was back, or what had made him return here, but it was apparent he wanted more than just to visit with the Ambassador, since he'd brought Rokai and the Elite Force with him.

It was more than a few minutes before Ambassador Karel with Lo'San, Rokai and their Elite security force finally arrived in

Karel's office. Synclare spent those minutes pacing back and forth, reading and rereading the letter that she shoved back into her pocket when she heard the door slide open and knew they'd arrived. Her heart jumped into her throat and adrenalin coursed through her veins.

"Can no one answer that com?" Karel asked, stalking over to it and pressing the button to accept the com.

"Ambassador Karel, here. How may I be of service?"

"What the hell is going on over there?!" Chairman Bartholomew demanded. "I've been waiting for an update!"

"Chairman Bartholomew! We are conferencing now, sir. We should have answers shortly, sir," Ambassador Karel said.

"Bart! How are you, my friend?" Rokai shouted.

"Who is that?" Bart asked.

"It is I, Prince Rokai!" Rokai said far too cheerily.

"Good gods," Bart mumbled. "I should have known you were involved."

"Stand strong, female. Any male would be proud to claim you," the quieter of her guards said to Synclare under his breath.

Synclare looked up to meet his intense gaze, then slowly turned at the sound of her name.

"Sink Lar!" Lo'San said, rushing toward her.

"Keep your distance!" one of her guards ordered, as both stepped in front of her to keep Lo'San from reaching her.

"Move aside!" Lo'San ordered with a snarl.

"No," the guard who'd told her to stand strong said, taking another step toward Lo'San.

"She is my mate, I would never do her harm!" Lo'San insisted.

"Yet you drugged her and left her here, claiming it was she who wanted away from you. We've heard your stories, and we've heard hers. We've seen what your actions have done. You tell lies," her other guard insisted.

"It wasn't me! Sink Lar! It wasn't me! I didn't bring you here, I didn't drug you. I had no knowledge of it at all! The moment I found you missing I began searching. Ko'San admitted what he'd done and I'm here. I'm here and I'm not leaving without you, my Sink Lar. I would never let you go, you know this!" Lo'San said, looking at Synclare standing safely behind the two guards that had been assigned to her.

"What the hell is happening?" Bart demanded.

Chapter 23

"This is all a huge misunderstanding, Chairman Bartholomew," Karel explained, watching the exchange between Lo'San and Synclare.

"Go back to your ship, Lo'San. I have nothing to say to you," she said, her voice just barely above a whisper.

"Tell him we do not hold you against your will, Synclare!" Ambassador Karel said emphatically.

"What?" she asked, at the same time Bart echoed her question.

"We've been accused of being complicit in your kidnapping! We have been no such thing!" Ambassador Karel insisted.

"My kidnapping..." Synclare said.

"Who was kidnapped?" Bart asked.

"My mother and Ph'eel arranged it. They coerced Ko'San who played his part, thankfully not to the fullest. He dressed in my uniform and carried you from the ship. He admitted that he brought you here."

"But the letter..." Synclare said. "I have the letter you wrote. And I remember you telling me we weren't going to try for children anymore. You said children with me were no longer important because you'd realized we should have just stayed as we were before."

"Exactly!" Lo'San exclaimed. "I meant every word of it! I cannot bear to watch the female that is my life suffer in order to give me young ones! I do not need young ones! I need only you! We should have never put your body through the pain and trauma of the treatments, we should have just remained as we were, you and I, no forcing of young ones upon your poor, sweet body, Sink Lar!"

Synclare stood there, realizing she'd misunderstood his words. "I thought you meant we should have remained friends," she said.

"Never! Do you truly think I could live one day without you at my side? Without knowing you were waiting for me to return to our home? To know that above all else in life, you value me?" Lo'San asked incredulously.

"But... you lied to me about the treatments, you didn't tell me it should have worked the first time I accepted the treatment."

"I knew how much it meant to you. And I kept thinking each time would be the answer to your prayers for a young one. But I cannot watch you suffer any longer. I need you, Sink Lar. Only you. Come home with me," Lo'San begged.

"This letter," she said. "You wrote this letter. And it says you don't want me. It says that I poisoned my body and cannot give you children through my own actions! Only you and a few others know of my past! And the credit band, it's loaded with your credits... Only you could have done that!"

"My mother did all of this. I do not know how she learned of your past. But it matters not! Your past has nothing to do with us or our future. We all have pasts, my Sink Lar. You know I never cared about any behaviors you took part in before me. It is no different than you disregarding my behaviors before you. Ph'eel found our letters to one another. They scanned them into her tablet, and had letters created for both of us. My mother's plan was for me to believe the letter I received from you, and for you to die from too much medication, but failing that, if you woke, to believe that I'd written the words in that letter. Those are not my words!"

"She wanted me dead?!" Synclare said, shocked.

"She'd instructed Ko'San to give you two more doses before leaving you here. Ko'San confessed all of it. She wanted me broken, returning to her and joining Ph'eel's household to take my rightful place in their society once more."

"Here," Rokai said, walking up to the guards who still stood before Synclare. "Move!" he barked out.

When neither of Synclare's guards moved, Rokai simply inserted himself between them, daring them to lay hands on him. "This is the letter they created for Lo'San," he said, pushing and shoving his way to reach out toward her while her guards attempted to shove him back.

"It's alright, let him through," Synclare said, reaching out for the letter Rokai offered her.

Synclare opened the letter and began to read. When she was done she raised her eyes from the page and looked up at Lo'San. "Why? What did I do that was so horrible?" she asked.

"Nothing, Sink Lar. Which is exactly why Ko'San didn't do what they told him to. He didn't carry out their intentions to end your life, and was filled with such guilt over their treatment of you that he sought me out to tell me of what they'd done. Ko'San left you here, not me. I will never live one moment without you by my side, Sink Lar. You promised forever, and forever is all I will accept — not a moment less, my mate. Please, Sink Lar, please, look at me. Remember our vows, remember how we love, do not allow them to win."

Synclare reached into her pocket and withdrew the letter she'd been reading over and over again. She stepped from between her guards and walked slowly past Rokai toward Lo'San.

Lo'San watched her approach, wanting nothing more than to snatch her up and run for his cruiser, but he knew she had to choose to come back with him.

Synclare held out the letter to him, waiting for him to take it and read it for himself.

Lo'San took it from her and unfolded it, reading the words printed there in what appeared to be his version of the English letters. "It even looks like my handwriting," he said. As he finished the letter he let it fall to the floor. "Not a word of this is true. I want you, Sink Lar. I've only ever wanted you. Please..." he said.

Synclare stood just in front of him, and a tear slid down her face. "It hurt so much to think I'd failed you, that I wasn't enough."

"It is I who failed you, my love. I got so caught up in my reunion with my family, that I let my guard down. I didn't put you first. Had I, they'd have never had the opportunity to carry out any of their nefarious plans. We'd still be happily aboard Command Warship 1, not standing here with me pleading with you to see that it was Ko'San, not me who brought you here, and for you to forgive me for my negligence. This should never have happened," Lo'San said. "I have vowed to love you all my life, and now I vow even more. I will never allow anything or anyone to shift my focus from you. You are my heart, my mate. You are my happiness. You are my reason for everything I do. I vow to you, you will never have an opportunity to believe you are anything other than the center of my life, Sink Lar. I only need your faith in me once more to prove it to you," Lo'San said.

Synclare threw herself at Lo'San who caught her and held her to him tightly, kissing any place he could reach as he apologized over and over again.

"I was so devastated," she said, holding onto him.

"We will never be parted again, Sink Lar. Please forgive me," he said again.

"Yes," she said. "Please forgive me for bringing them into our lives. I'm so sorry. All this is my fault because I insisted you give them a chance," she said, leaning back enough to see his face.

Lo'San shook his head. "You gave me back my father. That is something I've missed greatly. But it is on my shoulders that this has happened - I know what the females of my family are capable of, you did not. I should never have let my guard down. I never will again," he promised.

"Where are they?" she asked as he used his thumbs to smooth away her tears.

"Mee'ta, Ph'eel, and Ko'San are in holding cells on Command Warship 1. I plan to pursue charges and have Mee'ta and Ph'eel incarcerated for as long as possible. Ko'San... I've not decided his punishment — he could have killed you, but chose not to, then he came to me to tell me of their plan, but he will not walk away without consequence. My father is still onboard

Command Warship 1. I believe he had no part in it. I have no idea what he will do next. Once Ko'San confessed, I had the three of them arrested and rushed to come after you. There are details that remain to be seen to," Lo'San said.

Synclare nodded her understanding.

"Will you have me, Sink Lar? Will you forgive me and return home with me?" Lo'San asked.

"Yes," Synclare said, smiling through her tears. "I don't want to live without you, but I don't want them on the ship," she said.

"Not one of them will live aboard the ship," Lo'San assured her. "And you will never be without me," he promised.

"Then take me home, Lo'San," she said, wrapping her arms around his neck again as she pulled him down to her and buried her tear-stained face in the hollow of his throat.

"At once," Lo'San said, sweeping her up into his arms and stalking from Karel's office with half the Elite Forces following him and half staying with Rokai.

"Bart, Karel, and the rest of you dear gentlemen," Rokai said, bending over to pick up the letter Lo'San had dropped to the floor and folding it with the other he had in his hand, "it has been a pleasure. Thank you for your continued protection over the mate of General Lo'San. I will file reports with all pertinent parties, and make it clear to all those of the governing family of Cruestace that you were not involved in the taking of General Lo'san's mate, but have each gone above and beyond expectations in your services to us and her. Expect commendations, my friends."

"Commendations?" Bart said wryly.

"I should like a copy of the report you file," Ambassador Karel said.

"Of course, Karel. And I'm sure you'll be filing a report as well detailing how you mistook an impostor for General Lo'San, not asking for any identification at all before taking his word for his identity," Rokai said. "I will expect a copy of your report as well. But, in the meantime, I shall escort General Lo'San and his very traumatized mate back to our Warship. Do have a wonderful day," Rokai said, winking at the Ambassador. "Goodbye all, goodbye Bart!"

"Rokai, this is not over. You cannot simply arrive on the Consortium's satellite station without approval! You were expressly denied permission to dock!" Bart yelled.

"Of course not. We understand this. Under any other circumstances we would not have arrived without invitation, but, just this one time, we had to rescue Synclare. Come to visit us soon, or if you prefer, make plans to visit Cruestace. It is such a lovely place!" Rokai said, trying to deflect the issues at hand.

"I am with your parents now!" Bart said.

"Are you?" Rokai asked, knowing full well that Karel had said Bart was with his parents, but not imagining they could have been listening in with Bart. His voice did not give away a bit of the unease he felt at learning that they were most likely well aware of what was going on as it was happening. "Well, then enjoy your visit! Perhaps you can find a female to mate with there. It seems to have calmed Zha Quin — he bellows a lot less than he used to — perhaps it will calm you as well. Give my parents my love, I have a General who's just rescued his kidnapped mate to escort back to Command Warship 1!" Rokai said. He flashed a grin at Karel and the two guards, then hurried from the office to catch up with Lo'San and Synclare.

~~~

Lo'San strapped Synclare into the seat beside him, and began the process of powering up the cruiser. "Missy, please prepare the cruiser for flight. We will be returning to Command Warship 1 without further delay."

"Of course, General Lo'San. As I prepare for departure, Commander Tel Mo' Kok wishes to speak with you," Missy said pleasantly.

Lo'San sighed. "Wonderful," he mumbled.

"General Lo'San!" Zha Quin bellowed. "Do you care to explain to me why you and Elite Force Commander Rokai ahl have stormed the satellite station of the Unified Consortium Defense?!"

"Of course, sir," Lo'San answered, looking at the angry face of Zha Quin projected onto the white display across the windshield of the cruiser. "But please allow me to correct your assumption, sir, we did not storm the station. We simply landed, pled our case and gained access to my mate, sir," Lo'San explained, being more formal than necessary with the 'sirs'.

"Were you or were you not denied permission to dock?" Zha Quin demanded.

"We were," Lo'San answered.

"And yet you did it anyway! Are you aware that my Sirena and I were yanked awake after a stressful morning by a com from Chairman Bartholomew, accompanied by Sovereign Zha Tahl and Sovereigna Eula, demanding to know why two of our battle cruisers — not transports — battle cruisers, and two of them, insisted on docking despite the fact they refused to identify themselves and were denied permission!"

"No, I was not aware of that, Sire. I do apologize for the inconvenience, Sire."

"Inconvenience? How about the intra-universal incident you have caused. What about all the alerts that went out when it became clear that the Cruestaci were approaching on battle cruisers?"

"There was no incident, Sire. I give you my word, all concerns were addressed. We were given access to my mate, and all misunderstandings were explained. All is well, Sire."

A chime could be heard in the background of Zha Quin's vid com and he listened for a moment before giving his full attention to General Lo'San again. "Chairman Bartholomew is waiting for me on a different com. Standby," Quin ordered.

"We are departing now, Sire. We will be there shortly," Lo'San responded.

"Just standby!" Quin ordered.

"Yes, Sire," Lo'San said.

A few minutes later Quin was back on the vid com with Lo'San. "Kidnapping? You accused an Ambassador of the Consortium Defense of being complicit in the kidnapping of your mate?" Quin asked.

"No! I did not. I said she was kidnapped. Then Rokai implied that there may be a chance that anyone hindering us from saving her may be complicit. Neither of us directly accused anyone other than my family," Lo'San said.

Quin pressed his fingers to the bridge of his nose as he usually did when highly stressed.

"My mate was stolen from me, Quin!" Lo'San said, breaking from formality and addressing his Sire and Commander as his friend. "What would you have done if Vivi was taken from you? Even if by your own flesh and blood, she was taken from you and you were made aware of exactly where she was?" Lo'San asked passionately.

"You were denied permission to dock!" Quin insisted.

Lo'San shook his head resignedly, stared right back at Zha Quin. "What would you have done?"

Zha Quin stared back at Lo'San through the vid com and didn't reply at first. Then he simply gave a single nod. "Is she well?"

"Yes, we are both shaken, but well, and still mated," Lo'San said.

"Just get back here. We'll talk about it more when you arrive," Zha Quin said.

"Very well," Lo'San answered before Zha Quin ended the com on his end.

Zha Quin's chest rumbled as he locked eyes with Ba Re' who stood just behind him on the Command Deck. "Can you believe this?" Quin asked.

Ba Re' had a whole new outlook since finding, and being unable to claim his Ehlealah to date. He simply met Quin's gaze. "What *would* you have done?" he asked.

"Much worse, I fear," Quin admitted. He sighed as he returned his attention to the other active com on the viewing screen of the Command Deck where Bart waited for him to return to their conversation with Quin's parents seated beside him. "I am here," Zha Quin said, his voice still somewhat snarly.

"Have you spoken to General Lo'San or to Rokai?" Bart asked.

"Yes. They did not invade your station. They were on a rescue mission," Quin said, intentionally looking away from his parents' gaze as he spoke to Bart.

"No one needed rescuing, Quin," Bart snapped.

"They didn't know that," Quin insisted.

"Of course they did! No one under our protection, especially a female, is in danger," Bart said.

"Lo'San's mate was kidnapped! He went after her! What more is needed to understand his desperation?" Zha Quin asked.

"She was not in danger, and she'd expressly said she wanted no part of a visit from him, according to Ambassador Karel," Bart said.

"Are you aware of the details?" Quin asked, stepping closer to the viewing screen.

"I am. I heard their reconciliation. I am aware of the circumstances," Bart answered.

"Then what is the problem?" Quin shouted. "Explain to me the issue. No one was injured, no weapons were fired, and Lo'San and his female are reunited!"

"The problem is that two Cruestaci battle ships forced their way onto the dock of our satellite station, refused to be warned off, insisted the Elite teams they carried be granted entrance to our facility, and totally disregarded any authority the Consortium may have previously held. I have no doubt any respect we commanded has been brought down a notch, if not two! We cannot have this kind of thing happening, Quin! It simply cannot be tolerated!" Bart yelled.

Quin understood Bart's point of view. Bart had a position that demanded the utmost respect. He had a reputation and duties to uphold. Lo'San's and Rokai's assault on the Consortium's satellite station would have been seen as an act of aggression had it been on the Consortium's actual space station.

242

And it could feasibly be seen as such in this circumstance as well. Bart needed to save face and explain away the situation.

"I understand your situation," Quin said.

"Do you? Do you really?" Bart asked, beginning to pace.

"I do. How can we repair the appearance of our insisting on being granted entry to your satellite station?" Quin asked.

"How should I know?" Bart yelled, throwing a hand in the air.

"You are the Chairman of the Consortium, you would know best. Calm your mind, Bart. Think. What do you need us to do to help this look as though it is an acceptable event?"

"You could control your damned males! That would help immensely!" Bart snapped.

Chapter 24

Quin maintained his own control when he decided to explain once more from his perspective what had caused the breach in conduct for his General and well meaning brother who happened to be acting Elite Force Commander. "You have no idea just how controlled we all are. And allow me to clarify for the sake of argument, Lo'San's entire family with the sole exception of his father conspired to kill his mate. They drugged her, removed her from the ship...."

"How was that even achieved?" Bart interrupted. "Command Warship 1 has security most would pay to have. How was she taken off the ship without someone noticing? It makes no sense."

"Lo'San's brother could be his twin. He pretended to be Lo'San. No one questioned him. We are implementing new guidelines that will require double and triple checks of all flight plans and excursions. No one person will be given leeway simply because of their status. Even I will have to have the approval of several of my officers on my plan in order to commandeer a cruiser or a transport. This will prevent anyone getting off ship without proper approval and acknowledgment of their superiors and/or peers," Quin explained.

Bart just shook his head and continued pacing on his side of the viewing screen.

"I am aware of just how bad this could have turned out. If they'd been denied entry all together, and Lo'San was physically kept away from his mate, he could have lost control. Had it been another of my officers who is Cruestaci and their Psi took over, it would not have been so easily solved. Thankfully, Lo'San is more controlled due to his Eschina heritage, and the fact that he thinks on his feet, even when in emotional upheaval. Do not think I'm not affected by this. But, let me also make it clear, if it were my

Vivi, I'd have stormed the satellite station, found my Ehlealah, and blown it out of existence as I left if anyone thought to be stupid enough to keep her from me. I completely understand Lo'San's unwillingness to just turn around and come back without his mate."

Bart scrubbed both hands down his face, having calmed enough to see both sides. "I need to paint this in an acceptable light in order to maintain us all in a favorable status."

"Can we not just say that Lo'San's mate was kidnapped and you intercepted and gave her protection until he could arrive to save her?" Quin asked.

"There were at least forty soldiers standing them off when they docked. That's a lot of eyes to convince otherwise," Bart said.

"How many were witness to their reconciliation?" Quin asked.

"Your Elite Teams, Lo'San, Rokai, Ambassador Karel, myself via the com unit, and the two guards assigned to Lo'San's mate," Bart said.

"And us," Zha Tahl said. "We were listening as well."

"It seems to me, Rokai has provided us the opportunity we look for," Eula said.

Bart turned to look at Eula and Zha Tahl.

"He thanked everyone for their protection of Lo'San's mate, told them they could all expect commendations, and complimented them on their services," Eula said.

"He was not serious, he was being his typical smart-assed self. And because of that you're going to reward everyone on that satellite station for their part?" Bart asked.

"No, we are going to reward all who witnessed the actual reconciliation for their part in keeping Lo'San's mate safe until Lo'San could arrive. We are going to state that because you were on Cruestace, the communications were somewhat muddled, but that your Ambassador Karel was clear enough on the fact that the Cruestaci had reason to be aboard the satellite station that he allowed them to land despite the fact they were not cleared in advance. He alone provided the opportunity needed for our

245

General to have access to his mate that would otherwise not have been granted," Eula stated.

"Karel is an idiot," Bart mumbled.

"Even better. He'll happily accept the commendation and never tell of what really happened," Eula commented.

"You think that will work?" Bart asked.

"It's better than nothing, and we will provide the commendations, as well as make it a publicized event. It will promote the careers and increase the respect of all involved. Those on the flight deck will be none the wiser, they simply followed directions, and all was well that ended well," Eula said.

Bart turned to Quin. "What do you think?"

"I think it could work. It's the best option we have at this time," Quin said.

"Even if there are any rumors surrounding the occurrence, the hard evidence is that Lo'San and his mate have been reunited, and the warriors involved in guarding her while she was on your satellite station, as well as the Ambassador who granted our battle cruisers access, will receive commendations. That will far outweigh any rumors that may eventually surface," Zha Tahl said. "I think it's a good plan."

"Let's put it into place, then," Bart said resignedly.

"Excellent. Before I let you go work out the details, I will be calling a private vid com later in the month, I would appreciate all three of you making time for it," Zha Quin said.

"Is there a problem, Zha Quin?" Zha Tahl asked.

Quin shook his head. "No, I don't think so. But I am considering some changes, and may have news I wish to share at that time."

"Very well. Let us get this taken care of and let us know when you decide you wish to have us available for your vid com." Zha Tahl said.

"Thank you, Father," Quin answered.

Eula rose from her seat and approached the viewing screen on her side. "Quin, is all well?"

"Yes, Mother. Better than you'd imagine," Quin said.

"Very well, we'll speak later," Eula answered, a gentle yet surprised smile on her face.

"End com, Communications Master Vennie," Quin ordered, as he smiled at his mother, knowing she most likely had already figured out some of what he had to tell them.

"Com ended, Sire," Vennie responded.

"Thank you. Please confirm both battle cruisers are on their way back," Quin said.

"Confirmed, Sire. Both are on their way, no injuries, no fatalities," Vennie assured.

"Are you staying on deck?" Quin asked Ba Re'.

"Re'Vahl is on duty. I'll relieve him at the end of his shift," Ba Re' answered.

"Lieutenant Commander Re'Vahl, are you prepared to take the Command Deck?" Zha Quin asked.

"Yes, Sire! I am," Re'Vahl answered.

"Contact me if needed. I'm returning to my quarters," Quin said.

"Yes, Sire. I will," Re'Vahl answered, moving to take Quin's place in the command chair.

"Monitor both battle cruisers, if their path changes at all contact me at once," Quin said just before he exited the doors.

"Yes, Sire," Re'Vahl confirmed.

Quin strode down the corridor intent on getting to Vivi, but paused when he heard Ba Re' call out his name. Quin turned to find Ba Re' rushing to catch up with him. "Quin, is all well?" Ba Re' asked.

"Yes," Quin answered.

"Is there anything I should know?" Ba Re' asked, having heard Quin tell his family and Bart he wanted a private com with them.

"No," he answered, not wanting to tell Ba Re' anything his family didn't know yet. In fact, there was nothing to discuss yet, but hopefully there would be soon. "How do things stand with you and your Ehlealah?" Quin asked.

Ba Re' shook his head. "I've stepped away from her. I cannot function with this constant back and forth," Ba Re' admitted.

"I am sorry, Ba Re'. Surely all will work itself out," Quin said.

"I've suggested she petition for a position working with Bart under the Consortium's umbrella. I've moved into temporary quarters until she leaves the ship."

"Are you sure that's wise?" Quin asked, shocked to hear the news.

"I'm losing myself, Quin. I cannot compromise my wellbeing because she is unsure of what she wants. I will not force her, she will not accept my claim until she is satisfied with herself. We are at an impasse."

"If I can be of assistance..." Quin said.

"I will continue on as I always have. I will not be the first Cruestaci male unable to claim his Ehlealah. It will not kill me," Ba Re' said bravely.

"It is not yet done, she will eventually come around," Quin said.

"Perhaps," Ba Re' agreed.

"You know the politics between the Cruestaci and the Consortium as well as I. Feel free to send a formal request for placement with them for your female if you believe she could perform well. I will sign off on anything you suggest," Quin offered.

"Thank you," Ba Re' said.

"Do not spend too much time alone, Ba Re'. Time will drive you insane if you have too much of it," Quin suggested.

Ba Re' gave a sad laugh. "I am only too aware. I've been training with our warriors at every opportunity. It keeps my mind sharp and my body exhausted."

"Very good. I will take my leave now, I'm anxious to return to Vivi. But I will call you, as well as several others into the meeting I've requested with my parents and Bart. I'll let you know when to expect it."

"Alright. If you need me, call on me," Ba Re' said.

~~~

Quin very quietly walked into his quarters. All was still darkened just like he left it, which let him know that Vivi had managed to fall asleep. He went to his bedroom and found Vivi curled up with Kitty, soundly sleeping. He climbed over them and settled in behind Vivi, kissing her bare shoulder as he pulled the comforter over them.

She shifted against him before settling down again. "Is everything okay?" she asked.

"Miraculously, yes," Quin answered.

"Is Synclare okay?"

"She is. She is coming home with Lo'San. All is well," Quin assured her.

"Okay," Vivian answered.

"How are you feeling, Ehlealah?" Quin asked.

"Very, very sleepy. Just can't keep my eyes open."

"Rest, then. If you want anything at all, let me know, and it will be done," Quin said, stroking the skin on her back and her arms as he kissed the back of her head.

"We have so much to talk about though," she said on a yawn.

"It can wait. You need to rest. All you need to concern yourself with is knowing that whatever makes you happiest is what will make me happiest. All details can wait until you feel more yourself," Quin said.

"Good. I hired a nanny," Vivian said.

"Oh? And how did you do that from our bedroom?" he asked.

"Remember the girl that came with Lo'San's family to watch their kids? Au'revele? She came to me just after you left to go to the Command Deck, begging me to intercede on her behalf. Apparently Ph'eel sent word to her to prepare for someone else

249

to watch over the kids because she'd have to go to prison with her to tend her needs while she was incarcerated, and the poor girl was terrified."

"That is impossible. Ph'eel has no idea how her life will play out in prison. She will be just another convict, tending her own needs and praying for survival. She is a horrible excuse for a female," Quin grumbled.

"Agreed. Anyway, the poor girl has never known anything but servitude and was terrified she'd be held partially responsible for Ph'eel's actions. She grew up in Ph'eel's household as a servant and has never known anything else. I assured her she wouldn't be, but she was still worried about returning home with no position or way to make a living. She was concerned she'd carry the shame of being associated with Ph'eel's crimes and not be able to find a household to take her in as their servant. So, I told her she wouldn't be returning home if she chose to stay here, and I offered her a job as our nanny. I did say if we ever have children."

"I'm glad you were clear on the if," Quin said. "And she accepted despite the fact you emphasized the if?" he asked.

"Absolutely. I think she was just relieved to have the promise of a position. And if she hadn't, I'd have come up with something else. I need her to stay here for selfish reasons. I know not all my guard will come with us. But I'd like some of them to, and if she's with us, it will keep Zahn close. I like Zahn, his grumpy has grown on me," Vivian said.

"We have no way of knowing who will stay and who will choose to come with us. But regardless, why would it keep Zahn close?"

"Because she's his Ehlealah," Vivian said.

Quin burst out laughing, his deep, resonant laugh filling the bedroom. "Now it is all perfectly clear! That is why his behavior has been so out of character!"

"Yep. He stalks around wearing his battle helmet so she can't see him watching her, thinking that no one is aware of what he's doing, but we all know — except for Au'revele. He's more grumbly than usual, and suggests that I go exercise everyday, since that is where she is usually located with the children. Like I wouldn't notice that."

Quin laughed again. "He said he would not ever accept an Ehlealah. This will be interesting to watch."

"It will, but more importantly, I really like Au'revele. She's sweet, and kind, and humble, and the kids she was charged with obviously adore her, and were raised with love and I know that love didn't come from their mother. That makes me believe she's a good person. And I don't really think I'll ever need a nanny, but, it kept her here, and Zahn needs more time. So, I hired her."

"You have a soft heart, my Ehlealah."

"With you," she admitted.

"With many," Quin corrected. "You will be a wonderful Sovereigna to our people."

"I'll need help," she said. "Do you think your mother will stick around and help me once the time comes?"

"She will most likely need to be forcibly removed from your side when the time comes," Quin said, smiling as he kissed her shoulder.

Vivian smiled as she yawned. "Good. I love her."

"She loves you," Quin said. "And I love you, too, my Vivi," Quin said, closing his eyes and resting his cheek against her head.

"Love you, Quin," Vivian mumbled as she snuggled into his arms and settled down to go back to sleep.

~~~

Ba Re' stood on the flight deck as he watched the battle cruisers return to the ship. They both docked, the air locks released and the Elite teams, Rokai, Lo'San and Synclare exited.

As they approached, Lo'San with Synclare in his arms and Rokai beside him, stopped before Ba Re'. "Is all well?" Lo'San asked.

Ba Re' gave a single nod. "I believe so. And we have a plan to explain away the incident."

"Where is our Sire? I would appreciate the opportunity to explain my actions face to face," Lo'San said.

"It's not necessary, Lo'San. He fully understands. He has returned to his quarters. He said if he is needed to contact him, otherwise he is not to be disturbed. He is not available at the moment, unless it is an emergency," Ba Re' said.

"I will wait until he is on duty once more," Lo'San said.

"See to your mate, he'll certainly seek you out when he is ready to talk about the incident," Ba Re' suggested.

"There was no incident," Rokai defended.

"No, but there could have been. Believe it or not, you actually gave us the way to explain your actions, and save face for those on the satellite station," Ba Re' said.

"I did?" Rokai asked.

"Yes. We're giving them commendations and thanking them for protecting Lo'San's female until he could get there to rescue her. We're charging Lo'San's family with kidnapping and they will serve their time incarcerated," Ba Re' said, watching Lo'San for any objection.

"I have no problem with it. If they are locked away, it will tame the temptation to kill them myself," Lo'San said.

"And no one gives me credit for my diplomacy," Rokai commented, puffing his chest out.

"Diplomacy... no. But the ability to lie while looking anyone in the eye, and thinking fast enough to manipulate most... yes. You're very good at that," Ba Re' said on a laugh.

"What is diplomacy if not playing to the crowd you're facing," Rokai said.

Ba Re' nodded. "You're more accurate than you think, my friend."

"Wait, did you just call me friend?" Rokai asked.

"No, I did not," Ba Re' denied.

"You did! I heard you. You said, 'My friend'," Rokai insisted.

"I have business to tend to," Ba Re' said. "Be sure you do not speak of anything that happened until you meet with Quin. There is a certain picture that must be painted," Ba Re' said.

"Of course," Lo'San agreed.

"Rokai?" Ba Re' asked.

"I understand. I'll speak to my team as well. But, for now, admit that you called me friend," Rokai insisted.

Ba Re' shook his head. "I will speak to you later. I have responsibilities to see to," he said as he turned to walk away.

Rokai fell into step right behind Ba Re'. "What responsibilities? Do you need my assistance, my friend?"

"Go away, Rokai," Ba Re' grumbled.

"You see how I did that? I said friend. It is not difficult. Just say it... Fff..rrr... iiiend," Rokai said pronouncing it dramatically as they disappeared through the doors of the flight deck and into the ship.

Lo'San looked down at Synclare who slept peacefully in his arms. She'd been asleep for most of their trip back and even disembarking the battle cruiser had not awakened her. He wasn't sure that she'd not been affected by the additional medications that his mother had given her before Ko'San took her away. "We will go to medical, my mate. I wish to be sure you are well," Lo'San said quietly, and set his path toward medical.

"Missy?" he asked quietly as he stepped into the corridor.

"Yes, General Lo'San," Missy answered. "Welcome back," she added.

"Thank you. Is the Master Healer on duty?" he asked.

"He is," Missy responded. "Shall I tell him to expect you?" Missy asked.

"Yes. And my mate."

Chapter 25

The doors to medical swooshed open and Lo'San stepped through with Synclare in his arms. She'd begun to stir a little, and opened her eyes at the sound of an unexpected voice.

"General! Welcome and congratulations!" Doc said as he walked toward Lo'San and Synclare, smiling widely, clearly happy over something.

Lo'San's brow furrowed just enough to show his confusion. "Thank you," he said, deciding that perhaps news of his return with Synclare had already made the rounds of the ship's inhabitants. "I wished to be sure Sink Lar is well. I thought surely the effects of the medication my mother gave her would have worn off, but still she sleeps."

"Of course, General. What medication did your mother give her? She should not be taking any medication at all at this point. I'll be happy to examine her, but let me just say, additional rest is important for females like yours. She will know to listen to what her body needs. But come, I had planned to request additional examinations so that we could monitor her progress," Doc explained.

Synclare shifted in Lo'San's arms, and while still leaning her head against Lo'San's chest, gave Doc a sleepy smile. "Progress? We won't be having any more treatments, Doc. We've decided it's just not worth the trauma it puts me through," Synclare said.

Doc stood there, thoroughly confused. "Of course you wouldn't be having additional treatments. They're not necessary. Why would you continue with treatments when you've already conceived?" he asked.

Lo'San's face turned pale.

Synclare sat herself up in his arms, and blinked her eyes several times to be sure she was awake. "What did you say?" she whispered, afraid to believe what she thought she'd heard.

Doc looked from Lo'San to Synclare and back again. "Did neither of you get my message?" he asked.

"What message?" Lo'San finally squeezed through his tightening throat.

"You've conceived! The reason the treatments failed is you were already with young. Your body became so violently ill because it was actively ridding itself of the hormonal treatments we forced upon it. You are with young, Synclare," Doc said with a grin.

"I'm…" she said, with a catch in her breath. "I'm, I'm pregnant?" she asked.

"Yes. You are," Doc answered, glad to finally be able to deliver the news.

Synclare, still held in Lo'San's arms, turned her face to him. "We're going to have a baby," she said, as tears began to spill from her eyes.

Lo'San set her on her feet and took her face in his hands. He smiled down at her, as his own eyes seemed to develop a sheen. "We will have a young one, Sink Lar! Our very own," he said.

"I believe you were already expecting when you first came to me for treatments. I did perform our routine tests for enzyme levels that would indicate a pregnancy with any of the females we standardly treat. I did not think that the levels would be different for humans as it remains in such a predictable level for all the other species we treat. I was wrong, and for that I apologize. It wasn't until Synclare stated that with her overactive emotional state one would think she was already with young, that it occurred to me that it may be the very reason the treatments weren't working. I contacted the healers who work with the Consortium, then went a step further and contacted Consul Kol Ra' Don Tol. He put me in touch with several human healers. I sent the results of your last blood tests that I'd marked negative for the pregnancy enzymes we usually measure for. They came back positive. And I stand before you offering my sincerest apologies and thanks. You've suffered needlessly, and taught me much about your species, Synclare."

256

Synclare was laughing and crying. "It doesn't matter! I'm just so happy. And if I could help you learn more about our physiology, it's fine," she said, turning back to Lo'San. "We're gonna be parents!" she cried, throwing herself into his arms again.

Lo'San laughed and held her closely, sharing in her exuberance.

"I have but one more question," Doc said.

"Of course," Lo'San said.

"What medication was she given?" Doc asked.

"The same one that you prescribed for her reaction to the treatments. She gave Synclare double the dosage. I feared she was still suffering from its effects, causing her to sleep excessively," Lo'San said.

"I clearly stated in my message that she should not take any more of it! It could have been harmful!" Doc exclaimed. "Come, Synclare. Allow me to examine you properly."

"We never got a message," Synclare said, following Doc as Lo'San trailed along behind her, holding fast to her hand. "When did you leave a message?"

"I left a message on your com unit near the end of the day of your last treatment," Doc answered.

"My mother was sitting with you. I have no doubt she heard it," Lo'San growled.

"It may still be there, I haven't checked recently," Synclare answered.

"I checked. When I discovered you missing I checked the unit, hoping that you'd left some word of your whereabouts on it. It is empty, no messages at all," Lo'San told her.

"Have you experienced any pain, or any bleeding?" Doc asked.

"No, not since the effects of the last treatment wore off," Synclare answered.

"It is likely all is well, then. Let's confirm it, then we'll make all the observations necessary to log your progress," Doc said.

Synclare smiled as Lo'San lifted her and placed her on the examining table before she had time to even take her clothes off. "I'll need to put on a gown," she told Lo'San.

"I will help with that, too," he answered, reaching for the folded disposable gown that was lying on the small pillow at the head of the table.

"I can do it," Synclare said, still grinning. She'd not stopped grinning since she'd learned that she was indeed pregnant.

"I will do it. You grow our young one, I will do all else," he said as he reverently placed his hand over her lower belly when she unzipped her jeans.

"Even undressing me?" she asked on a laugh.

"Even undressing," Lo'San answered. His gaze moved from her belly up to her face. He looked lovingly into her eyes. "I am the most gifted male in all of existence. I have you, and we will have our young one. Nothing will ever compare to the joy you bring me."

~~~

Ba Re' stood in the serving line in the commissary alone. He stared at the food and waited his turn to be served. He didn't notice anyone around him, nor did he make any effort to interact.

"Sink Lar, I will ask Ba Re' to eat with us," Lo'San said.

Synclare glanced up from her plate and looked around the expansive commissary until she found him standing in the serving line. "I still can't believe he and Elisha didn't work out. I hurt for him."

"As do I," Lo'San answered. "Shall I invite him?"

"Yes, please do," Synclare said.

Lo'San rose and walked toward Ba Re'. He was standing right beside him and actually had to call his name to be noticed. "Ba Re', will you take your meal with Sink Lar and myself?"

Ba Re' looked at Lo'San, and it became immediately apparent that he had no idea what Lo'San had asked.

"Sink Lar and myself would like your company for lunch today," Lo'San repeated.

"I am not very good company," Ba Re' answered.

"You do not have to be, we are," Lo'San answered with a grin.

Ba Re' gave a half-hearted chuckle.

"You will join us, yes?" Lo'San pressed.

Ba Re' looked over toward Synclare who offered him a little wave.

"Very well," Ba Re' agreed.

Lo'San stayed beside Ba Re' as he worked his way through the line, and then escorted him back to the table.

"Hello, Ba Re'," Synclare said brightly.

"Synclare," Ba Re' answered. "You look well. You both do," he said.

"Thank you. I'm still so tired, but I don't mind it all that much," Synclare answered.

"It will not be long and you will get no sleep at all. Best get it while you can," Ba Re' teased with a sad smile.

"How are you?" Synclare asked.

Ba Re' looked up from the food he'd begun to push around his plate and shrugged. "I am waking up every morning. I am performing my duties. I make myself eat, then I go to bed to start again the next day. It is all I can do," he answered.

"I'm sorry, Ba Re'. I'm not going to tell you you'll get over it. You most likely won't, but with time it will get easier," Synclare said.

"Is she hurting?" Ba Re' asked.

Synclare looked from Ba Re' to Lo'San. "I... I don't know. I haven't spoken to her since she left for the Consortium. But I do know she wasn't as happy with the situation as she wanted everyone to think she was."

"It was her dream to work with the Consortium as a translator, or liaison for foreign dignitaries. It is why I asked

Quin to speak to Bart and ask for her to be given the opportunity," Ba Re' said.

"Sometimes we don't know what we want until it's taken away from us," Synclare said.

"I know that humans do not feel the same recognition that we do when we find our Ehlealah, but do you think she notices that I am not part of her life anymore? Do you think she feels the loss?" Ba Re' asked.

"We may not have that inborn instinct that screams he's mine! But, there is no denying I was drawn to Lo'San even before I knew he wanted me, too. And the same with Rosie, and for Vivian. Even Ada Jane was sad to leave Kol behind when she went home without him. We may not have the exact same reaction you do, but to some degree, there is still a connection on our side. And once it's established, it's as strong as yours is to us. So, yes, I think she's acutely aware of the fact that you're no longer beside her. I'd bet she's second guessed herself a dozen times each day since she's been with the Consortium," Synclare said.

Ba Re' nodded and looked down at his food.

"You should reach out to her," Lo'San said.

Ba Re' shook his head. "I insisted she accept my claim. I tried everything I knew to make her accept me. I tried to tempt, I coerced, I became angry, I insisted, and finally I just withdrew. A male can only be rejected so many times."

"Surely she wanted you to claim her. She came to this ship with you. She knew your intent," Lo'San said.

"She said I did not give her a chance to be herself. She kept insisting she needed to establish herself first. She said she'd always stood on her own feet and paid her own way and she would not be a kept female. I only wanted to keep her at my side. I didn't mean to keep her from her dreams."

"Maybe she'll be back," Synclare said.

"The night before I asked Quin to make arrangements for her to work with the Consortium if it was at all possible, she returned from her girls' night having had far too much to drink. She called me by a silly name and offered herself to me. She told me it was now or never, but even I, as much as I'd pushed and tried to make her accept me, could not take advantage of her vulnerability. She was not clear headed. When she woke the next day I asked if she still wanted my claim. I told her I could not continue as we were. Either I claimed her, and she me, or other arrangements had to be made. She refused and said she had no knowledge of offering me the opportunity to claim her. I moved my things into temporary quarters that day. Several days later she was hired by the Consortium on Quin's recommendation and then she was gone."

"You didn't even tell her goodbye?" Synclare asked.

Ba Re' shook his head. "It hurt to even look at her. I simply gave her her dream and let her go."

"You have my deepest sympathies, Ba Re'. I cannot imagine the difficulty you endure each day," Lo'San said, reaching out to take Synclare's hand in his. "The nights are much harder than the days," Ba Re' admitted.

"Any time you want company, you know where to find us. Any time you want to talk I'm here for you," Synclare said.

"Thank you, Synclare. It has been a relief to speak of it to a female who might understand her," Ba Re' said.

"I'll reach out to her, see what she has to say," Synclare said.

"It matters not. What's done is done," Ba Re' said.

"That's not true. I know she cares for you. She talked about you all the time. I know she cared!" Synclare said emphatically. "I'm not sure why she thought she couldn't have both you and her work, but it's ridiculous for her to insist she can't have you until she's established herself professionally."

"She has said I was... overbearing. It means too hard, yes?" Ba Re' asked.

"It means you are too pushy. It means you wanted things your way only and expected her to be okay with that," Synclare said.

"It is my way! I meant no harm. I wish to be valued for me, as she wishes to be valued for herself!" Ba Re' objected.

"I know, I know. I'm not saying you did anything that you need to apologize for. But I'm beginning to think you both need to learn to communicate," Synclare said.

"I told her what I wanted," Ba Re' said.

"And when she told you what she wanted, what did you say?" Synclare asked.

Ba Re' lifted his chin slightly, a sign of defiance.

"Did you tell her that you would do anything you could to help her get all she wanted and you'd support her in her dreams?" Synclare asked.

Ba Re' looked from Synclare to Lo'San who watched him, waiting for an answer. "No," he finally said.

"What did you say?" Lo'San asked.

"I told her that her life would be full, as would be mine, whatever it brought. That she was my Ehlealah and we were meant to be together. Anything that took her away from my place on Command Warship 1 was not feasible within our bond."

"So basically, you said, too bad, you're stuck here and you're going to have to learn to like it," Synclare asked.

"No. I told her of my feelings for her. I told her of how very much I valued her and cherished her!" Ba Re' said defensively.

"But you gave her no hope for the things she wanted out of life," Synclare explained. "You didn't try to compromise. That's most likely why she didn't accept your claim. She wanted more for herself than just hanging around this ship day after day waiting for you to return to your quarters. And she wanted you to be proud of her, too," Synclare explained.

"I was very proud of her," Ba Re' said. "She was training to be a liaison here on our ship," he insisted.

"She can't very well be a liaison if every time she leaves your quarters you hound her with where she is, what she's doing, who she's speaking to. You never let her out of your quarters except for that one night she went out with us, unless you were with her," Synclare said, trying to make him see it from another point of view.

"We were not bonded! I couldn't have her walking the ship at will — there are too many unmated males about!" Ba Re' said.

"Did you tell her why you didn't want her outside your quarters?" Synclare asked.

"I'm sure she understood," Ba Re' said.

"Maybe. But maybe she just thought you wanted her kept at home all day and that would be her life if she were to accept you."

"It does not sound like she expected a very happy life, Ba Re'. Perhaps you should reevaluate your expectations and communicate with her," Lo'San suggested.

"Exactly. Reevaluate your approach, your needs, and contact her. Communication is key. You have to learn to compromise. You give a little, and she gives a little, and you keep doing that until you meet somewhere in the middle. Each of you give up a little of what you personally want, but you both get so much more when you compromise," Synclare said.

Ba Re' sat there, still pushing the food around his plate. "She did not even say goodbye," he complained.

"And neither did you," Synclare reminded him.

"I do not think she will speak to me," he finally admitted.

"She may not. But, she might. I could reach out to her and see what she says if you like," Synclare offered.

Ba Re' looked up at Synclare. "I would very much like that."

~~~

Elisha paused outside the conference room where she'd act as interpreter for one of the visiting dignitaries. She saw her reflection in the highly polished metallic surface of the corridor wall. Even on this imperfect surface she could see the dark circles under her eyes from lack of rest.

She just couldn't sleep. Every time she closed her eyes she saw Ba Re's face. She'd relived all their moments over and over again, and it always ended the same. It was all about what he wanted, and she was expected to just sit home and be the little wife waiting for his attention. She'd worked too long and too hard to just let go of her dreams. She'd realized he didn't want her for herself, or even love her for herself, he wanted and loved who he wanted her to be, and she could never be happy or satisfied being who he wanted and letting go of who she really was. When he gave her the ultimatum, mate him or walk away. She walked. She took advantage of the opportunity that Commander Zha Quin had told her about, and left Command Warship 1.

She closed her eyes and leaned against the corridor wall, her heart breaking a little more at the thought of Ba Re'. Despite their inability to agree on most things, she loved him. And she missed him terribly. She startled when a voice spoke very near her face. "Are you well, female?"

Elisha opened her eyes, and reached toward the male. "Ba Re'?" she said, stopping just short of touching him, when she realized he wasn't the male she wished for.

"I am not Ba Re'," the male answered. Then he looked at her more curiously. "Who are you?"

The pain in her eyes as she looked at him more closely was easily seen. "I'm sorry. I thought you were someone else. I'm a Liaison here, I'll be helping with translation today. I've only just started last week," she explained. "I apologize for my forwardness. As I said, I thought you were someone else."

"What is your name?" the male asked.

"Elisha," she answered.

The male smiled slowly. "Hello Elisha. I know of you."

"You do?" she asked.

"I am Jhan Re' Don Tol — brother to Ba Re'."

Elisha's eyes rounded, she knew Ba Re' had a brother but had never met him, and hadn't been told how much they favored each other.

"Tell me, Elisha, why are you here and your male is on Command Warship 1?"

"He didn't want me anymore, so I took a job here. I think I disappointed him one too many times."

Jhan's face showed a momentary expression of surprise, then he shook his head. "I can promise you he still wants you.

264

But come, our meeting waits. We will speak when it is finished and you will tell me of how my bother managed to drive his Ehlealah away."

Epilogue

The smaller of Quin's conference rooms was filled with people all looking at one another speculatively as Quin And Vivi sat holding hands, waiting for the vid com to come on line.

Ba Re', Lo'San, Rokai, Re'Vahl, a very haggard looking Zahn, Rel, Asl, and Kail.

The holovid had been set aside in favor of the standard vid screen, and there were three views sharing the space on the large screen at the moment. One of them flickered, coming into focus with a large, blue Cruestaci warrior smiling at them happily.

"Blue Dude!" Vivian cried out happily.

"Vivi! Zha Quin! Is that Ba Re'? Everyone is there! Hello!" Kol said, waving animatedly from the privacy of his office.

"Kol! It is good to see you my friend," Quin said. "You have been too long away."

"I have, but, life is good here. Perhaps soon we can come for a visit," Kol said.

"I thank you for being here, Kol. I know this would not normally be a meeting you'd have to attend, but it will soon become apparent why I asked you to join us," Quin said.

"I am always available to you, Quin," Kol said.

"How are the boys?" Vivian asked.

"Most days they drive me insane," Kol admitted, shaking his head, "they never, ever stop! But it is an insanity I welcome. They are strong and smart. They are adventurous and kind. As my Ada Jane says, we are blessed."

"I look forward to meeting them," Quin said, just as another view began to flicker and an image of Sovereign Zha Tahl and Sovereigna Eula came into focus.

"Good morning," Zha Tahl said.

"Good morning," Quin answered.

"I trust all is well," Zha Tahl said. "I hope the update from Eschina is a positive one."

"It is. We shall get started as soon as Chairman Bartholomew joins us," Quin said.

"I am here," Bart said as his image came into view on his own screen.

"Thank you for joining us," Quin said. "Now that we are all here, let's get started with the first business at hand," Quin said. "Now, as all should be aware, commendations were presented to those aboard the Unified Consortium Defense Satellite Station in recognition of their assistance to and protection of General Lo'San's mate. It appears all was well received. Bart, do you have anything to add there?" Quin asked.

"All is well, and if there have been any grumblings about the issue, they've not reached my ears or those of my people. I think we covered it well," Bart answered.

"Excellent. Further to that subject, are those who caused General Lo'San's mate to be aboard the satellite station. General Lo'San has given his testimony in the trials of his mother and sister-in-law. Both were convicted of kidnapping and attempted murder of his mate, as well as charges of theft and fraud. They have been remanded into the custody of the Unified Consortium and have begun serving their time. When it became clear the conditions under which the males on Eschina lived, Lo'San and I discussed offering options to those who wished to take advantage of them. As Eschina is under the protection and governing of Cruestace, with the help of Sovereign Zha Tahl, we've instituted changes that are available, but not required, as there will inevitably be those who wish to continue in the old ways of Eschina. I'll turn the floor over to Lo'San at this time to update everyone on the occurrences on his home planet before I take a moment for matters of my own. General Lo'San... if you will," Quin said.

"Thank you. Let me say first, I am very satisfied with the outcome. I would be surprised if either is ever released," he commented, "and I have no problem with that at all. The trial was quite sensationalized on Eschina, and as would be expected with any society, there are strong opinions on both sides. We took the opportunity of both females being removed as head of their households, to turn both households into examples of changes that are available to any who are interested. Basically, any male who feels he is held in a household against his will, cannot be forced to remain by his female. He is free to leave that household, reenter the claiming events — with his young ones if he should have them, or take one of two additional options. He is free to join a working produce farm as an equal partner.

To clarify, there have been several males who decided they wished to establish their own farms, free of female rule, with each having an equal ownership of the land and the profits. They are happily providing for themselves and the young ones they took with them from their prior females' homes. The other option is even more unique to them. My father opted to hire other males to work our family farm. Only my father owns his farm, but each male is paid a fair wage. In return, they work daily, and are even offered housing if they'd like to take advantage of it. For my family farm it seems to be working well. In either circumstance these males understand they are responsible for their own lives. If they wish a female, fine, but they need no longer accept multiple husbands for one female if they don't wish to. Some of the males in neighboring areas have spoken to him regarding their situation and the idea of working for fair wage and hoping for a single female and male family seems to be taking hold. Of course there will always be those who resist change and will never change their living situations, and that's fine for them. We intended only to make it known that there are options for those who are unhappy with the old ways. Ph'eel's household has been disbanded. All males were given the choices I've just outlined. Some have chosen to remain and look for a female to replace Ph'eel, one has requested employment from my family's farm.

We are satisfied with the results we are seeing. At the very least we have made it clear that no male should have to continue to live a life as dictated by anyone — not even his female — as many thought they had no option to."

268

"What of your brother?" Kol asked.

"Ko'San is serving time as a coerced accomplice in Sink Lar's kidnapping. He will be freed in three months time. Because of the fact he came to me willingly, and refused to harm Sink Lar, I pled for leniency. It's been granted. He will return to Eschina upon release, where he will take employment on the family farm and raise his young ones. His young ones are currently with my father until his release."

"I am happy that all seems to have played out better than expected. Even happier that the males of Eschina now have choices," Zha Tahl said.

"As am I," Lo'San agreed. "Thank you for your support as we instituted these changes."

"You are most welcome, General Lo'San," Zha Tahl said.

"Is there anything else that needs to be addressed?" Zha Tahl asked.

"I see no point in delaying our news any longer," Quin said. He looked to his left and reached for Vivi's hand. Vivian looked at Quin and offered him a shaky smile before placing her hand in his. Quin kissed her knuckles then rested his hand still grasping hers on the table top for all to see as a sign of their unity. "For those who are not aware, General Lo'San and his female are expecting their first youngling. We share in their excitement of the impending birth.

Their path was not an easy one, and was in fact the catalyst for a change in our lives as well. While watching the medical treatments Synclare underwent, it became a subject for much discussion between Vivi and myself. We have never considered having younglings. It was not possible because of physical scarring that precluded any chance of conception. I knew this from the moment she was first healed when arriving on Command Warship 1. Vivi knew as well, but we didn't spend a moment thinking of it. We had one another, that was all that mattered.

But, watching Synclare and Lo'San gave us hope. Vivi decided to undergo procedures to remove and rebuild the damage her body had borne. She is healed. We are healed.

Successfully so. I am happy to give each of you the news that we are expecting our first youngling as well."

Congratulations, cheers, squeals from Eula, and hugs from Rokai who jumped up and rounded the table to hug and kiss Vivi, and grumbles from Quin as he tried unsuccessfully to push Rokai away before he landed a big kiss on his cheek, causing everyone to laugh filled the room.

After all was again quiet, Quin continued. "As we will be welcoming our first youngling soon, we have decided a change is needed. We have decided — Vivi left it to me actually — and I have struggled with the issue for several days. Now that the decision is made, I am fully at peace, and know it is the right decision."

"I cannot believe it," Kol muttered under his breath.

Quin met Kol's gaze and winked at him. He'd had no doubt Kol would figure it out before he even had a chance to announce it.

"Believe what? What decision?" Rokai asked, still standing behind Vivi and Quin with his hands on his hips.

"We will be returning to Cruestace to raise our youngling. It is time I took the mantle of leadership from you, Father, as you've long asked me to do. I will not give up my place as Commander of our military forces, but another will actively command this ship and its warriors. All my leadership will come from the palace on Cruestace," Quin said.

Everyone began talking at once, Eula was telling Vivi excitedly that she'd begin redecorating their wing of the palace at once, Bart was asking who was being left in charge of Command Warship 1, Kol was smiling ear-to-ear, Lo'San was happy for his friends but worried about who his new Commander would be. Rokai was looking like a deer in the headlights, truly a stricken look on his face, and Vivian's guard were worriedly whispering amongst themselves.

Quin knocked his knuckles on the tabletop to regain everyone's attention. Once they all quieted down, he spoke again. "There are many details to be decided upon and laid to rest. We will not be leaving the ship this day, this week, or even

270

next, but it is time to begin preparations. In the meantime, transitions will begin to take place. This ship will become known under a different name. It is no longer a warship, and as everyone is aware, it is being used instead for diplomatic missions. Let me be clear, it will be changing in name only. All its current capabilities will remain intact, only for the sake of its new path, a new name should be chosen. Command Warship 1 will not be reassigned, and will instead be held unused in the event it is ever required to once again be known as a warship. Its warriors will continue to be the top of our military as it is subjected to any number of accessibilities that our warships have never been before. Because of this, it must maintain the most efficient warriors. As far as guidance... I've appointed my replacement as Commander of this ship." Quin looked at Lo'San. "Commander Lo'San, congratulations on your new position."

"Oh, thank the gods," Rokai mumbled, dramatically leaning against the back of Vivian's chair. "I did not want that job," Rokai said, looking down at Vivian while she grinned up at him.

Lo'San broke out into a wide smile he just couldn't hide.

"You have long ago earned it, my friend. Everyone respects you, your even temperament and quick mind have served us all well. Your loyalty is exemplary. You know this ship and all aboard it as well as I do. I will rest easy knowing she is safely under your command. May you command for a very, very long time, should you decide to accept the position," Quin said. "You are expecting as well..."

"I will happily accept," Lo'San said quickly. "Sink Lar and I have discussed the possibility of moving planet side and we both dismissed the idea as soon as it occurred to us. This is our home," Lo'San said.

"I am happy to hear that," Quin said. He returned his attention to the remainder of the people in the room. "As Commander Lo'San takes over this ship, his former position is left open. Ba Re' Non Tol, I've recommended you as General, second to Lo'San if you will accept the position."

"Humbly," Ba Re' said, nodding in a dignified manner as he met Quin's gaze.

Quin gave Ba Re' a nod before moving on. "Re'Vahl is finished with his training and is officially Lieutenant Commander and will continue with his duties as such. Rokai ahl will begin training as a Lieutenant as well."

Rokai's eyebrows scrunched up as he thought about what this might mean for him. "I don't want to leave my team!" he objected.

"Rokai, you will maintain in the position Kol left vacant when he accepted the Ambassadorship on Earth. You will remain Elite Force Commander, you will, however, begin your training to support the Commander as one of his Lieutenant Commanders, in the event you may be called upon for assistance."

"You didn't ask if I wanted that position," Rokai grumbled. "You asked the others."

"Rokai, would you be interested in maintaining your position of Elite Force Commander, while learning to support your Commander and General as a Lieutenant Commander?" Quin asked with a hint of sarcasm in his voice.

Rokai looked at Quin and made a show of considering the offer. "You know... I think perhaps I would enjoy this new opportunity," he finally said.

"You cannot take the ship out of orbit," Bart added forcefully. "I do not want to get word that Command Warship 1 has landed on Earth!"

Rokai raised an eyebrow as he pinned Bart with a pointed look. "You cannot take the ship out of orbit, Lieutenant Commander!" Rokai corrected.

"Quin..." Bart said.

"It will be fine," Quin answered before launching into the end of his presentation. "There are many changes coming into play. Decisions will have to be made to determine which of our personal guards will accompany us planet side, and which prefer to stay aboard this ship, or others for that matter. Command Warship 2, Command Warship 3, and some of the smaller more active vessels are options as well. Our move to Cruestace will give opportunities for those who've guarded us to move up and over throughout the rest of the force as positions are available if they'd prefer that to following us. While we'd like nothing more than to have no major changes in our guards, it is not necessary for everyone to accompany us if their aspirations lead them elsewhere.

Personnel exchanges will be taking place as we find just the right combination to keep all personnel in the arenas they wish to be in, and all moving smoothly, but I feel these few changes I've specifically outlined here will be most effective to cover my absence from Command Warship 1. There will be time for all to make their preferences known. In the meantime, I wish you all well in your new roles," he said, looking at Lo'San, Ba Re', Rokai and Re'Vahl. I thank you all for giving us these few moments today to let you know of our future plans, and I thank each of you for your loyalty and support as we embark on this new adventure and the next phase of our lives."

"Congratulations Zha Quin! Vivian, I wish I was there to hug you. You will make such a wonderful mother," Bart said.

"Thank you," Vivian answered. "I wish they could see me," she said, referring to her uncles.

"I have no doubt, they are smiling down, or up, you are pretty high up there," Bart teased.

"I thought that once we're on Cruestace, maybe you could bring Samuel to visit," Vivian said.

"I'm sure he'd love to come. We both would," Bart said. "If I'm welcome back," he teased.

"Absolutely," Eula responded from her vid. "You made quite the impression when you were here."

Bart immediately blushed and Quin looked from his mother to Bart trying to figure out what they were talking about.

"I was quite impressed as well," Bart responded.

"Wait, did you meet someone?" Vivian asked, directing her question to Bart.

"Isn't this an official meeting?" Bart asked, trying to duck Vivian's questions.

"Gentlemen, you may return to your duties," Quin said, realizing it was turning into a family visit.

After much shaking of hands and repeated congratulations to Quin as he saw them off, all that remained in the conference room were Vivian, Quin, Kail and Zahn, as Vivian and Eula discussed Eula's idea for preparing the East wing of the palace for them.

"I have several excellent ladies maids that I encourage you to meet. You should hire one to help you with the children," Eula said.

"I won't need a nanny full time. I want to raise my children myself," Vivian answered. "But, I have already hired someone that will accompany us to Cruestace for whenever I need an extra hand," Vivian answered.

"Oh, is she one of the females from Earth? Do I know her?" Eula asked.

"No. She's from Eschina. She was a servant in Lo'San's brother's household. She raised his children," Vivian said, watching Zahn out of the corner of her eye. "Her name is Au'revele. I'm very fond of her."

"Send me her information and I'll obtain resident papers on her at once. I'm excited to meet the female you trust so well. I'm sure she's a very sweet girl," Eula said.

"She really is," Vivian answered.

"Sirena, I would like to declare my intention to accompany you to Cruestace," Zahn announced.

Vivian turned her chair and smiled innocently at Zahn. "Are you sure, Zahn? I know that life at home is much less exciting than life aboard the ship."

"I am very sure, Sirena. If it is acceptable to you, I will be most honored to continue as the head of your personal guard," Zahn said.

"Accepted. Thank you, Zahn. I'm very happy you'll be staying with us," Vivian said before turning around and giving Eula her attention once again.

"I cannot wait for your arrival, my daughter! I have waited for this day for a very long time," Eula said.

"I'm excited for it. And a little scared. But," she said, pausing to take a deep breath, "we're coming home to Cruestace."

The End — for now.

From The Author

Thank you for purchasing this book. I hope that my stories make you smile and give you a small escape from the daily same ole/same ole. I write for me, simply for the joy of it, but if someone else also smiles as a result, even better. Your support is greatly appreciated. If you liked this story, please remember to leave a review wherever you bought it, so that more people can find my books. Each review is important, no matter how short or long it may be.

See you in the pages of the next one!

Sandra R Neeley

Other books by this author:

Avaleigh's Boys series

I'm Not A Dragon's Mate!, Book 1

Bane's Heart, Book 2

Kaid's Queen, Book 3

Maverik's Ashes, Book 4

Bam's Ever, Book 5

Vince's Place, Book 6

Whispers From the Bayou series

Carnage, Book 1

Destroy, Book 2

Enthrall, Book 3

Lore, Book 4

Murder, Book 5

Aubreigne, Book 6

Haven series

Haven 1: Ascend

Haven 2: Redemption

Haven 3: Transcend

Riley's Pride

Riley's Pride, Book 1

Richie's Promise, Book 2

Travis's Gift, Book 3

Variant

Beginnings, Variant 1

Standalone Novels

WINGS

Short Stories and Novellas

CAT

Only Fools Walk Free

Safe On Base: A Howls Romance (loosely connected to
Riley's Pride series)

Blessed Curse
(Released as part of the E.V.I.E. anthology)

Halloween Treats, An Avaleigh's Boys Novella

About The Author

My name is Sandra R Neeley. I write Paranormal, SciFi, and Fantasy Romances. Why? Because normal is highly overrated. I'm 57, I have two kids, one 34 and one 14, one grandchild, one husband and a menagerie of animals. I love to cook, and was a voracious reader, though since I started writing, I don't get as much time to read as I once did. I'm a homebody and prefer my writing/reading time to a crowd. I have had stories and fictional characters wandering around in my head for as long as I can remember. I'm a self-published author and I like it that way because I can decide what and when to write. I tend to follow my muse — the louder the voice, the greater the chance that voice's story is next.

I am by no means a formal, polished, properly structured individual and neither are my stories. But people seem to love the easy emotion and passion that flow from them. A bit of a warning though, there are some "triggers" in them that certain people should avoid. I'm a firm believer that you cannot have light without the dark. You cannot fully embrace the joy and elation that my people eventually find if you do not bear witness to their darkest hours as well. So please read the warnings supplied with each of the synopsis about my books before you buy them. I've got five series published at this time, Avaleigh's Boys - PNR, Whispers From the Bayou - Fantasy PNR, Haven - SciFi Romance, and Riley's Pride - PNR, Variant - a dark genetic manipulation romance, a couple of standalone novels, several short stories, and much, much more to come. I'm always glad to hear from my readers, so feel free to look me up and say hello.

You can find me at any of these places:

authorsandrarneeley@gmail.com
https://www.sneeleywrites.com
https://www.sneeleywrites.com/contact
https://www.sneeleywrites.com/blog
https://www.facebook.com/authorsandrarneeley/

https://www.facebook.com/groups/755782837922866/
https://www.amazon.com/Sandra-R-Neeley/e/B01M65OZ1J/
https://twitter.com/sneeleywrites
https://www.instagram.com/sneeleywrites/
https://www.goodreads.com/author/show/15986167.Sandra_R_Neeley
https://www.bookbub.com/authors/sandra-r-neeley

Stop by to say Hi, and sign up to be included in updates on current and future projects.

Printed in Great Britain
by Amazon